MARIA YING

The Grace of Sorcerers

This book was professionally typeset on Reedsy.
Find out more at reedsy.com

Contents

Prologue

Gabrielle Sejana is walking to the King Street Market for lunch when she first sees the woman.

A tall blonde in a tailored suit, ice-blue eyes and vivid red lips; the woman catches and holds attention. But Gabrielle is busy, and a little hungry, and certainly isn't impolite enough to stare. By all rights, the stranger should simply have been an attractive woman she notices for a moment, considers briefly as she eats her burger at the market, and then has forgotten by the time she leaves work that evening.

But as she passes on the sidewalk, the woman looks at her and says, "Gabrielle Sejana."

The way she says the name makes it clear that the stranger knows her, so clear that Gabrielle can't question it. On this woman's lips her name is an old friend; when she utters it, Gabrielle has to find out how this woman knows her so completely.

"Follow me, Gabrielle Sejana," says the woman, and turns on her heel. Gabrielle follows. She could hardly do otherwise.

She's led to another office tower, a block or two away: the guard at the lobby barely looks up as they cross to the elevators together. The woman hits the button for the fifth basement level with one long, manicured finger.

"What's going on?" asks Gabrielle, confused.

The woman smiles. "Don't be afraid. It won't make a difference, and you'll be happier if you're not afraid, so don't be."

"What?" says Gabrielle. The woman's smile grows wider, more malicious; Gabrielle is suddenly terrified. The confined space fills with the cloying sweetness of decay. Several options occur to her—the emergency button, the emergency line. The woman is between her and the panel and she cannot bring herself to attempt either.

The doors open to a whitewashed concrete hall, the same sort of half-industrial bareness that underpins most of the buildings in the city. The woman strides out of the elevator. Gabrielle slams the ground floor button. "Follow me, Gabrielle Sejana," says the woman without even glancing back, and Gabrielle follows. The elevator departs behind them with a little ping.

The woman opens an undistinguished gray metal door that leads into an empty concrete room. There is a dry metal drain in one corner and a naked light bulb hanging above: it looks like a garage that has been cleaned out, part of some underground parking complex snipped off as a separate room for... something else. Panic is rising fast in Gabrielle.

"Be bound, Gabrielle Sejana," says the woman with a gesture. Shackles of green light spring into being around her wrists and ankles, pulling her spread-eagled where she stands.

"What—what?" whimpers Gabrielle.

"I've been studying you," the woman says, smiling. "I have need of someone with your skills and your connections, and when I found you I studied you and examined you until I learned your True Name, Gabrielle Sejana."

The name is a blow, the name is a lash, the name is a knife flaying Gabrielle open before this monstrous attention.

"Please, I'll do anything," begs Gabrielle. Tears stream down her cheeks.

"You probably would," agrees the woman. "Things you never would have imagined doing ten minutes ago. But, also, you might not. I didn't get where I am by trusting others to do the right thing, Gabrielle Sejana."

Gabrielle screams at the name and tries to flinch away. She can turn her head, but her limbs are as good as useless.

"No," the woman continues, ignoring Gabrielle's reaction, "what we need, if this little partnership is to work out, is a whole lot more of *me* and a whole lot less of *you*."

"Please—" says Gabrielle again.

The woman reaches into her own mouth. And then keeps reaching. Her hand goes in, past the wrist, halfway up the forearm, her face slack and her jaw distending with soft cartilaginous pops. Gabrielle cries out and gags. The woman pulls her arm back out, and in her slim, elegant fingers there is a spiny, teardrop-shaped slate-blue worm, squirming and thrashing. Gabrielle screams again.

This time it earns the woman's attention, or at least her irritation. "Silence, Gabrielle Sejana." Gabrielle can no longer make noise. The woman gestures and the glowing bindings pull Gabrielle flat on her back, suspending her a meter off the ground. "I want you," purrs the woman, stepping closer. Gabrielle's eyes are riveted to the worm in her hand. "I want everything you are. Your memories, your personality, your talents, your *life*. I want to *use* you, to wring you dry and throw you away. I want you and I am going to have you. But Gabrielle Sejana is in my way."

Even under the agonizing horror of the name, Gabrielle still cannot move or speak or react. There is nothing in her universe but the woman, and the worm, and the fear.

"I know your True Name. But I'd rather not have to keep spending *my* time dragging you around. So I'm going to put this little piece of myself"—she *licks* the worm like it is a lover's throat, and the worm wriggles happily between her long red nails—"inside of you, and I'm going to eat your name. And then, when you're nothing but an empty shell, I can use you the way I want to, without any effort at all. Won't that be lovely?"

Gabrielle can't respond.

The woman gently untucks Gabrielle's blouse from her belt and pulls it up to reveal her belly. She holds the worm lazily suspended over Gabrielle's navel. "Any last words, before I replace you with more of myself? Thank me, Gabrielle Sejana."

"Thank you for destroying me," Gabrielle rasps.

The woman smiles beneficently and lets go of the worm. It lies cold and prickly on Gabrielle Sejana for a second, and then squirms into her navel, the skin and fat of her belly twisting to allow it passage. Then it is in her, in a place that isn't simply her abdominal cavity or even nestled among her intestines but much deeper *inside*, and after a moment it begins to eat.

3

The thing was once a person, and *almost* still is—but there is nothing inside it now, nothing but an aching, unfillable void where Gabrielle Sejana once was and where a slate-blue worm now lurks.

It sits up from where it fell, the bindings of Gabrielle Sejana extinguished along with Gabrielle's personhood. The one that owns it is already leaving the room, with no need to speak to or even acknowledge the creature. The nameless thing straightens the clothes it wears, carefully checks its makeup to ensure there is no sign of the ordeal Gabrielle suffered, and then leaves as well.

An observer would see Gabrielle walk out of the office tower, smiling and a little lost in thought, just as she walked down the street barely a half-hour before. The nameless thing smiles its empty, meaningless smile, and sets off.

It exists now, after all, to enact Cecilie Kristiansen's will alone.

One: The Warlock and Her Armor

VIVECA

To be a warlock in this age is to know patience, to trade in powers and promises and poisons, to bind demons and men to your will, break them as you see fit. Silver and gold, pewter and silicon, brimstone and depleted uranium—the list of reagents has grown with the generations, but such work as mine has always required preparation. And now I stand on the edge of a binding circle—behind me, years of toil and seas of blood, and ahead of me a few uncertain minutes that will change everything.

It has been a long war between myself and the killer of my kin, spread across a hundred halls of power; tyrants and presidents and executives are our pawns, and history our board. My nemesis Cecilie Kristiansen may be the most powerful woman in the world, having taken that distinction from the still-warm hands of my late mother. For years I have sought to return the favor, and for years have I failed. But by the reckoning of mages, I am young yet, relentless, and not alone; my sister Olesya is a powerful sorceress in her own right, taken now to the art of assassination and subterfuge. When we work in tandem, no foe can stand against us; together, we will see Cecilie Kristiansen broken and the Hua name restored.

And now, beneath the din of a freshly won battle, I may have found the key to our victory. A rumor of a weapon too powerful for Kristiansen to wield, a tool she grew to fear and stashed away; I broke nations, decimated armies both loyal and foul, all to create an opportunity to steal into a far-flung repository and take that which I needed.

My loyal homunculus, hide of stone and eyes of emerald, finishes the preparations with mechanical precision. The automaton is the last gift my mother left me—an implacable, impervious protector of granite, a guardian and companion both. But it will crack and wear with time, as all stone must. As all legacies will, if they are not forged anew. My mother's gifts cannot protect me from every mistake, cannot make every mistake for me. It is time I crafted tools of my own, and I must succeed or fail here, alone; I will the homunculus away and begin the incantations.

Before me a shade flickers and flows, sometimes like smoke and sometimes like flame, until it finally coalesces into the shape of a woman, taller and wider than me, dressed sharply in a suit of Stygian black. The demon is not as imposing as my homunculus' stone, at least not at first look. But she cuts a striking figure of her own, shadows twisting at her feet and miasma bleeding from her tailored shoulders. She radiates the confidence of a storm rising on the horizon, a distant and peaceful visage that hides a roiling fury; her eyes flash like lightning. Red flickers in the black of her hair, cinderous.

The first thing that comes out of her mouth is, "I didn't expect you to have an office."

I didn't transport her as such—in corporeal form, that is, for some measure of the word. What my raid secured were rites of ancient power, metals of impossible and evil provenance, and most of all—a *name*, a True Name, recorded in cuneiform and vinyl and laser etching all. I use it now: "Did you want to meet me in a dark dungeon, ███ ██ ██?"

She flinches when I speak it, and my lip splits; even her name is anathema to reality. And then the demon smirks and slowly pans her head up to look at me. There is no surprise on her face, as I must have known her Name to pull her into this plane of existence. But her gold eyes still glow bright with malice; by their very nature, demons despise being bound, a trait I can appreciate.

"You may call me Yves, if you like," she says, then deliberately turns back toward the demarcation of her prison. I watch as she measures the perimeter with her steps, long fingers grazing the invisible bars I have forged to contain her. The deliberation with which she plants her feet, the angle of her

6

shoulders, the thin smile that splits her face—she stands apart from her kin, possessed of troubling intelligence and burning calm.

I must watch myself. I will power into the enruned jewelry I wear on my wrist and neck, reach into the wards that surround her and check my defenses for any fault. My magics keep both of us safe, in a way: even as it contains her, the summoning circle is its own hellish terrarium, a slice of the infernal realm demons are yanked from. Without it or a binding to anchor her to this reality, a demon will burn away like fog before a rising sun.

This one, though—if she were to break free, I am certain she could rip my heart out before vanishing back to nothing.

The demon stops her pacing, seemingly satisfied with her cage. "And no. A dungeon would be ill-suited for someone of your standing, Ms. Hua." I thrill as she says my name—but she looks past me, gold eyes flitting across the massive windows that surround us. "This place is beautiful, if a little Nordic. Wintry."

Twenty-eight stories up, this should be an impressive view of the Hong Kong skyline. Instead, we look out over a scene of driving snow—the glass serves as a portal to a barren Antarctic escarpment. One creates the landscape one wishes to inhabit; sometimes I step through and, in the moments I have before my body succumbs to frostbite and death, find calm in the desolation.

She turns back to me, her faint, thin-lipped smile giving her expression a sardonic edge. "Why am I here?"

"To make a bargain, of course. I learned of a great weapon that the thaumaturge Cecilie Kristiansen found but locked away. Anything that scares her, I want."

"Ah." Something shifts in her eyes. "Your nemesis thought she had found something worth possessing, too. She was… disabused of the notion soon enough, and dispelled me in time. You must have gone through great effort to secure my True Name."

"You're a remarkably surly demon, for someone who is negotiating a partnership with the warlock of her age."

"Which is it, possession or partnership?" Her words taste of ash and petrichor, the charge in the air before a rain of fire. "A sword can be either, but the distinction matters to me."

I smile, magnanimous. "I understand you killed Kristiansen's first protege, Tristan Philipe. Is that right?"

"He grabbed the wrong end of the sword," she says with a dry chuckle; my body heats from the noise, the unaffected confidence. "A complete sadist. He wanted to impress and intimidate people with his kill count; I disagreed, and made him part of mine."

"Then help me add Cecilie Kristiansen to that sum, too." The pleasantries are over; the time of binding is at hand.

The demon stops and stares at me, the shadows around her stilling, as if in thought. Finally, she replies, "I tire of being a weapon, warlock; I have lost my taste for blood. I politely decline."

"The night is young and we have much to discuss, ███ ██ ██." I use her True Name again, impossible consonants that rip at reality and tear at the tongue.

This time she stumbles, as if hit with a hammer, and when she rights herself, she smiles with her fangs. "You shouldn't have done that."

A binding is as much a negotiation as it is a contest of wills; to threaten her so overtly was an escalation, but she needs to know my mettle. I flash my bloody teeth back.

I see Yves place her hand against the magic wards, but I *feel* her will run up against mine, testing me, eldritch power washing over pewter and rune and incantation. Powerful, but I am a greater warlock yet; my defenses hold without effort.

The demon does not seem perturbed. "You have made," she says, very slowly, keeping her hand raised, the lightest touch against my barriers, "one critical error. Your nemesis had hoped to use me against you. In our time together, she shared with me those secrets of yours that she had gleaned. To acquire them, she consorted with far darker powers than I, seers that read the past in newborn blood and witches that feast on the flesh of kin. I know far more of you and your life than you might think. Your strengths, your weaknesses, the nature and texture of your life. All the tiny facets that go into an identity, meticulously gathered by an enemy who wants to see you completely and irrevocably undone."

My blood runs cold. "Wait—"

"What I'm trying to say is that I know your True Name, Xinyu Hua."

My Name doesn't rend the air like Yves'. It doesn't throw me back, or bruise my face, or make me spit blood. It's so much worse. It feels like the sun on my face, during that last picnic. It sounds like the whoop of triumph, that first summoning. It tastes like the long loneliness of each night.

My birth name is not a closely guarded secret, easily enough found after an afternoon's research; I choose to do business as Viveca out of personal preference, not obfuscation. But it isn't the Name that holds the power, it's the *knowing*, and this demon speaks true—and with that knowledge comes power, if only for a moment, over myself and my works.

The wards shatter.

I scream out with every ounce of power I can wield, lash at her with word and will, but her hand is around my throat before I can finish. She lifts me up and back, driving me against the glass windows, and then through them. We explode out of the building—not to a twenty-story fall to the pavement below, but into the ice and fury of an Antarctic waste in storm.

"I told you," the demon growls, pinning me beneath her, hand still around my neck; her voice is colder than the gale we have tumbled into. "I told you that I would not be your weapon. You should have listened."

In this place, nature abhors us both equally, and we are each unmade. Yves is already eroding, her demonic nature unmoored and antithetical to the stuff of reality; existence tears at her edges. As for me—well, a human body was not meant to be propelled through a sheet of magically fortified glass into a subzero hellscape. An arm is bent beneath me and blood dribbles from my mouth; from the corner of my eye, I can see the snow, red like a bed of velvet.

Between the cold and my wounds, I'll be dead in a minute, two tops. Enough time to negotiate.

"Yves, you won't die here. But you will disintegrate, and then my homunculus will destroy every shred of your existence. No knowledge of you will survive its wrath—it will be as if you were never born, and no human will remember your name."

"You know that isn't how it works," the demon says. "True Names return to the world; I will be summoned again." The tie around her neck is caught in the storm, dissolving like a dandelion on the wind.

"Of course." I can no longer feel the ice beneath me. "In what, a thousand years? Ten thousand?"

"Time means nothing to one such as I."

When I smile, the frozen blood at the corner of my mouth cracks. "But it matters to Cecilie Kristiansen."

Her eyes flicker, and I drive home my advantage. "She killed my mother, Yves. I don't know what she did to you, but I know what she is capable of. This is your one chance for vengeance. We can kill her togeth—"

"Terms, warlock. *Terms.*" Her voice is fraying, and mine is gone; when I try to reply, I cannot push air from my lungs. When I realize what has happened, I cannot even laugh: my heart has stopped.

Warmth suffuses my neck, reaching down into my chest. Whatever power Yves yet retains over the physical world, she has poured it into restoring me to life, if only for a moment. "If I take my hand from your throat, you die." It isn't a threat, or even a statement of fact, but an entreaty. "For both our sakes, lay out your terms or never speak again."

"No weapon, Yves. I need armor. Stand by my side in battle, protect me from harm, swear that you will guard me and mine. Help me kill Kristiansen. Otherwise, you are free to do anything else, travel through the world as you see fit, anchored to me for as long as I might live."

It is poorly worded, lacking in the specificity we would otherwise each demand; we will simply have to trust the other, or twist the pact to our own selfish ends when the need arises.

"I accept. Seal it in blood."

I chuckle, mirthless; what I have already spilt is frozen solid, and I have no more to give. A contract failed, for lack of ink; as these things go, it's a fitting end.

Yves looks down at me, a shadow in driving snow, and it is only now, at the end of my life, that I do not feel alone: all that remains of me, held in the hand of someone that knows my name, completely. *What a thing we could have built*, I think. *What a waste.*

She pulls me to her, and our lips meet. Her touch is impossibly soft, warm, the gentle heat of laundry dried in the sun. And her taste! Like shadow, like victory, like blood—

Blood.

The last vestige of her warmth melts the blood frozen to my lips, the iron tang filling both our mouths. And then there is not warmth but *heat*, harsh and intoxicating, radiating out into every limb. I cry out in the pain of life restored, but I do not pull away; I drink deeper, feeling her become corporeal atop me. Hale and firm, her body wraps around mine; she holds me as my broken arm violently mends, as my lungs burn with the cold air.

And still I drink, my tongue finding hers, my hands running down her neck, my nails clawing at her back. It feels, for a moment, like we are pouring into each other, lashing ourselves together. Binding each other, more intimately than I have ever known before.

After what feels like an eternity, we pull apart. Yves kneels before me—apparently solid, but the snow that lands on her doesn't stick so much as disappear, as if she was less a thing and more a hole in reality, threatening to consume all she comes in touch with. I must watch myself with her, I remind myself, more than ever.

For my part, I am restored. Not even the cold can hurt me now; I feel as if I am wrapped in the most gentle of blankets. And I can feel Yves, too—sense where she is beyond just sight or touch, a gentle pressure on the psyche that I know will always point toward her. It is... discomfiting.

"I have been bound to items before," she says, as if reading my thoughts. "Never a person. This will take some getting used to."

Then something catches her attention, as if she has suddenly tasted poison on the wind. She cocks her head, staring at me hard, golden eyes unblinking. "You deceived me."

I smile back. "Whatever do you mean?"

"You... you were never in any danger, were you? You baited me into forging a pact with you."

"If it's any consolation, my heart really *did* stop. But it does that on occasion; I have many contingencies to avoid a more permanent expiration." It's not a lie, but it's a bit of a bluff, too—I do have pacts with other entities, and there are contingencies for my eventual physical death. But when that day comes, the price for those agreements will be high, and today's adventure was a close thing, closer than I'd like to admit.

On the other hand—I do love to be underestimated, and she underestimated me a hair more than she ought to have; she will not do so again, but what's done is done. "And it's not as if you were exploited," I continue. "The terms of the covenant are remarkably generous. Let's just call it the first test of your dedication, hmm?"

I don't wait to see how she responds; I pull myself up and march back toward my office window, still suspended in space; through it, I can see Antarctic snow melting in Hong Kong light. "Come along now," I call over my shoulder. "We do have an enemy thaumaturge to kill."

Two: The Sorceress and Her Tiger

OLESYA

Attending the auction is an obligation I could not refuse without insulting certain people, and my existence as a Hua is already insult enough; my powers are not what they once were, and I must keep my few allies happy. But for all the touted uniqueness of this event, I have not been impressed—the conversation is droll, this year's fashions even droller, the wares forgettable. I wish my sister Viveca were here; at least then I could voice my commentary.

Onstage, the first two items wheeled out are a gazelle and a swan, prey animals both; weak and insipid. Caged, too—unnecessary, I would think, but I have heard that swans can be murderous. In neither can I glimpse any sort of sapience; I wonder how they have been forced to stay in animal forms—drugs, perhaps, or arcane items, alloy acupuncture cleverly hidden—or if they are really wereanimals at all.

The received wisdom is that wereanimal parts confer all sorts of virtues (or vices), that some of them can guide you to the world's mysteries; any rumor you can think of, one has sprung up around shapeshifters. It's a lucrative market, hunting things that look human but are not quite; mages like to imagine themselves as just one potion away from obtaining the swiftness of a gazelle or a… I'm not quite certain what a swan would confer. Obstinacy and an unhealthy love of bread? But the common wisdom has some truth to it: wereanimals are often centuries old, their very names ringing with promise—vessels of power, excellent reagents for certain rites.

I sip the provided wine—my alchemist Chang'er has checked it for poisons and curses—and attempt to appreciate it. Very vintage. Red, though, where I prefer white. That surprises most people.

"You're not having a good time, Ms. Olesya," says Chang'er, a little amused. Few look at her and think alchemist: too sleek, too much like a fox, none of the mustiness most associate with someone who spends all day with mortar and pestle and alembics. It can take a lot of arguments to even convince people she's entirely human—there's something of the deep forest in her gaze, the canopied depths in her voice. Before she came into my employ, it was said that she had a cannibal habit, with an especial taste for livers.

I nod at her. "Do either of them strike your fancy?" She likes being spoiled, and I can afford to indulge a woman who's both my alchemist and bedmate.

"No." She sniffs. "Most of what they say about wereanimals is superstition, you know. Besides, I don't want you to purchase some pretty fawn of a girl and give her all your attention."

"You'll always have my attention." I cup the back of her head, stroking the fine hairs at the base of her skull. She closes her eyes and nearly purrs. Most alchemists are the glum sort; Chang'er is anything but, though she can shade into petulance if she thinks another woman has caught my eye.

I'm thinking of leaving when the third item is wheeled onstage.

Contained, like the rest, but in a cage that looks even sturdier than the others: thicker bars, stronger base, and much larger. The monitor gives me an up-close look, such that I can delineate every tuft of fur. They've cleaned her up, but there are gouges under the striped, gleaming coat; there are marks of a battle hard-fought. Her eyes are this peculiar, harsh green that cannot be found in any human.

She is a tiger of unparalleled beauty, crowned with a majesty exclusive to queens and apex predators. I wonder how many she took down before she was captured; how many bodies she crunched in that powerful jaw. I want to see her teeth.

My fingers tap lightly on the touchscreen.

Next to me, Chang'er makes a face. "Really, Ms. Olesya?"

"Maybe I want to harvest her for parts."

The alchemist's pout is very pretty. It's an art form she has perfected,

14

almost more than alchemy. "We know you're not going to do that. She's too expensive."

I win the bid without effort.

My warlock sister is a specialist in rituals of containment, and it's in one of the chambers she has built for me that I have placed my new purchase.

Outsiders believe that practitioners are unable to touch technology, or that our proximity alone breaks their circuits, as though our existence is an electromagnetic disruption. We've let the notion lie; the more we're underestimated, the better. And what we have built here, my sister and I, is a fine blend of magic and technology, designed to contain the dangerous and the beautiful.

My prize is both.

On the CCTV, the tiger—now a woman—is eerily still on her bunk bed, gaze steady and straight on, not in the way of resignation or defeat but in *patience.* I would have expected a tiger to be bulkier in human form, but the way she occupies space is more length than breadth, defying the conservation of mass. Long-limbed, long-backed; I imagine her spine would be a sinuous thing, a curve into which I can fit my hand when I press into her skin the ink that'll bind her against doing me harm.

When the tiger arrived, I found her hide pierced by dozens of tiny needles, the method by which the auctioneers kept her contained. I removed them one by one with gloved fingers. Chang'er was muttering that the tiger would eat me whole.

"You're not going in there, are you?" my alchemist says through my earpiece. I can almost hear her moue.

"It is rude to keep a guest waiting."

"Don't come crying to me, Ms. Olesya, when that creature mauls you right open."

The door unlocks at my authentication. I shut it behind me.

Inside, the air is frigid. Viveca's work will keep the tiger weak, but her penchant for cold gets a little much. My guest does not seem greatly bothered by the temperature; she has put on the provided trousers but lies on her back bare-chested. Nudity probably doesn't mean much to her.

"What kind are you?" she asks, without getting up or even looking at me.

I spread my hands wide. "You'll need to be more specific than that."

"They told me who bought me," she replies, still watching the ceiling. "I've heard your name before, out in the city. For some reason, I thought you'd be… older."

"Well, do go on. Feel free to continue your frank assessment."

Now she sits up. Even in this form her gaze is lambent, her mouth unexpectedly quirked. She looks me over, thoughtful; despite the imbalance in our power—me the captor, her the half-naked captive—I feel as if I'm being put under the scalpel, exact incisions made into the crux of me.

"I think," she says, "that you look hungry."

Heat coils in my stomach, near-instantaneous. I have never *quite* been seen through like this. I step a little closer. "Your name?"

"Dallas Seidel."

"Like the city."

"Sure." She shrugs, light, as if it were just as likely that the city was named after her. "What do you want with me?"

Now it is my turn to study her, more than I already have. For all that she is slender, there's muscle to her—her stomach is hard, not the ladder of ribs one might expect; her breasts are small and inviting, and what I can see of her narrow hips intrigues me. Atop her head, wild hair as dark as her stripes, except where light gathers and makes it shine an impossible gold.

"What if I tell you I don't want anything?" I suggest.

"Then you'd be lying." Said quickly, easily, by a complete stranger.

Faintly I imagine sinking my hand into her black-and-gold mane. The texture looks so luxuriant, for all that she needs a haircut and a haircare routine. Perhaps I can persuade her to let me brush it. "I saw you on the stage. A creature like you shouldn't be held in a cage."

She snorts. "Well, in *that*, we agree." In both her forms, she moves with grace and purpose. She begins to pull on a shirt; her back is a work of art, sculpted planes and sharp geometry, tightly gathered muscles. "The flesh

16

market—I plan to kill everyone involved. Am I to count you among that number, or will you stand aside?"

It is my turn to snort. "You have remarkable confidence, for someone who started the day in one cage, and is ending the day in another."

"Ah, the mercy of cages," Dallas growls, so low the air seems to tremble; she has turned back just enough to fix me with one jade eye. "How readily they make mortal men feel *safe*."

Despite all my training and power, I am still a woman, still flesh and blood—some atavistic part of me freezes in place, torn between disabling fear and overwhelming arousal. An image seizes me, of her crushing me in her jaws.

And then she flounces back onto the bed, cool and collected, a detached smile on her lips. Mercurial like a cat, or the performative predation of an apex hunter; I should not be drawn into fascination. "Eight guards, give or take, conventionally armed. Two mages among them, including a naga. And I'll remember the scent of the warehouse when I am at the docks."

"You *let* yourself be captured." There is admiration in my voice.

She looks very satisfied, to be recognized so. "It's a good way to get the measure of a place. Or a person."

I think to ask her, *And what could you have learned about me in this short a time?* Instead, I answer the question she has asked of me: "I will not keep you here, but I am not stepping aside, either—I'm joining you on this hunt."

This, finally, genuinely startles her. "I'll pretend that is a serious proposal. What will you ask of me in recompense?"

"That you accept a binding." I hold up a vial of ink, blue-black, the shade of hadopelagic depths. "It spells out a promise that you cannot harm me or mine, and lasts for a year. That's it; you are free to do anything else. After I've put this on you, we leave this room together."

Her stare goes on a little longer, unblinking. "I'd accept, but that isn't what you *really* want."

"I—" My cheeks color slightly. "Explain."

"If you wanted safety, you'd get a nice little kitten; if you wanted a leash, you'd get a trained dog. I think you *want* to be bitten. So let me: I will take your blood," she says, as casually as she might ask me for water or tea, "and you will have my loyalty."

My mouth widens into a smile. Oh, if she thought this would fluster me. "As you like."

Another flicker of surprise, but she hardly misses a beat. "From where would you prefer?"

Now I'm grinning, showing her my teeth. "Can you manage a thigh without hitting an artery?"

"I have the incisors of a surgeon."

Which does not actually make sense, but I accept the assertion in the spirit it is meant. I join her on the bed. There is every chance that she *will* penetrate an artery and I'll die here of hemorrhage, barring Chang'er rushing in with help and an I-told-you-so. But I like to think I am a fair judge of character, and Dallas strikes me as honorable in her own fashion.

They say that tigers owe a debt to the one who's freed them from their chains. They say that blood makes an unbreakable oath.

I hike my skirt up, not far, above my knee. A modest distance.

Dallas says, "Higher."

A dare. I oblige, lifting the fabric until it is nearly up to my waist, raising an eyebrow at her. "Normally I make women wine and dine me first."

"They weren't tigers, were they? It seems," she adds, bold, "that I'll be your first in that regard."

Her head lowers. Her breath grazes my knee. She inhales deeply, as though she means to gather all that I am into her lungs, until my scent is a permanent part of her memory. She licks and I discover that, while her tongue is not as rough as a cat's, it is more so than any human's.

Dallas pierces skin. Pain flares, then slows to an even throb. The wound cannot be so large, and yet when she descends to it, it feels enormous. Her golden head brushes against me, and I cannot help myself; I run a hand through her mane, eagerly confirming that her hair is a delight of texture, finer to the touch than any silk.

She parts my legs a little wider as she sucks. I grip at her shoulders, conscious that a tiger's instincts may drive her to tear out actual flesh, telling

18

myself that I am holding her back to keep myself safe, not pulling her closer
to—

But she is able to restrain herself; her mouth latches on, catching every
drop, but does no more. Very gently, she runs her tongue along the wounds.

When she's finished, her head rises, her gaze meeting mine. Her eyes and
lips are bright, and her breathing fast.

So is mine. I smell my own blood, but underneath that there's something
else—a tiger's musk, earthy. The punctures have already closed. I cover
myself up, smoothing out my skirt. "Does that suffice?"

"Yes." She licks her lips. Her nipples are hard little points against the white
shirt. "You heal fast."

"Personal protection. It deals with scratches." It deals with more than that,
but no point revealing all my secrets. "Now let us get you dressed properly
and fed. We have a long night ahead of us."

The meat plated before Dallas is variously beef and pork, all of it raw. She
declined the wagyu I have in stock, citing that it is too soft, too fatty. I
half-expected her to dig into her dinner with her hands, but she keeps to the
civility of utensils. It is an interesting spectacle, to watch the raw proteins
seep and puddle, and then to watch her spoon up even the blood: this is a
woman who doesn't like to waste.

For myself I have nothing but jasmine tea, warm and diluted. Attempting
anything more substantial while Dallas carves through kilograms of meat is
too much, even for me.

Halfway through demolishing the meal, she pauses to say, "I figured out
what kind you are." The category of practitioner, she means—the very first
question she asked me, when I stepped into her cell.

"Oh?"

"You're the woman mages hire when they want to kill other mages. I've
been wondering how you have gotten away doing that year after year, and
with what appears to be a high success rate too." She puts down her fork.
"There's something in your blood, isn't there?"

"I'm afraid the secret to my success is that I have very good snipers." Hand-picked, loyalty fostered over years. They are nearly extensions of me.

"What kind of ammo do they use?"

I laugh. "Rifle rounds. What else? You can't possibly think I dip every bullet in my blood before sending them out."

"It took a lot of self-discipline," she says, holding my gaze, "not to take more from you than I said I would."

So far she has not even glared at me threateningly. Tame as a domesticated cat, or putting up a good pretense. "I must be especially delicious."

"A forest of tigresses would fight to close their jaws around you. Your taste is… potent, like light—like how you think warmth and summer days should feel." Her face darkens. "And shadow, too, like poison and occultation."

My jaw clenches tight, impotent fury ill-contained. This, I did not want a stranger to know. Even my sister is ignorant—how dare this tiger see so much, and how dare she speak of it. "Ah. So you can taste that, too."

She stares at me, hard, like she is hunting for a wound in my flesh, trying to find what is wrong with me. I feel naked before her; I have known this beast for only hours, but to her I am as glass, transparent under her forest gaze.

"I don't know," I finally admit. I try to keep my voice light, even wryly detached. One day I was hale. The next I was not. The vector of contagion, the mechanisms of it, whether it targeted me specifically: all of these remain mysteries. "A wasting disease of sorcery, it seems—a curse that feasts on my magic when I draw it out." Feast it does. It is consuming me, this affliction—slow when I do not use my magic, fast as wildfire when I do. "Only my alchemist knows of my unique ailment, so I would appreciate you keeping this to yourself."

She starts to say something, and I cut her off. "Enough of your flattery." I motion to the wall-mounted monitor. "You've already earned your dessert."

On the screen, a view comes to life, visual and audio both clear—a result of mixing scrying and conventional cameras. A dark alleyway: a man is emerging from the back entrance of a club, lit in red neons. The asphalt gleams from a fresh, warm rain.

Dallas draws herself straight. She recognizes him—but of course she would, he was one of the hunters who captured her. I wait for her fangs to come out, for the tiger to emerge piecemeal. This doesn't happen; her control must be iron. Hard-earned, perhaps.

The man in the monitor takes a step, looks around, lights a cigarette. The cinderous point of it is like a demon's eye.

It is also like the red laser dot that appears on his temple, a few seconds later.

One shot. He drops. Mages can be difficult to kill—most have woven into what they wear, or into their bodies, armor against mortality. They can take terrible gut wounds, even head injuries and bullets. A conventional sharpshooter would need to fire twice, thrice—or more—if they want to end the mage before the mage can come end them.

The rounds my personnel use are made differently, though. A single bullet, aimed well, typically does the job. I did not lie to Dallas: I don't dip the ammo in my blood. It's more a matter of anointing them in the *concept* of what I carry, of infecting them. Subdividing your vitality is a draining matter and shortens the lifespan. Transmuting it into something more like a contagion, and the process turns much easier, is less demanding on my body, becomes a materiel that I can use.

"Each kill," Dallas says slowly, "what does it take out of you?"

"Less than you think."

Her brow furrows. "What is your life expectancy?" It is as if the man on the screen is already forgotten, and her only concern is me.

"More than you think. The curse in my veins is nullified by… certain processes." Overseen primarily by Chang'er, by the fact that I use magic as little as possible, by the restorative techniques I've learned—teeth gritted, furious that I have to—over the years. "What's released in the world is not subjected to such constraints."

"But this is not how you should be," she says. "You are a woman made to burn bright."

I shrug, feigning acceptance. "I've gotten most of what I wanted out of magic." My body, to be specific. I finished reshaping it in my early twenties, well before the curse came along. What good fortune, I keep telling myself. How much worse it could have been, to be imprisoned not just within this affliction but by the vagaries of my birth.

"I hear," she says dryly, "that the heart and brains of a tiger can confer immortality."

"I have no need of it. I'll live out the terms given to me, or I'll break them with my own hands. You're too handsome to cannibalize." A thought my sister would disagree with: if she finds a demon who can give her immortality, she would strike a deal without hesitation. Warlocks are a different breed, but then she was the one to inherit our mother's mantle, with my full support—I never wanted the weight of that particular crown, and these days I have forged myself into a different sort of weapon, to spread a different sort of fear. Fear: it'll protect you until it no longer does.

"All right," says the tiger. "I'm in. We will see what happens afterward." She cocks her head in sudden thought. "But why did you kill just the one hunter?"

"Dallas, haven't you ever scared your quarry back to its den, the easier to slay the whole damn pack?"

The surprise with which she looks at me is priceless.

We're coming through the door of the warehouse when a half dozen mooks open fire.

There is a precise art to disrupting the trajectory of a bullet. It travels so fast that it leaves behind the sound of its own discharge; you will be dead before you finish hearing it.

Of course, spells exist with comparable penetrative force, without the hassle of carrying a firearm. But guns are such a convenient tool that modern mages employ them freely; let it never be said that non-practitioners have never invented anything useful. Such a simple instrument, but terrifying in its potency and its finality. Once a bullet leaves a muzzle, there's not much you can do to prevent its impact; you cannot rely on eyes or ears—both are too slow.

Two options remain: erect a barrier of such resilience that it can absorb and deflect the bullet's force, or create one that nullifies vectors beyond a certain speed within your radius. Nothing reaches you, that way. My mother favored the first, but the latter is my preferred method.

Dallas is already on the move. The golden vector of her cuts through the lavish dining room, opening crucial seams: the throats, the stomachs, the femoral arteries. The rank, dark fluids of the human system spill in her wake.

I follow up with exacting, surgical lines of force. One must take care, with a body like mine, to expend power in the most efficient manner possible. Inside me, the curse blooms. It pulls my gut tight. It clenches, a vise, around my heart. For me, to use magic is to tempt fate; it is to invite agony. But magic is the moment when I feel alive. It is the moment when colors return to my world.

But I'm used to it. I'm used to moving past the knowledge that I am inching a little closer to my end. And violence grants me an outlet. The poachers and sellers of the flesh market didn't expect it, either—the mage-killer rarely leaves her lair, delegating violence to hired help. I am not a face most anticipate in public, let alone doing my own wetwork. All the same, I take satisfaction. One day it'll be one outing too many; for now my fortune and my physique hold, and the curse will not yet breach the line.

And so today, the bullets fall at our feet, harmless as pebbles. Noiseless, because the carpet is so plush, so luxurious that it's swallowed up all sound save the gunshots. The tiger lifts her paw from a throat, the movement almost delicate. She rises, and becomes a woman once more, nude and wearing the gore like a rich, savory suit.

Around us, the dead are still.

"I can smell your mortality's edge," says Dallas, no tact, no diplomacy.

"How dare you, when I have so effortlessly vanquished our enemies." Sometimes I wonder whether I might have been the sorceress of my age, but the back of my mouth is burning—the sour, vile taste I get then the curse flares up, acid bubbling up my esophagus. I don't allow it to stagger me. I do not permit myself any outward sign.

But she can see, or scent; tiger senses must be many times more granular than human. She reaches for me, then draws back; self-conscious, perhaps, that she's about to stain my clothes. "You did not have to do this—to come personally, to test the bounds of your affliction."

How do I explain to her what it is like to sit in my estate day in, day out, as outside my walls the world moves on without me? How do I tell her that without the curse I could have been my sister's equal, practicing in my own field and honored for it? In the afterglow of combat, adrenaline still pounding, my affected detachment slips. "Tell me how it'd feel if you've been forced to stay in your human form for years. Would it chafe?"

"It'd drive me to insanity. I—"

I sweep my hand across the corpses. "Have we got them all, the hunters who wronged you?"

She barely looks at them—she'll already have counted them off by smell and visceral certainty. "Yes."

Victory intoxicates, every time—it affirms to me that I remain capable, that I may still assert myself upon the balance of things. When we were young, that's what Viveca and I talked about with children's solemnity: who will make a mark on the world more, the warlock or the sorceress?

We return to my stronghold clothed in our enemies' blood.

Strange that a sense of *our* can so swiftly cohere. Dallas trots by me, once more on four legs, as we enter the estate grounds.

Chang'er fusses over me as we come in. She is a little angry, and she pointedly ignores the enormous beast at my side. "You didn't have to go to the frontline *yourself*."

But the truth is that I am uninjured, not even a scratch. Supporting fire from my snipers, yes; more than that though, it was because Dallas as much avenged herself as put her body between me and harm. "I am fine." I bend to kiss my alchemist on the mouth, careful not to get gore in her hair. "Come to my room tonight."

She scowls at the tiger, and when she tiptoes to kiss me back, she bites, as if to remind everyone present who has the prior claim.

Dallas, like any housecat, follows me into the shower. It is there that she retakes her other form, and watching the quicksilver matter of her flow and shape into bipedalism is an intriguing sight. She kneels before me, naked and wild and gorgeous. Blinks as water gets in her eyes before she draws to her full height. "Did you do all that so I would be in your debt, sorceress?"

"To what end, tiger?"

"Practitioners always have a motive." Her head cocks. "What do you really want?"

I touch the side of her neck—she does not flinch from the contact—and once more enjoys the texture of her hair. There's so much of it, an endless mane. "I told you. A being like you should not be in a cage."

She fetches the soap bar from its marble holder. "And you—are you in a cage, Olesya?"

My affliction is a chain that binds my every waking moment, a shackle that keeps me prey, weak and insipid. Less of me, each time I breathe; less of me, each time I weave my magic.

But I'm less frank with my next words. I don't want to be that transparent, to admit that at the auction, sympathy drove me. The mage-killer experiences no such emotion. "The world itself is composed of prison bars. That's what most mages seek—to escape its perimeter, to seek what lies beyond."

"It's not an answer." But she shrugs, relenting. "Does your alchemist have something against tigers?"

I relax. "She has something against butches, and she's possessive."

"I don't mind sharing."

I snatch the soap from her. "Who said there's anything you get to share with Chang'er?"

"You fed me. We fought together, and you went above and beyond. I owe you much. But what we did is as good as a courtship ritual for tigers, and—unless your feelings have changed in the last few hours—I have been able to smell your intention from the start."

She is so simple, so frank. I can't help laughing. "Then you're staying with me—the mage-killer, the scourge of polite arcane society."

"Then stay I will. Why would I care about sorcerer mores?" Her eyes take in the whole of me, and now her expression changes, darkening to a hunger that matches my own. Her hand, wet and very warm, slides up my hip; she leans over, her mouth at my earlobe—the same mouth that, not so long ago, ripped flesh apart and splintered bones. "But first," she growls, "I'm going to finish what I started, Olesya. How much do you like teeth?"

I wind my arm around her neck, pushing her toward the cold, wet wall. The negotiation has reached its immediate conclusion. Down the line, the terms may alter and solidify. In the meantime, we are about to mark each other—in more ways than one.

"Oh," I say, cradling her hardening length in my hand, "we're going to get along. Bite as much as you like, Dallas."

Interlude: The Heirs of the House of Hua

TO: Sealing and Containment, Analytics Department

SUBJECT: The Hua Family, In Legend and Truth

As a condition of my continued employment at Shenzhen University, I have been tasked with aiding S&C's efforts in compiling a history of the Hua lineage. Under duress, please find attached my report on the matter.

Unlike some families of renown, the Huas do not shade themselves with cadet branches; their name winds through history like a singularly resilient vine or a lonesome snake. Each generation has two offspring at most, and between them there is only ever the one heir. It follows, then, that even as the Hua name has grown in renown, the Hua powerbase has stayed rooted in the personal, prone to misfortune and upset, and the Huas themselves are unfailingly singular figures, often alone, often pitched against a world hostile to their desires.

This lends itself to an air of the heroic, even the melodramatic. I have done my best to capture that element in this report—neither a conventional biography nor a history, but a romance to be contrasted against the records. I think this is the only way to get at the unblemished truth at the heart of these legends, the solitary fact that unites these lies of triumph and woe: in their time, each Hua is presented with a choice, a great and impossible question—and each time, they have answered correctly.

- Professor al-Kattan, Dept. of Theory and Epistemology, Shenzhen University

The first recorded warlock who would come to take the name Hua was said to be a queen.

She was not born into the idea of thrones, with her hands grasping at a future of scepters. Rather she strode into the court of a prince, who may or may not have been just, and said, "Your house is henceforward my house, and your treasury my treasury."

The prince's army roused with blades and arrows. She turned the first to slag, the second to kindling. In time she'd be called a tyrant, but she was practical: she offered continued life to all who would surrender. But that was before the fame of her family took root, and so to a man they fought to the last.

In the aftermath, she stood over the corpses and the blood. She did not regret. It was precisely slaughter of this scale that she required. With the tools she brought, she arranged the bodies, made use of the gore. Such excess should not go to waste.

She spoke her incantations. She invoked a True Name. Her mouth blistered in the pronunciation of it.

The prince's corpse juddered and listed this way and that, a puppet under the hand of a poor puppeteer. She spoke the name again, and blood seeped from her mouth and eyes. This time the corpse split, disgorging from its bones and tissue a thing that had no resemblance to man—

—a vastness of geometry, in form resembling no living thing ever born of this earth. It filled the prince's bloodied throne room; it outsized his palace, half-corporeal, occupying dimensions beyond the one of flesh and linear temporality. The creature held in its breath the cold of forever.

You have committed a great offense, it told the warlock, the first Hua.

"You were observing our world as this prince, but it must have gotten dull for you, watching the coming and going of witless courtiers. What if I propose something more interesting?" She smiled and wiped her blood from her own face, extending a hand gloved crimson.

Eldritch depths hovered close, sleeking through the air, but did not bend to taste. *What could a creature as transient as you offer a being such as me?*

"I have heard," she said, "that you came to this world not out of boredom or in search of novelty, but to monitor a being whose existence itself pushes against yours like thorns, and whose emanations bleed through our world into yours."

The demon that took the prince's form lowered its head. *And what of this being?*

"We can declare a contract, with clauses and terms as specific as please both of us. But the substance of it will be this: if you work with me, I and my heirs will take care of your anathema, by binding it to dim its light so its fire can no longer singe you, and in time destroying it completely."

You believe a thing such as you, as weak and brief as mayflies to my kind, have the reach and might to suppress our enemy.

"What we lack in longevity," said Hua, "we make up for in ingenuity and speed of innovation. How else did I force you out of that carcass?"

The being stayed inert for several moments more. Weighing the facts, the potential. *Declare your terms, and we will see if we can forge a covenant that suits both our purposes. What is it that you desire, warlock?*

She nudged one of the bodies with her foot, idle, in thought. "Very simple, demon. I'm not after immortality for myself, or unimaginable wealth, or even unmatched might. I want my line to endure. I want a legacy that weathers countless generations."

The third Hua warlock was said to have delved deep beneath the earth, arriving at a secret armory of fire the color of gold and pearl. She had won the map that pointed there, solved the puzzle of its cartography; she had wrested the key from a general of the infernal realms. Of her own familiars, none had come with her—the succubi and imps, the hellhounds and eldritch beasts. There was a light, here, that they could not bear, a brilliance that lashed at their substance, that dissolved it from this world despite the anchors put in place by the warlock.

But she knew this already. She knew that, to uphold an ancient contract, whatever she faced here she would have to do so alone. She knew, too, that she had ensured her successor—both ends of that old promise would be kept.

Perhaps she would die here, but her line would endure.

She, who often had to ward herself against the cold and grasping dark, now warded herself against the hot and hungry bright.

Everything within the armory was the strongest steel that could be tempered, the best that this place's wardens could have forged. Thick, strong bars to cage the object at the heart of it all—a slim white blade, whose metal itself had begun to melt, fusing to the plinth on which it rested.

All around the cage, the wardens lay dead, their skin cauterized and their skeletons blackened. She was the first living human to set foot there in what must have been months. The thing within the sword was in the process, slow but inexorable, of breaking free.

She touched her fingertips to the cage. The heat threatened to scorch, to sear the flesh from her bones.

You serve one of my enemies, hissed the being within. *If you think you can stop me here, then you've overreached yourself more than any of my jailors.*

"That is because they have bound you in the most rudimentary of manners. Really, they could have come to consult me. People always think they can do *so* much better than warlocks." She drew her hand away; not a centimeter of her was burned. "We've spent generations looking for you. It is fortunate that all the forces and denizens of hell hate you desperately."

The brilliance, growing more blinding by the moment, pulsed and sang. *Then let me be. I despise the coarseness of this realm. I have long wished to return to the silver arches and ivory trees of my nativity.*

"But that won't do, will it? Once you're back there and have healed, you will descend again to smite and incinerate. And you consider my family accomplices to your foes, and so my heirs down the line will have to deal with you in the fullness of your might. You must understand," said the warlock, "that I would rather not have that."

You do not have what is required to pin me to this world.

But the Hua only laughed. "In that you are wrong. I have brought my greatest tool: myself."

By the time she was done, there remained in the cage a single white sword, whole. The heat had cooled, the light dimmed. There was no body: human flesh was not made to withstand so much, even warded as hers had been.

And a few years later, the next Hua would come of age and arrive to take custody of the weapon, and what had been sealed within it.

The sixth Hua sired a child pallid of flesh and brittle of bone, born under the cursed light of a blood moon. The warlock thought to dash her progeny to the rocks below, hated herself for it, thought again of the price she would pay for a child hale and sound.

"An easy offer, easily made," came a voice from the tree line, deep and rich like a vein of gold. Eldritch the speaker was, and evil in the way of all predators.

"I have no need of deals this night," the Hua snapped.

"Your heir will die before the morning sun crests the ridge," the thing said.

The warlock stayed silent, furious at the truth this monster spoke.

"And your family has a burgeoning reputation for deals of great import with my kind. So consider this: rid yourself of this blight, and in its still-warm blood write a new compact. With my assistance, you may yet forge the heir your family deserves."

The Hua thought on this, and hated herself more with each moment; listened, with sadness, to the struggling breaths of her dying daughter. "The lifeblood of a Hua," she finally accepted, "for a child of great power and intelligence, who succeeds where her mother failed and surpasses all that came before her."

"On the condition that it is I, and no other, that carries your heir," the twisting monster agreed.

"The terms are acceptable," the warlock said through clenched jaw and with clenched fist.

"I'll give you the time you need," was the reply. "Find me in the woods when you are done."

"Oh, you needn't go too far," the sixth Hua said, and hurled herself from the cliff.

A noise of breaking bone and ruptured flesh below, and then a long silence.

"Ah," said the beast, staring at the child it was now sworn to carry to greatness. "This is very inconvenient."

The seventh Hua warlock grew up fast, under the tutelage of her surviving mother, a woman who came from a line of illusionists. The mother wore mourning clothes every day of her life. The young Hua did not ask about the clothes; she understood, from a young age, what her birth cost.

Her other teacher was the gold-voiced beast.

The girl first saw the creature in her nursery, a shimmering shadow limned in red. Sometimes it arrived as a human-shaped hole; more than once it warmed her limbs, returned breath to her lungs, ensured she would not perish in the night. Her remaining mother understood its purposes. Nevertheless, she gave it wide berth; she was not herself a warlock and grasped the contract as best she could, but she did not like that in place of her wife there was an entity from beyond raising her little girl.

By the age of three, the child had grown less weak, though she'd grown less human too: a pinpoint of red resided in each of her pupils. Her mother noted this, distrusted it, but she had no other option. She herself was a master of illusions and transfiguration, and neither art aided her in dealing with an eldritch nurse. All of the estate's demonic servitors had left with the previous Hua's demise; this one alone remained, bound to an oath that lasted beyond the warlock's death.

When the seventh Hua began to speak, precocious beyond her years, she asked the demon, "Should I call you my mother as well?"

The beast, four-legged at that time, did not respond at first. "I advised your warlock mother to throw you down a cliff, runt."

"Yes," she said, patient. "I already know that. So what is it that I ought to call you? Uttering your True Name is beyond me yet."

"I respond to your wails out of obligation, not parental affection. You would be wise to learn well what contracts mean, and give no more than you ought."

"So 'mother' it is," the seventh Hua said, "as we do not always get to pick our family, and no contract can contain all which we owe them."

The demon said, "I will not answer to that."

"Yet you must answer to *something*. I hear you are to make me great, such that I surpass all previous generations of Huas—even our first, the queen. When will that start?"

By the time she was ten, she was as hale as any child blessed from birth with vigor. She ran in the sun, under the watchful eye of her enchantress mother; she studied the archives that were her birthright, and listened when she was told which tomes were too dangerous for her, and must wait for when she was older, surer in her ability.

It was a time of peace that she was born into, and though her family was little trusted, mage society respected might more than it respected any other vice or virtue. The seventh Hua developed a face of sharp angles and cutting eyes. It did not invite softness from those who gazed upon her, but all agreed she was striking, and most polite company did not remark on the red pinpoints that'd settled deep in her pupils like embers.

Her first act of summoning was of a minor hellhound. Her second was a shifting mass that sometimes seemed a shark, other times a serpent. By every rubric, she had outpaced her warlock mother, and the other Hua warlocks before that. Still she was discontented. Greatness was prophesied for her, or at least promised. She wished to do more, to innovate, to bring to the arsenal of her family a new and hitherto untried technique.

And so of her demon mother she asked, "Teach me how to capture a part of hell and bring it to earth."

The beast's outline simmered and hazed. "That is beyond the accomplishment of a human—any human, no matter their hubris."

"Am I not meant to exceed the achievements of all my line?" She widened her eyes at her eldritch tutor. "And I have seen how you look at the dark depths of the ocean, and at the sky when fired with sunset. You have given much to me; let me bring a part of your home to you, if only for a time."

"The infernal realm will erode your body if you're exposed to it for even a heartbeat."

"If that is the case," the girl continued, "is my home not as painful to you, as yours would be to me?

"The weight of my pact crushes all other considerations," growled the beast. "The trick is focusing on something even more bothersome, like the chitter of a runt begging for knowledge beyond her ken."

"I'll have you know," the seventh Hua said, preening, "that I'm a runt no more—I won the school race by half a lap! The other girls look at me with trepidation and envy."

"Oh! Is that so?" The demon's affected disinterest slipped for a moment; they had an obligation to fulfill, and in their own way took great pride in the seventh Hua's achievements. "Fine. Then tell me more, as I gather the reagents."

"There's this girl—she has the prettiest brown eyes. I think she's afraid of me, a little, because of the family name. But I'd like to make friends." She chattered on about school, about the girl; about other families beginning to send overtures to her illusionist mother, well in advance. The seventh Hua was not yet of an age, but in a handful of years she would be.

By and by, over months, the demon taught her the secret of transporting to the mortal realm a fragment of inferno. The Hua braided and wove protections about herself, on her demon's instructions, to guard against each strain of ill that would corrode her life and flesh and breath.

Those first few attempts fizzled out. They frustrated her, who was used to success without effort. Still, she kept at it. She exercised the utmost care.

When finally she brought forth a part of her demon mother's home to this world, it did not last long. Mere seconds, then gone.

"Satisfied?" said the beast who'd seen her to greatness. "This is a feat no other mortal has ever managed."

The Hua said, "Your home—it's beautiful."

Her third parent was startled. "That's not a common human perception of it."

The girl laughed. "I'll make it last longer, next time."

Years passed. They always do; there is no way to prevent their march.

The seventh Hua courted and was courted in turn. She liked the daughter of this or that clan well enough, but did not make her choice for a long while.

Finally she brought home a woman with sweet brown eyes, the disposition and mien of a gazelle, introduced her first to her human mother and then to the demon one.

The Hua's would-be bride did not flinch. She curtsied to the demon, gave them the same respects she accorded the enchantress. And the Hua warlock said, "I have asked and received the blessing of my human mother; I wish for your blessing on our coming nuptials, too."

"What—do you expect me to raise your get too? You greedy child. The contract's good for one generation and one only."

The seventh Hua bowed her head. "I'd never ask you to oblige yourself more than you can. Even a parent or a grandparent must eventually depart the life of the ones who love them—to our afterlife or your hell, no one stays on this earth for long. But in the time we have, could you give your blessing to this marriage, as a parent would, and sometimes visit? You are under no obligation to me any further, and I under an unfathomable obligation to you, and yet all I can find myself doing is asking for more."

"That is the nature of Huas," the demon groused. And then, softer, "And of daughters, too."

Of the tenth Hua, little is known. She was born into a time of war, in the shattered remains of a once-great estate. The records that might enumerate her great deeds are gone; no pacts of renown gild her legacy, and no scrap of her name survives. But *she* survived, if only for a time, and that is a victory itself.

The twelfth Hua had an easy strength and a dangerous charm, a jaw like diamond and eyes like gemstones. By her hands and will alone the House of Hua thrived more than ever, its lost knowledge found and its scattered artifacts, save one, recovered.

She made many enemies, too; moved too quickly for her peers, in this one life we each have. And so her enemies conspired to rid her of that life, and very nearly did. Perhaps it was luck, or ingenuity, or sheer stubbornness that allowed her broken body to cling fast to this world, to keep within her heart a single spark of animation.

But a Hua cannot stay a spark; they must perish or conflagrate. And so the twelfth Hua, broken in body but indomitable in mind, turned her efforts to new pursuits. In the depths of the earth, in hidden caves and mines long forgotten, she entreated with stone and shadow, intent on filling the parts of her that had been torn asunder. Easy strength sloughed away to hard effort and bitter toil, and through agony untold, the twelfth Hua learned how to cast her spirit from her mortal frame and into her surroundings. With effort did her jaw again become diamond and her eyes gems, and again she strode the earth like a colossus, flesh turned to impenetrable stone. It was thus that she carved anew a place for the Hua name—or, at least, bought herself enough time to see her daughter thrive, and even her two granddaughters take flight.

A final thought, for the members of Sealing and Containment that have made it this far.

I imagine you are reading with an eye for prying open the secrets of the warlock family—how their rites may be subverted, their legacy broken, their ancient covenants shattered. If you wish to do so, you will need to take up their ways and reach into the infernal realms, to bargain and make brittle the oaths and pledges the Huas have extracted from those places.

I imagine none of you would be quite willing.

You can burn down every last warlock's atelier, dig up the very foundations of the Huas' estate and scorch them, and still in a year or two there will be a mage who seeks to call to our world a being from the realms beyond. The world's constant is that knowledge cannot be contained. The seeking of what is forbidden will always continue—this is not a threat, but a truth, one that the Huas understand most ably of all. Theirs is the work of the impossible.

- Professor al-Kattan, Dept. of Theory and Epistemology, Shenzhen University

OLESYA

We meet in a venue of Viveca's choosing, which means a hotel in the Arctic, one of those properties that can charge an arm and a leg for the ambience—a location that will kill you in minutes, but a view gorgeous enough that you won't mind. Of course, my sister adores the sheer desolation of it, the endless expanse; there is, she insists, catharsis in bleakness. And sometimes I can be persuaded to the concept—it centers you, like meditation, like facing oblivion.

I've preceded my sister in the suite we've rented: a conference room; a dining room; two bedrooms, each enormous enough to accommodate five. Not that we'll stay overnight—each of us has our reasons for preferring home territory.

The decor is warm, expensive: African blackwood has been transported here, its grain exposed in the tabletop. Counters in heartwood and ivory, preserved so that it will never yellow. An arrangement of corals, drawn from some brilliant shallows close to the sun, held now in a glass terrarium. Schools of fish, but in ghosts only—an interesting bit of minor illusion. Fragrance in the air, orange blossom and jasmine, and not artificial; either another piece of sorcery, or a truly pricey air freshener.

"I wonder what this place would look like torn up," says Dallas behind me, idly. "It's too much civilization for me, sorceress. Supposed mastery, erected in the face of freezing entropy; built to last yet, like all hubris, ephemeral."

"I think your objections are of a more personal nature," I tease, poker-faced. "The clime here is far from your native one, isn't that right?"

She glances at the window, grimaces. "It *is* too fucking cold."

I quirk a grin at her. "You could fuck me against the glass. That will warm you right up."

"Woman, do you never get enough? I thought I was the beast here." But there's a feline purr to her amusement. "You're in an odd mood. Don't get along with your sister?"

"On the contrary. She's the one I prioritize the most in the world."

Dallas places one hand in the small of my back. From anyone else, presumptuous; from her, the touch is pleasing. "But?"

In too short a time, she's read too well my glossary and indices, every page thumbed through. "But nothing."

"What is she like?"

"You no doubt know her by reputation. The warlock of her age." I flick my head. "She'll be here in a minute."

Viveca walks through the door not long after: we compete in the sport of punctuality. She has brought what must be her newest familiar. This, in and of itself, is not unusual; she does like to show off her toys. What *is* unusual is that Dallas stiffens at the sight of Viveca's companion, a demon of height—though no taller than I am—and light-eating shadow, with the sort of face for which Viveca has a vice: handsome, sculpted planes and golden eyes.

My tiger's reaction has not gone unnoticed, either by my sister or by the demon herself. But no one passes a remark. Viveca takes a seat. "Room service, Olesya?"

"I've eaten. Something from the bar would be nice—dealer's choice."

She laughs and nods to her demon. "A bicicletta for each of us, please, Yves. There should be fruit in the fridge."

The demon—Yves—raises an eyebrow, but gets to it as if she's been ordered to mix cocktails often enough. She is efficient about it, too, selecting from the rack a bottle of Gruner Veltliner and Campari, then from the fridge fetches the ice cubes, an orange, soda.

Two tall glasses are brought to the table, one placed in front of me, the other in front of Viveca. None for Dallas. My tiger's expression is carefully blank.

I wonder how they met, and where, and in what context. No matter. There are only so many types of relationships that engender this sort of reaction, and soon enough I will have an inkling.

"She is my new colleague," Viveca says, far more diplomatic than she has ever been about any other demon she's pacted. Yves stands back, assuming the position of a butler or bodyguard. My sister suddenly smirks. "I stole her from Cecilie."

"Oh?" I lean forward, playing the part of the proud co-conspirator. And there is an artifice to it: of the two of us, it's Viveca—the fourteenth warlock of Hua—who has taken up the lion's share of avenging our mother. I have helped as I could, hid my debilitating illness from the one person who would worry the most, so that she might focus on our family's victory. But I am truly powerless to assist in the ways I can and should, and every day it is a struggle to not drown in bitterness.

(And I love my sister, you see; I have tried to be her sanctuary, in that way. She may show it little, but she misses our mother desperately—she misses having someone be proud of her. And so I am proud of her, would still throw my body in the way of the mortal shot, would still give my life for hers. I just wish that *my life* was not this slow, creeping death in her shadow.)

"She obtained Yves' rites at one point," she is saying, "but chose to seal her away—coward. But then Cecilie's never been a real warlock." She is preening a little, but she deserves to; this is the most injurious strike she's made against our enemy to date. "And who is your new friend, sister?"

"Dallas Seidel," my tiger answers. She too has remained on her feet, and now bows to Viveca with an antique courtesy. "I met your sister at a business event."

"Ah." Viveca sips from her drink, not missing a beat. "It must have been very fruitful, for her to have brought you here with her. So, Olesya, since it doesn't look like you want Dallas here to leave the room…?"

I shake my head. "What I have to say is plenty fit for her ears. I asked to meet because I have heard, from reliable sources, that Sealing and Containment is poking around our family history again."

"Ah." This time it is a grimmer utterance, quickly masked with affected disdain. "They're so obsessed, and so boring. What sort of dog have they sent to sniff around this time?"

"An academic." I slide across a piece of paper. "Her curriculum vitae, up to her posting at Shenzhen University. I don't believe she is necessarily hostile—what she's obtained for Sealing and Containment is, quite literally, ancient information about our forebears. All the same, I'll keep an eye out for her movements; she's risen in station these days, even as her academic appointments have frayed, and I believe she'll be a free agent soon."

Viveca tucks a strand of her hair behind her ear. "You have the best information network, sister."

I have been distracted—ice moves in my glass, melting. The bicicletta is growing diluted. I drink anyway. The Gruner Veltliner is very passable, and the slice of orange must belong to an exotic cultivar—it tastes almost spicy, like someone's infused its originating soil with cinnamon, or crossbred it. Such botanical marvels are possible with specialized sorcery. Could I manage—but experimentations belong to the past. These days the closest I get is Chang'er's workshop; shame I'm not much good at alchemy. Not that the act of mixing this or that, of refining solutions, brings me the exultation of true sorcery at my fingertips.

But I can contribute, I tell myself. I *am* contributing; I move in the shadow of my sister's light. "Well, hold your praise until you've heard the next piece of news. A development more relevant to our war against Cecilie Kristiansen—her one and only protege is coming to an event in two weeks, presenting herself to high society. Goes by the name of Maria Ying. It's neutral ground, so it's not as if you can publicly act against either of them." I can't help but smile. "And despite your *notorious* reputation, I managed to secure you an invitation."

Viveca smiles, bright and devious, and then pouts. "I can behave when I want."

"See that you do. Inspector Budak will be representing Sealing and Containment at the gala."

My sister blinks, once. "That would be… awkward. I will be on my best behavior, fair? Now, shall we stay to take a tour, or have lunch?"

We do that so rarely anymore; I have avoided her, mostly to hide my affliction. But as it was once, it can be again, at least today: "Yes, that sounds like an excellent idea. Tell me about their restaurant's menu."

Three: A Love of Bargains

There is one name I swore never to utter again. I would sink it into the depths of the ocean and blot it from my brain if I could; the memory of her hangs on me like a manacle.

But needs must. Olesya Hua is dying, slowly—a wasting illness that has made using magic anathema. Though I have known her for such a short time, I am entranced by her beauty, feel a crushing heartache at her tragedy. I told myself I would do anything to save her—and now, with bitter humor, I commit to the one *anything* I never wanted to evoke.

I'm in a public park, the city vertical and vertiginous around me, never sleeping. Once, this sort of beauty would have been the exclusive demesne of royalty; now, an ambulance screams in the distance. Nocturnal birds hoot; no chrome and steel can keep them out—every human city is full of wilderness, little specimens. Squirrels, mice, owls. Not enough room for something like me—to fit into the human definition of order, you have to make yourself small, to become a scavenger.

It's late enough that no one is here to see, practitioner or not, and I need not keep secrets from the moths and the ants.

"Yves." I shape the syllable just so, breathing it into the night the way you might uncap a bottle of poison. It is not the name that has power over her; she may choose to hear me, or not.

For a moment, no response. And then she is here.

Exactly as she was in the Arctic, exactly like she was, before: broad-shouldered and densely made, clad in that light-drinking suit, inferno's red in her hair and devil's gold in her eyes. The same as ever; the same as she will always be until she chooses another form in which to manifest.

"Dallas." Her mouth is a thin line, and her expression as she regards me is not precisely a glad one.

It is not really my name, of course, much as 'Yves' is not really hers; my true one is a thing of growls and hisses and long susurrations, bound to my birth-soul. And we have called each other many things over the years, a hundred names in a thousand tongues. But 'Dallas' and 'Yves' suit us best, embody a part of who we are in a way that other aliases have not.

Idle musings. I make an expansive shrug. "The one and the same. Haven't changed it or anything. How have you been?" We didn't have time to chat when the Hua sisters met in the Arctic. In fact, we studiously said nothing to each other.

"The Huas conversed and you were not deaf. I'm sure you know exactly how I have been." Yves' voice is precise, unfeeling. No matter the language she is speaking, she infuses it with disdain, whets her consonants and vowels to an edge. "I am astonished that you've agreed to become a sorcerer's housecat. How the mighty have fallen."

"What can I say. She has a pretty face, and you know how I get about those."

The demon doesn't rise to my bait. She did, once. It's true what they say—familiarity really does breed contempt. "I'm busy, tiger."

Tiger was said in a much different tone, too, years ago. "It's about Olesya Hua."

"If the elder sister has anything she requires from me, the warlock would've conveyed to me the request or exigency."

"That's the problem. The younger sister doesn't know."

Yves grunts. "*What* doesn't she know? I swear, if this is some trifling matter—if the holder of *your* leash has a woman she needs to charm or some thug she wants disposed of—"

"She is dying of a curse. I want you to help undo it."

42

A bar, the sort that serves mages, so it doesn't matter or draw much attention that Yves obviously looks inhuman. (She can appear mortal, if she likes. She doesn't like, most of the time. This is a demon who flaunts the truth of her nature.)

Amber lighting. The sparkling clinks of glasses, the more liquid sound of vodka or whiskey being poured, water meeting water. Sometimes—very sometimes—if I try hard I can sit in a bar and imagine that I am in the jungle of my nativity, because it is quieter here than out in any park or even nature preserves. The Botanic Garden bears no resemblance to where I was born; to return home, I only need near-silence and running water and imagination. The only way, in fact—it's more than a hundred years gone, burned down and shorn through by human greed. Once I understood the jungle to be eternal. I was disabused of the notion when the trees began to fall and scorch.

We take a corner booth. Yves erects around us a barrier of secrecy. No one will hear us until she lets go of it, and even seeing us will require a certain acuity of sight. Seers are uncommon enough.

"So you believe," she says in a low voice, "that the younger sister isn't aware."

If you listen carefully, or if you have a tiger's senses, you can hear distant thunder when she speaks. Smell the ozone, a little. It's not all brimstone in there. "You tell me, Yves. If she was, she'd already have compelled *you* to fix it."

"What makes you think she can compel me to do anything?"

"I'm not privy to your covenant," I say placidly, "but I understand she is intoxicated with power."

A snort. "She's a—never mind. Did your sorceress put you up to this? Am I the *only* demon anyone in this region knows?"

"Olesya hasn't the faintest that I have come to seek you out." I pause. "She noticed how we both stiffened, back in the suite, but she hasn't pressed, and I haven't told."

Yves watches the other tables, but her interest is desultory. Demons have many hungers, the same as tigers: violence is an attractor, because in the moment of bloodletting all kinds of vices erupt—passion, primal impulses, a loss of control. She does also like the taste of souls, on occasion. None of that tonight, though; in this bar, there's just people being drunk, venting small grievances to friends or drowning their solitude in rum.

Her gaze returns to me. "You have not contacted me for over fifty years. And now you reach out on behalf of a woman you've known for *how* long—a month, two?"

"I have been busy." It's the wrong thing to say, of course, but I want her to see how little I think of her. And I did try to reach out, for a time; gave up, when my calls were never heeded. As far as I knew, she'd disappeared from the world—it wasn't until that moment in the Arctic that I learned she was corporeal.

Her hand shoots out and seizes my jaw. I used to believe demons incapable of true emotion, the sort we of flesh and blood experience. Yves dispelled that idea entirely, and then also the idea that her kind can only feel bloodlust and rage and spite. *"Five decades.* The lion's share of a mortal lifetime." Her voice slices through the air. Static electricity crackles. "I've never known you to be stupid enough to trust mages."

"She shattered a cage that held me." I do not try to break free from Yves. "Tigers owe a debt for that. It's not a pact, but my mother raised me better than to ignore the basics."

"There was a time when I would have done anything you asked. You spurned the offer and you spurned me. And now here you are." Her grip tightens. "You'd never willingly come back to me. Has this sorceress enchanted you?"

If I pretend enough, I can almost imagine her voice having its old concern. Still I don't struggle. I am capable of contesting her might, but we'll level the bar and it'll get back to Olesya, when I'm *trying* to keep my effort to lift her curse a secret. "She cares for me a great deal. She makes me feel—"

Beneath the cadence of Yves' speech there is the fury of a sea. *"And I did not?"*

Sentences paralyze in my throat. I want to explain to her that in the short time we've spent together, Olesya has come to feel like home; has eased the place inside me that misses the jungle and its green-black shadows. That

Olesya, instinctively, understands. "You met me when I was young," I say, which is not an especially good excuse or concession. Yves is hurt; she is angry. And I was the one who left her, who betrayed her in the worst possible way.

The outline of her distorts. With effort, she solidifies and lets go of my face. "You were well into your first *century* of life. You were supposed to know what you wanted, Dallas."

"Well, I didn't." She's not the only one who is angry. All of this was so long ago; I hoped the demon would have moved on, but I also knew she would not. Time doesn't mean the same thing to her as it does to me. Demons can hold onto grudges, and other things, for eternity. "I *am* sorry how that turned out. I should have… communicated. I shouldn't have done to you what I did."

"You're only saying that because you need something from me." Her golden gaze roves across the bar; perhaps she is wishing that alcohol did something for her. From any angle she is handsome, but in profile especially so. A memory rises, tactile, of being drawn into the shadow-matter of her, buoyed within it.

"Describe the curse," she mutters.

"It struck her, I guess, less than a decade ago." Which is around when her reputation as the mage-killer arose. "Twists a practitioner's core. She can't use much magic, or it'll kill her on the spot. But it's killing her anyway, slowly. She won't tell me how long she's got left, but I have tasted her blood—twenty years at most." Olesya deserves more than that.

Yves glances at me sideways. "And she's tasked you with resolving this?"

"She hasn't." That is why I have stayed: she does not ask anything of me, is content to have me as her companion. Sometimes she bathes me in my tiger form, brushes my pelt down, and sleeps curled up against me. Her enormous beast in her enormous bed. Not a single demand, and not a single question.

Yves grows silent, then still; I know she is reaching out with her power—doing for me what I asked, despite her reservations.

The ground around us shimmers blackly. Wherever she goes, she changes the landscape, little by little. I've seen places where she has abided so long that the effect is permanent, the soil shaded unnatural, the air impregnated with inferno's breath.

"I know something of her curse," she says, at length. "I cannot remove it."

I start. "Why not?"

"The reason isn't for you to know. But you also know that I do not lie."

I delude myself into believing that there is a touch of pain in her voice, but it's just the past I'm hearing; her speech is unforgiving steel. But I also know that Yves does not lie—or that if she has, she has only ever lied to herself. If she says she cannot, then she cannot.

Still, I make my tone as contemptuous as possible. "Is it because you're jealous?" Because that was all we were good at, toward the end, goading each other until we got what we wanted. Teeth and claws and blood's spill.

Her laughter carries with it the echo of avalanches, so lifelike that it pushes some of my more primal buttons. Tigers may be masters of the jungle, but we're not much good in the face of mudslides; have to run away from it, the same as any fawn. Gravity is the great equalizer, and Yves a terrible weight. "You think so little of me," she growls. "There's much I would do for you, against my better judgment. I am incapable of lifting this curse. I can no more dispel it than I can shift this world's axis."

"Why—"

"Dallas, a long time ago I tracked down the company that deforested your home. I killed the owners. The stakeholders. The foremen. The workers. Not a single one of them survived."

I draw a harsh breath. "You didn't tell me."

"Because you would have spat on it and told me it wouldn't bring your home or your family back. You would have said you wanted restoration, not vengeance." Her golden eyes brighten. Her fingers, black-tipped, dig into the table. It creaks. "You wouldn't have understood. So go back to your woman, Dallas. Enjoy your two decades together. That's longer than most human marriages."

"Yves, if—please do not tell the sister." I am surprised at how plaintive I sound. "I told you only because I was confident in your abilities. It was her secret to keep; Olesya will tell her sister whenever she is ready."

"'Her secret to keep,'" Yves echoes. "Maybe someday you'll learn to hold on to things that aren't yours to give away."

The demon doesn't walk out. She simply disappears, returning to Hong Kong or perhaps materializing elsewhere, a spot where she can brood alone.

I don't expect to see her again.

Olesya is awake when I return. Reading in bed, which emanates a perfume not her own—Chang'er has just been here, taking advantage of my absence. The alchemist's libido is something else. I'm not sure how Olesya can keep up with both of us.

She looks up when I come in, setting the book in her lap, a copy of *Four Reigns*. Her attention for me is total, immediate, and consistent. I will not say that she has eyes for me alone, but when I'm in her line of sight I know I am noticed, that she looks upon me with tenderness. Where I have hitherto only known turmoil, this is comfort.

"You smell of soot," she says.

"I *should* have showered before coming in here. But I missed you."

She tosses her head back and laughs; the cords in her throat are mesmeric. "We last saw each other ten whole hours ago, and most of those because I was working. Come here."

I shrug off my coat; my shoes are long behind—in this house, you take them off at the door. The bed bows under my weight as I put my head in her lap. She smells wonderful, always, despite the poison that bides its time in her blood. I could find her scent in a packed train, the North Star to my compass. She could be half a world away and my senses would point me toward her, tug me there inexorably. Even tigers must submit to our neurochemistry, the same way demons submit to pacts.

"How was your day?" I lay my hand against her belly, feeling its warmth, the vitality that remains yet, despite the curse's worst efforts. Her skin is firm, with few blemishes. A hint of lemongrass clings to her.

"The usual." Her voice is wry. "People want to buy my ammo so badly. The answer is always no."

"Has anyone tried to turn it against you?"

Olesya sinks her fingers into my hair, lightly scratching my scalp. "Yes. It doesn't work, though."

I nuzzle her stomach, rumbling from the back of my throat. She does like that. Normally I don't play the tame cat for anyone. "Good."

"Shall I ask where you have been?"

"Ran into an old—" My expression is hidden against her skin. "An old acquaintance."

Her strokes are long, even, the same way they are when she's brushing my coat until it shines like the vault of a queen. "And?" Maybe she can even guess who I met with. Olesya's thoughts run deep, the sort of water that quickly wears down stone.

When I was with Yves, I resented what felt to me like probing questions. They were never actually that, at least not most of them—they were expressions of concern, said in too clipped a tone. But what I did not realize then aids me now; I lean into the appreciation. "An ex-lover. I have a few of those, I'm afraid."

"Dallas, you're a tiger who found her way to a human form. I am aware you're centuries old. Unless you have taken a vow of chastity, I'm certain you've had many lovers. You don't need to pretend you didn't have a life before meeting me."

"Maybe I was trying to be your pretty young thing." I laugh, but the sound crumbles to ashes in my mouth. "It's just—I want to stay with you for a long time."

She kisses my brow. "Well, let's start with getting a good night's sleep. I'm not going anywhere."

"My ex." I don't know why I tell her. "She's your sister's new demon. Yves."

"Is that so?" Her voice stays level, but something stirs inside her. "What a coincidence."

And then she laughs, holds me tighter, crushes me in her embrace. "Oh, my tiger, how much you must care." When I pull back to look at her, confused, she clarifies. "No doubt you went to her, looking for a cure."

I flush slightly, embarrassed to be read so easily, then nod. "I asked her not

48

to tell Viveca. I don't know if she will. I am sorry; I betrayed your trust for nothing. Yves cannot heal you." I bury my face back into her chest before she can see the emotions that seize me.

She chuckles, genuine. "How could I rebuke you, when you were so brave for me? Some of my exes, I would literally die before talking to them again."

I laugh through a sob, and she continues. "You care about me, you took action on my behalf, you are honest in deed and in word. I could ask for no better mate. As for a cure—I resigned myself long ago. Think no more of it, lest we cheapen the time we have together now."

After that, she holds me, and I hold her. She dozes off in little time. I listen to her breathing, evidence that she is strong and hale. Usually she doesn't sleep much, but when I'm next to her she seems able to take her best, deepest rest.

With Yves I let go too easily, allowed myself to shed what we had because I was a fool, because I feared falling too far and too fast. With Yves, I did not know the value of what I held, and too readily threw it away.

This time is different. This time, I will do better. With Olesya, I'm going to hold on until I no longer can.

The truth laid down by Olesya's curse is not immutable. We will not have forever, but we will have more than what her misfortune has allotted. I will find a way.

Interlude: The Tiger and Her Shadow

In the seventeenth year of the Jiaqing Emperor's reign, the Eight Trigram Sect raised their banners in rebellion and stormed the imperial palace. Aided from within, the brotherhood fought their way to the throne room, where they—inevitably—were slaughtered to a man.

But one of their number was not a man, and stalked through the shadows alone.

"You do not belong here," chastised the shadow. "You smell of the wild jungle, and this is a place of cobblestone and shingle."

"Well, neither do you," replied the tiger. "You smell of ash and thunder, and this is a place of people."

"Those who came with you are already dying," warned the shadow. "You may be fast and sharp of claws, but the Crown Prince has a gun of foreign make, and he will shoot you dead."

"And those that came before you are already dead," again replied the tiger. "And though no mortal blade may harm you, you must know that if you stay here, you will someday join them."

"But I must stay here," said the shadow. "I must be tied to something, and in this life I have feet of stone."

"Then let's fix that," said the tiger, and began tipping over statues.

Another empire, another revolt; the whip-crack of rifles as sandstone crumbles.

"We cannot stay here," yelled the shadow over the tiger's wail. "The Rani is

50

dead, and with her Gwalior Fort falls."

"Then heal her," cried the tiger back, cradling the still-warm body. "Undo the work of this gram of lead."

"I have no more power over life than you," said the shadow, stooping low. "And it is for that reason we must flee—you will die if we stay, and that I cannot stop."

"You must never have loved like I have," spat the tiger, "or you would know that I would sooner die than leave her here."

"Then bring the corpse along," replied the shadow, and pulled the tiger up.

A shout from the rigging—a pod of rorquals to port! The crew yells and the ship cries out, flesh and timber straining together toward the bloodshed to come.

In the rigging above, the tiger perched, almost at home, beams like limbs and masts like trees.

"A sailor now," said the shadow, "but a hunter still."

"I wanted to see the world, and every crew I sail with believes me good luck," replied the tiger. "Last I heard, you were in the Americas."

"A civil war they called it, though far from polite," sighed the shadow. "Battle has never been pageantry, but this heartless ferocity was something new."

"Then you must have taken to it easily enough," rebuked the tiger, still furious. "You have the soul of a field marshal."

"I took no life and saved those I could," said the shadow. "I met an army surgeon, and for a time, we fought against death side-by-side, she and I."

The tiger looked askance, as if evaluating troublesome prey.

"You told me not to see you again, until I had learned something of the healing arts," explained the shadow. "And you, too, have kept the silver to which I am bound."

"You know very well I cannot simply break it," muttered the tiger, touching the unadorned bracelet. "How else would you return to me?"

A capital boulevard with a capital crowd, strolling along a capital river in a capital town. The shadow held a parasol, the tiger a little brochure.

"It's made of puddled iron," read the tiger. "Very modern, very strong."

"Yes," groused the shadow, eyeing the tower beyond, "but does it *look* like anything?"

"That's very short-sighted," needled the tiger, "for someone who may take any shape at all."

"And for a Fauves," countered the shadow, "you are very quick to admire iron beams."

"You certainly taste of iron," murmured the tiger, leaning in, "but I've come to quite like your strength."

"Strong things can be quite brittle, and tall things fall hard," the shadow whispered back. "I won't land on my feet like you."

They bleed over old rocks, impossibly old, the roots of great mountains ground to nothing, filled with the power of ages. The tiger hunts with a long gun, an irony lost on the dead.

"You got a new face," said the shadow, over the thunder of gunfire. "It looks good on you."

"She ran ammo to the miners and took a bullet to the throat," replied the tiger, aiming down the sights. "I liked the cut of her jaw; a shame to lose something so handsome."

"There's no way we can win this," said the shadow, eyeing the aircraft coming over the ridgeline. "But I know how you get about final acts."

"That's the problem with life," joked the tiger. "You have to see it through to the end."

The sea, a final time.

"A more human look for you," said the tiger with a smile. "You look hale. You look *here*."

"I'm trying something new." The shadow preened. "Humans are so limited, but I am enjoying the shoulders. And I found a name I like in the pockets."

"They have a certain charm we do not," said the tiger, glancing inland. "Can you really never see yourself loving a human?"

"They are so small, and the world so big," said the shadow, eyes to the water beyond. "Whatever I love, it needs to be my match. In that, I think I have only ever found a few, or even just the one."

"I have loved many of them, and quickly, too," sighed the tiger, oblivious. "You must think me a fool."

"You have a large heart," replied the shadow. "You love deeply and widely, like every shore the ocean touches."

"I do not believe I could ever love the ocean," said the tiger, touching the collar at her wrist. "It is too dark. It drowns you in its depths."

"Ah," said the shadow, and turned from the realization.

A bar, anywhere. A woman of long lines and hard angles, crumpled around a bottle in the back. On the wall, a television flickers: a man on the moon, they're saying, the future arrived—and the rest of us trapped here on this earth, weighed down with a past that never ends.

Another woman, tall and dark and deep, like a night in storm. "I've looked everywhere for you, Dallas. I could not hear you, I could not find you."

"And yet here you are, Yves," slurs the first. "Like a bad penny, or a shadow I just can't get rid of."

Yves ignores the brambles and reaches to pull her partner up. "Let's get out of here. Let me get you home. We can—" She has done this for years, sees no reason she won't do it once more—until she *does* see it, and freezes with sudden realization.

"Where's your bracelet?" she asks, voice sharp with fear.

"Oh, that old thing?" Dallas half-laughs, half-sobs. "I pawned it off for a bit more booze. Figured I'd shut you up and get buzzed at the same time. But here you are, and the beer's all gone."

"It was a gift," Yves says, slow and cold. "It was a sign of my appreciation. Of the trust—"

"It was a fucking manacle I've worn every day since I met you," Dallas snarls, a fury long denied. "Years of it, years of being loved by shadow and bound by silver. How oppressive your attention, how toxic your concern."

"It's just *out* there, for anyone to use." Yves' voice is the hardest Dallas has ever heard it, the hardest Dallas has ever heard any noise, like the rumbling of a kraken rising from the deep. Fear bleeds the alcohol from her system, and it is her secret shame that she will remember the betrayal in Yves' voice with sober clarity.

"Why?" Yves asks, and something *cracks*, brittle and hard. "I'm the only living thing that knows who you are—who knows your name, who—"

"That's the problem, Yves. Names change. They're supposed to, at least. Marry, take a new family name. Grow old, and give away a part of your name to your cubs. But you—your name is constant, ███. And you can't build a life on such an uncaring and unmoving foundation, demon."

And so something in the shadow cools, and hardens. She steps back, no longer touching the tiger. "Very well."

Four: Monster Without a Name

YVES

Century after century, and humankind has changed little.

Chandeliers above. Clinking glasses below. I observe from a somewhat unorthodox vantage point: my warlock is wearing me, a dress of high collars and long sleeves, in hadopelagic black and cinderous red. The colors are my choice, the design hers—surprisingly modest, but she is not a woman who likes to show her skin.

Most of her fellow mages have donned much more ostentatious affairs—ensembles of glistening bone and slick metal, gauntlets and bodices made of fluid alloys that bend light, diaphanous fabric that emanates cold. Their familiars perch on wrists or shoulders, wrap around them in serpent-shaped haze, glint from their heads like crowns. There are even epaulets present; I think one has a breast of medals.

"I've been meaning to ask," Viveca says. "You know my sister's new associate."

Tempting to not respond—answering her questions isn't part of our pact, dredging up this piece of my history especially. "What of it?"

"Dallas Seidel. Is she trustworthy?"

Half a moment passes before I realize the direction of her interest: she's not asking about Dallas' connection to me, she's asking whether Dallas is good for her sister—whether the tiger can protect Olesya and facilitate her business. What a mundane concern. I'm both disappointed and relieved. "Do you mean, will your sister be safe around her?" If only she knew what

Dallas asked of me on Olesya Hua's behalf.

The warlock draws a flute of fruit punch from a passing tray held aloft by an ethereal servitor. She does not imbibe alcohol in public. Good sense, given that her peers are as often as not her enemies. "Dallas is some wild thing. It'd be nice to know she isn't prone to mauling the only kin I've got left in the world."

"On that count, you have nothing to worry about. Dallas falls in love deeply, and she is loyal beyond reproach; she would sooner cut off her own hand than harm your sister."

And I do speak true—for all my faults, I can admire the strength of the only steel that has ever truly pierced my hide. And for all her faults, Dallas *is* loyal. That makes her betrayal of me sting that much more; these years on, the knowledge of how she threw me aside weighs heavy on my heart, a feeling like guilt.

But I've said too much: from my admission, the warlock will easily guess what my tie to Dallas is—was. But Viveca merely mulls over the information before she says, "Good to hear. I trust your assessment."

I give an affirmative *hmm*, lost as I am in my own thoughts. Dallas' reappearance in my life is like a splinter under the skin. It frustrates me, too, that the first thing the tiger did is to call on my powers... and that I was then immediately found wanting. My inability to do as she requested rankles. I *ought* to have been able; while I cannot restore the dead to life, I have worked to become an adept healer, and the stuff of this earth is typically so malleable to my touch—

—it matters not. I will look into it when I am able, but first comes my pact—my warlock, and our shared mission of vengeance. The issue of me telling Viveca about what ails her sister—the issue of me betraying one trust for another—will be something I confront in due time, too.

Viveca is sighing. "I do hate these functions. Olesya is so much better at attending them." To the side, her homunculus rumbles, a noise that may mean amusement or nothing at all. "As a subculture, we have some of the worst fashion sense in the world. Mages don't know when to *stop*."

It is true that next to most attendees, her presentation is subdued. If not for the fact that my matter distorts her shadow, she would appear to be wearing an ordinary dress, albeit more haute couture than fast fashion. "And why are you attending? Are you not," I add, allowing the faintest edge of mockery into my voice, "the warlock of your age, and thus do not need to care what your peers think?"

She merely laughs. "A lieutenant of Cecilie Kristiansen's will be here. Her new protege."

The sisters did discuss that over bicicletta. "So? Will you butcher her here and command me to devour her soul, Ms. Hua?" My voice resonates with a touch too much hunger; I very much want to hurt Kristiansen, and her apprentice is a start.

"You tease." Viveca grins. "But I'm not looking to be struck down for violating neutral ground laws. Speaking of which…"

Through the mingling crowd comes a handsome woman in a sharp black suit, powerfully built. Graying at the temples, a face scarred like bronze armor of yore, pitted but unbroken—she is a warrior, and experienced at that. She draws up to the warlock, towering over us both, and with a touch of deference gives a small bow to my master. "Ms. Viveca Hua."

I feel Viveca draw up to her full height, but feel no uncertainty, no jockeying effort at bluster. No, this is not a need to appear more imposing, but the way a young woman might straighten her collar and stand taller when greeting a respected elder. I am surprised. "Inspector Budak," the warlock replies, nodding back.

Budak. *Fahriye* Budak. Among my fellow hellions and all the dark things that walk this earth, the name is known—a remarkable feat in itself, considering the inherent transience of human life. She is an inspector with Sealing and Containment, and despite her association with that august and much-reviled organization, she has a reputation as a fair and impartial arbitrator of justice. Respected, if not loved, she is often relied upon as a neutral adjudicator of magical disputes, a constable capable of keeping the peace at events of supernatural import.

Ah, so this is what that is about. The bad blood between Hua and Kristiansen is legendary. Even if our nemesis is not scheduled to appear tonight—as I understand the courtly nature of mage society, it would be a terrible faux pas for a master to overshadow her protege's cotillion—it'd be assumed that Viveca would attempt to avenge herself on the next in line. And here Sealing and Containment has sent their best to seal and contain that hatred.

"The warlock of her age, come to the debutante ball of her nemesis' apprentice." A thin smile flashes on the inspector's lips as she looks over the hall with her eyes of deep green—the eyes of a hunter, or a tracker, seeing past deceit to find the truth of all things. And then, incongruous: "'The founders of a new colony, whatever Utopia of human virtue and happiness they might originally project, have invariably recognized it among their earliest practical necessities to allot a portion of the virgin soil as a cemetery, and another portion as the site of a prison.'"

"Hawthorne," says Viveca. "How is a woman so well-read and so handsome still single?"

I glower at the comment, surprised at my own possessiveness. In response, I can almost hear the warlock laugh; she is needling me as much as she is teasing Fahriye.

"Your mother once lent me a copy. Something about the Hua name and scarlet letters." The inspector turns back to us and gives another slight bow. "Don't make of this a cemetery, and there will be no need for a prison. A pleasant evening to you both."

"She *recognized* me," I mutter once the inspector is out of earshot.

"At least someone else here can admire you as yourself," the warlock says, conciliatory, smoothing her hand down her bodice. I don't need to feel it, but I choose to. Her flesh produces interesting sensations, and I have enveloped her in her entirety.

"That one in the turquoise dress and the pearl earrings is the apprentice," she continues. "Her name is Maria Ying."

A young woman, younger than Viveca, in a dress that appears to have been sewn from mermaid scales. Dawn-pink pearls at her earlobes and nacre at her throat. Her smile is bright and very sharp: I can see, at a glance, that she and my warlock are of a kind—humans who will trade anything, breaking as many as they must in their climb, to gain supremacy over others. Where Viveca is here with only her homunculus, Maria has come with a retinue: two surly women in black, a semi-formless thing that flits about her ankles, and a man whom I can tell at a glance is a hanger-on.

"Ying is after my time," I admit, the fabric of me susurrating against the warlock's skin. I can manifest separately, more person-shaped, but Fahriye Budak's perceptiveness aside, there is value in merely appearing to be a dress. "What does she do?"

"Hunts mermaids. Or anything that looks like one, anyway; the meat is supposed to make you immortal, but they're just about extinct, so it's a tricky claim to prove." Absently Viveca touches me again, playing with the skirt; I don't think I have ever seen her fidget with her clothing so much. "Otherwise, Ying specializes in aquatic sorceries. Her familiar's some sort of deep-sea horror. Nowhere as powerful as you, of course."

Obvious, but it's not like her to flatter me. I consider whether I appreciate that. "She's coming toward us."

The girl motions her retinue away as she approaches. A few paces from Viveca, she drops into a deep curtsy; I can hear the sea whispering in her steps. "Ms. Viveca."

Her business alias, a thin veneer of defense between the world and her True Name, Xinyu. Except Maria must know the latter, or something close, thanks to her master's hunt for knowledge; this is a pretense at business and courtesy.

My warlock regards the sea witch in kind, all smiles and false sweetness. "Ms. Maria. To what do I owe the honor?"

"I wanted to make the acquaintance of Hong Kong's most powerful warlock." She bats her eyelashes. "Possibly the most powerful in Asia."

"Europe and North America haven't produced anything worthwhile in generations," Viveca says dryly. "I trust you and your master are well."

Maria shows her teeth. "Never better, Ms. Viveca, even if my master is a product of Europe. I am here in her stead—one must keep up the social niceties, and this is something like my debut. I'm to be her presence in Hong Kong."

This young thing tastes of arrogance and youthful folly; I want to watch as her pride snaps like kindling under me. And Viveca is tensing—I can feel it in her nerves, muscles pulling taut. She is thinking of strangling the younger woman with her bare hands, of ripping out Maria Ying's spine: I'm close enough to her psyche that I can nearly share the visualization.

"How wonderful," Viveca says. "Most practitioners in Hong Kong are so ancient, the old guard; it'll be good to have new blood. Perhaps I can help you look for mermaids?"

"That would be *lovely*. To have the close guidance of Viveca Hua herself. Why, I—"

The chatter slows, then mutes. My line of sight is not limited to Viveca's and so I see, before she does, Cecilie Kristiansen entering the hall, as cold and imperious as when she bound me those years ago—beautiful in the way locusts descending upon a field of wheat might be. But I have been the wheat and she the horde, and in recompense for her delicate touch I will yet flay her alive.

She is alone, unlike her protege, and clad in a long coat. I can *hear* the low buzz of what now makes up her body—this close, I do not know where she ends and the hive begins.

Kristiansen wasn't invited; the formalities of this pageant aside, no one is foolish enough to have her and Viveca in the same location. But Viveca is not surprised when I alert her to Kristiansen's arrival; perhaps she always suspected it would come to this. Maria's expression, however, gives away that she did not expect her master, and the corners of her mouth tighten—I can read, easily, that she wanted to establish herself, make her mark in her own right. And here arrives her teacher, her owner, to tarnish the evening. Now she must scurry to Kristiansen's side, pay obeisance, and shed her pretense of independence.

Kristiansen draws close, and all eyes turn our way. I can feel Viveca's muscles coil, feel her heartbeat rise. But to an outside observer, one not intimately close to her skin and welded to her mind, she appears as serene as ever. Bored, even. "Cecilie," she drawls. "You must've come from a long way off; last I heard, you were holing up in Siberia. Fancied a change of weather?"

The older woman grins down: she has at least ten centimeters on Viveca, and has not yet begun to stoop with age. Her eyes remain the same harsh, unforgiving blue I remember without fondness. "I see you've got something that belongs to me."

Viveca laughs. "She's mine now, actually. Don't be a sore loser, old woman. I'll take much more from you before the end."

Kristiansen's mouth stretches a little tight. A rictus. I am close enough to reach out and reach in and crush her heart, except of course she doesn't have one anymore, not in a body like this. "Is that so? It seems you are not aware of what I have taken from you. You should check on your elder sister more, little girl."

"My sister—" Now Viveca's expression shifts. Her pulse pounds. "She's in perfect health."

The old warlock chuckles. "You think? But I'm not here to deliver meaningless barbs. Maria, come behind me and stay close."

I hear it. Viveca does too. I am already her armor and she'll not be touched, but—

The swarm that spreads from Kristiansen's body is fast—Maria cries out, for all that she is exempt—and Viveca lunges, slower than the insects but quick enough to put her hand through the old warlock, her physique enhanced and subtly guided by my strength.

We tear through nothing. Larvae seethe against our skin. A thousand wings beat against our wrist—Kristiansen's mastery of embodiment and her command of insects has grown in the years since she imprisoned me, becoming something truly inhuman.

Around the hall, screams. A fine mist has hazed the air, thin and gold, and even as I move with Viveca I *know* what that is, this curse Kristiansen is unleashing; I know because I cannot possibly be ignorant—

Viveca digs her fingers into Kristiansen's skull, crushing what she finds there pointlessly. What she destroys is releasing insect lymph, poisonous; the carpet beneath us corrodes. Maria is shrieking as part of the swarm lifts her up and bears her away. Her entourage is not so spared.

The other mages are beginning to mount a response. Too slow, too late—whatever curse Kristiansen has cast is already twisting through their veins, suborning their magic, turning it against its wielders. I have seen a version of this, I realize, when I reached out to Olesya Hua at Dallas' behest, and I see now what happens when the curse metastases: these vaunted masters of the world begin to drop where they stand, scorched from the inside by the very sorcery they've mustered to defend themselves. I care nothing for them, but their fate is instructive; with all my might I concentrate on Viveca's body, to both augment and protect.

"I should have known," Kristiansen speak-buzzes from the mandibles of her parts, "that it wouldn't take with you—after all, you're *wearing* the petri dish in which I bred this curse. But don't worry, little girl. When the enforcers come, it'll very much look like your new demon pet killed all these assembled mages. Such a blatant disregard for the rules of neutral ground—"

What remains of the swarm is beginning to disperse, Kristiansen escaping. Viveca knows this too. She grins—I can taste her blood on her lips—and says, "If I go down here, Cecilie, I'm taking you down with me. I know exactly what you've made yourself into, and *I know how to contain you.*"

Viveca snaps her fingers and the banquet hall *shifts*.

A sky of ash and rent souls. A ground of ancient soil in which nothing has ever grown, nor ever will. I laugh, loud, a howl; might courses through me as it never can in the mortal realm. I am shocked; I am elated. Viveca has summoned to earth a slice of hell.

In the humans' world, I am severely limited—the substance of me fights constantly against a reality that rejects it; even when I am not actively *doing* anything, my core itself must work to keep me corporeal. Here I have no such constraints. This reality is *my* reality.

My shadow rises, a tide; the true mass of me expands and expands again—a leviathan ascending from the depths. I run down each and every piece of Kristiansen, crumpling them to fluid and exoskeleton dust. Here a bug that was her eyeball, here a worm that was her tongue. There the filthy flies that formed her fingers.

I stand in triumph, each part of my foe obliterated. Then I turn to find my warlock fallen to the ground, coughing and hacking. The ease of being has made me forget: that here she cannot thrive, and she has lasted this long only because I clothe her.

I pull us back to her reality, immediate, and lift her in my arms.

The hall is now a charnel house, limbs feasted upon by the insect horde, melted from within by Cecilie's curse, and charred under the touch of hellfire. A noise from behind us, and we turn to find Inspector Budak standing alone amongst the ruins, coiffed hair only slightly ruffled; she is lowering a magical shield, and at her feet is a perfect circle of untouched carpet. To have survived both Kristiansen's poison and my hell, she must be a mage of incredible, if overlooked, puissance.

At the moment, that is a little beside the point; the good inspector's hand is resting on the grip of her handgun, as yet undrawn. "Ms. Viveca Hua," she says for the second time this evening, her tone now far more dire.

"I didn't do it," Viveca gasps. "You know I didn't."

"They won't see it that way." How convenient, that the inspector may distance herself from her compatriots and masters as the need arises—*Though I might believe you*, her body language declares, *they will not, and my hands are tied*. I bristle, prepared to fight; time is of the essence, and for my warlock, I will tear even the vaunted Fahriye Budak limb from limb.

But to her credit, she does not move to draw her gun—just stands as still as stone, hunting for a way out of this. "I can," she finally says, "buy you a few hours, a day at most."

I nod. To Viveca, I say, "Your orders, warlock."

"Take me home." Her breath is short and fast. Blood flecks her eyes. "Or you're not going to have a warlock for much longer."

Viveca's apartment is a place of jungle shadows and ophidian ferns, the light fixtures a warm gold; all of it is in sharp contrast with her glacial office, located several floors up, nearly the habitation of a different person. The homunculus, teleported alongside us, positions herself in a corner, emerald gaze straight ahead, unblinking.

We should be running; we should be attacking, finding the lair of our foe and breaking her before we are broken in turn. In one night of woe, Cecilie Kristiansen has framed us for her massacre and turned the hands of Sealing and Containment against us. A masterful touch: the only organization with the resources to uproot Viveca from her seats of power is now our mortal enemy.

But in place of fight or flight, I am instead laying my warlock gently on the divan and examining her—even a time this brief in my home realm has damaged her badly, nearly enough to burn through her personal regenerative protections. Her skin is burned, even her optical nerves are fried, but luckily there are no brain injuries. I reseal internal organs and reknit soft tissues, redirect blood flow and restore her vision. Normally it'd be a delicate process, but I'm bonded to her deeply, more so than I have been to any prior summoner. I can work fast. The perks—and peril—of being anchored not to steel or stone, but to her very flesh.

"Thanks," she mutters, head lolling, still out of it.

In this moment, I'm acutely conscious of how fragile she is, how close she came to mortality's terminus. Every pulse of her body's processes is visible and audible to me. The lymph, the blood, the gossamer mesh of nerves. She is as easy to break as any human. I feel the sudden impulse to sink my teeth into her, to enter her, to possess what I have restored to wholeness. "I'm fulfilling the terms of our contract."

She laughs, eyes half-shut. "You know we didn't get her, don't you? Or not all of her. That was a false body. Still a setback for the hag—not like she can make one of these every day—but we're going to need to find out where she stores her real one. Good time to do it though; she'll have to stay put until she can assemble her fucking bugs into a new avatar. Press the advantage."

Her voice is slurring. I lick blood from her mouth; I have tasted it before, but it's a nice treat. As compensation, I pour a little more vitality into her. She sighs, relaxing into it.

"I'm getting clean," she says once she regains the wherewithal to sit straight. "Then we can plan."

I could tell her she's in no shape, but I'm preoccupied with my own thoughts. Kristiansen called me her petri dish, and the magic she used to destroy the other mages... it tasted of me, of my power. Torn away, no doubt, during the experiments she subjected me to; she tortured me extensively when I was bound by her. A few grains of captive power, maintained against all odds, used to incubate and breed pestilence. No wonder I couldn't touch the elder Hua's curse, I realize in a moment of cold clarity—the thing that is killing her and slaughtered the mages at the gala *is* me.

A demon is rarely moved to consider something unholy, but what Kristiansen has committed is a violation most profound. A pact involves me, directly, in accordance with primeval laws. Theft is different.

My thoughts veer, inevitably, toward fighting with Viveca. In my long existence, I've participated in all sorts of violence; until now I have not fought as one with a human, have not united with another in flesh and soul. Her display was impressive, but more than that she entrusted herself to me entirely. Were we less harmonized, the combat would have been halting, her movements blunted by doubt. But from her, not a speck of fear. She must truly believe in our shared wish to see Kristiansen dead.

Viveca emerges from her bathroom in a light robe, pale green to match the decor, shaking her wet head like a—but I do not want to think about *her* tonight; I have enough on my mind. And if the tiger wants me to change so much, to leave her behind—

I swallow back my bitterness. The warlock meets my eyes and I almost think she must have caught the edge of that thought, of my acrimonious history. But she only says, "We should be preparing for our egress."

Sensible. I wait for her command.

"I'm not at my full strength yet." Her hand flexes. "Your healing was flawless, of course, but the human body has limits yours doesn't. Take a solid form, will you?"

"Why?"

She doesn't respond as she heads to the bedroom. Mentholated radiance slants in through the window; as with her office, this too doesn't overlook a view of Hong Kong but a view of a forest, evergreens crusted in frost. Her taste for frigid locales seems nearly compulsive; it's a wonder she hasn't asked me to drape her in snow and glaciers.

Finally she settles on the bed, shrugging off the robe without any self-consciousness; reasonable, seeing I've already been her dress and she's been naked inside me all this time. "My homunculus used to speak, back when my mother was alive. Not the best conversationalist, but better than nothing." Her gaze turns to the wintry image she has made a destination for her window. "I suppose that I hate sleeping alone."

It seems a non-sequitur. Demon kinship is a peculiar thing—I have only one being I call my relation, an eldritch being of great vastness and age, but we are in fact not even the same species—and every one of us is essentially endless. There to see stars birth, here to see the sun die. Entropic decay will never dissolve us. I have not made much effort to understand human emotions; they have always struck me as trivial, limited in range. But perhaps it does not hurt to attempt. Is that not the point of entering the human realm, to experience something new, movement contrasted against the eternal stasis of the infernal world?

"In a few hours," she continues, "I will be a wanted woman, *persona non grata* in every magic port of call." A *very* generous estimate of how long we have. "At least give me a little reprieve before we flee."

"Very well." Against my better judgment, I acquiesce, gathering my shadow into the form in which I first appeared before Viveca—a suit of blackest night, eyes gold and hair cinderous, as if I am the pulsating heart of a cooling kiln. And it is the same form that I chose so long ago to please another, almost like a second human skin, the pinch of the comfortable.

But the tiger is not here, and the warlock is; all old things may be made new again, and desires long frozen might flower come spring. Something within me is awakening, not just tonight but even earlier, from the first moment I laid my eyes on this woman—a hunger I have not felt in decades, and only once or twice in the long eternity that is my existence.

Come what may, whatever forces are arraying against us beyond our walls—for whatever my warlock asks of me tonight, I will find the time. I will *make* the time.

I climb in. The mattress dents. Her back is very still against my chest, slightly tense; she is considerably smaller than my manifestation, and soon I become certain she's not going to fall asleep. The scent of her brims with power, her own and mine. To a tiger's nose, we would smell indistinguishable now—and this close, the smell of her sinking into me, *becoming* me, my judgment grows even less reliable. "Tell me, warlock," I murmur into her ear, "is rest the only thing on your mind?"

Viveca laughs, half-muffled by her pillow. "When did you notice?"

"You kept caressing the dress."

"And did you like that?" Her voice is low. No longer exhausted. "Did you enjoy touching every centimeter of me? To have the total measure of my skin, and hold it within yours."

I run a finger along her nape, her fine hairs; I let her feel my claw. "Do you think you're the first summoner to try to seduce me?"

"Of course not." Mimicking my tone, she adds, "Tell me, demon, am I going to be the first to succeed?"

My palm passes across her flank, the bare skin smooth and warm, beating with arterial percussion. "What would be in it for me?"

"Oh, I don't know. Reducing *your* warlock to a quivering mess? Proving that, contract or not, you are much more than the tool in the equation?"

Women have tried to get me in bed throughout the ages, for most have heard of what a demon lover could do. With a few I have obliged; with warlocks, never—it upsets the legalistic language of the covenant, and it gives them the wrong idea. The memory of Viveca sheathed in me is fresh, though. I find I want to chase that again.

And she is exquisite, in the glacial illumination.

I touch her with my hands, then with my mouth, and then with the rest of me—the advantage of a malleable shape. She gasps when she feels my mouths on her nipples, a third one between her legs, my fangs on her neck—I do mean to test the pact's boundaries, see if a little pain in the act of carnality would violate it. A little pressure, and nothing. A bit closer to breaking skin and I can feel the contract tighten around my core. Off-limits, then.

"*Are* you taking off your clothes?" she asks, fingers tugging at the collars of my suit.

To that I nibble at her earlobe. "I think, Ms. Hua, your libido responds much better to me clothed."

"What would you know about my—" Her breath rasps through her teeth as one of my tongues laps at her clitoris. Her arousal darkens her smell. "Do that again."

The human body is an easily manipulated instrument. I can bring her to climax fast; I can give her one that'll feel as if it never ends. Her senses are joined to mine, after all. Instead I take my time. I want to hear her mewl and watch her writhe. The light makes her seem a thing of marble, stunningly sculpted by the finest chisel. But no sculpture moves as she does; no statuary claws at me as if she could carve open my substance, bathe in the heat that I offer.

When I ease into her, she clasps her hand over her mouth. I pry the hand off, immobilize it against the sheets. "You wanted to have me," I growl against her skin, "then you'll have to let me hear you."

She gasps. Bites down on her lip, teeth tight on her own soft flesh. "Or I could just be quiet."

Viveca makes good on that threat for a time. Not for long. Her nails dig deep into my back. Her legs clasp around my hips, and her motions become erratic. She comes like a wave crashing against shore, her cry jagged.

I hold steady: I am not brittle stone that would give before the sea. But I'm careful, too, as I slip out of her. She shudders and makes little noises.

"This is the first time I've had a demon," she says once she recovers her command of language.

I should not indulge her more than I already have. But I stroke her spine, cup the small of her back; I do have a fair idea of what mortal women like, the gestures that make them feel safe. "You must have summoned very many."

"They weren't like you." She bites one of my fingers. "Oh, you taste interesting. Very... burnt toast."

Amusement ripples through me, despite myself. "What did you expect, sulfur?"

"What else?" She wraps herself around me, as if I am no more threatening than a human bedmate. "We do have to do something about Cecilie, though."

"Later." I cradle her against me. "Sleep, warlock. I'll keep watch over you."

And I mean it: I would sooner blot out the light of the sun, pull the moon down from the sky, than see her roused before she is rested. She will awaken to a new world, one in which we are pariahs—but until then, a full night's sleep it is.

Five: A Mercy of Cages

DALLAS

My treatment of Yves must seem cruel by human standards. No, no *must* about it—I have lived with humans long enough, walked amongst them on two feet, been greeted as a friend in a dozen of their languages; I understand the general contours of what they call love, affection, obligation. By these standards, I have treated Yves... poorly.

But in my defense, these feelings, this way of being—it isn't my home. It isn't *me*. It isn't what my heart feels.

My heart is a jungle that no longer exists, an untamed wilderness free of law and responsibility. I was mighty there, unfettered. No borders contained me, no weapon could hurt me. And I am who I am, *what* I am, because I grew long of tooth and sharp of claws in that place, because I feasted on enough human hearts that I could, in time, cloak myself with human likeness, emulate their passions and their vices.

Yet humanness will always be a foreign land. This is what love feels like, to me: a tightness in my chest, a hum in the air, a growing itch to run. Love is the burst of blood that comes with a fresh kill; love is the wild panic of a tiger gnawing through her own leg to be free.

I've eaten every heart that has ever loved me. Yves' was no different.

Each morning, I awake beside Olesya. Sometimes I wake as myself, and sometimes I wake in the human shape I took a century ago, a fighter with flashing eyes and a sharp chin. Yet Olesya is always wrapped around me, face buried in my neck or in my fur, and however I look, her eyes light up the same; I am undone anew with each sunrise.

And each morning, I wait in that first moment of consciousness—wait for the terror to grip me, wait to be overcome with dread; wait to leap from this bed, to rip apart this woman while I scramble for the door. And yet...

...it doesn't come. It still hasn't come. *Why* hasn't it come?

I pad around Olesya's estate as both myselves, hunting for the unease. Instead, I find contentment and I find *purpose*. I am not some hanger-on, much as Chang'er's glare would indicate. An assassin steals onto the grounds, light and shadow wrapped around them like a second skin—dead, before they manage to cross half the lawn. An arms deal goes south—a bullet finds my shoulder, but not before my claws find all their throats.

And there is the curse. Twenty years, my senses tell me—ten, before the first signs of degradation become too obvious to hide. It may as well be tomorrow, the way I viscerally react. After all these centuries, I finally feel death's gaze, like a predator watching through the tall grass.

But the hunt for a cure is still a hunt, and I am a tiger of unparalleled skill and determination. I slew mortality once, when I shed my stripes and became something more; for the one I love, I will slay mortality again

OLESYA

As a girl, I did not daydream of romance. I had more pressing matters, like my studies and my growing mastery of transmutation. Some are born into the body they wish to possess, ever lucky; others achieve some modicum of contentment through exercise or fashion. That was not the case for me, and my youth had no time for love or courting, torn as I was between two warring truths, each of equal importance—that I was the loving son of Elizaveta Hua and the loyal brother of Viveca; and that I was most certainly *not* a son or a brother.

The only solution, then, was to pour myself into my studies, to push myself harder; to excel in transfiguration and fleshcrafting, for my family and myself both. I could have gone to another sorcerer, of course, paid the necessary fees—it's not a rare procedure, and Mother had plenty of gold to spare—but I wanted to rebuild my body on my own, to ensure every part would be guided by my will alone. That is the shape of perfection, the sum of grace, sculpted by my own hands.

But if I'd been given to adolescent fancies, I like to think I would have visualized something quite like Dallas. It pleases me to look at her; I enjoy the long lines of muscles, the leanness that hides her true strength, the well-made and handsome face. The hunger, most of all.

I watch her move around the estate, and in her beauty find only more questions, an ever-deepening desire to know. Where has she gone, what has she lived through? Where has she left her claw marks on history, and who has she loved?

In this last subject, I am surprised that of all the beings in the world, she has been involved with my sister's newest demon. In the little she has said, I can feel my way through the texture of their past relationship; it is easy enough to infer that their farewell was not precisely amicable. A demon and a tiger is an unusual pairing. What brought them together? And while Dallas is not eternal—Viveca's demon is—they must have spent more time together than I will ever live. A century, two centuries? I should not pry: it's no crime to have a past, I told her that myself—and yet it piques my curiosity, suggests a channel through which I might understand Dallas better.

I tell her as much, one afternoon when we are taking tea on the veranda, watching Chang'er collecting roots and seeds along the forest edge beyond the lawn.

Dallas tenses; I watch, patient, as she wills her shoulders to droop, as she unclenches her fingers. Finally, once she has convinced herself that this is not a trap and she is not in a cage, the tiger opens up: "We were together for a century and a half, give or take. Not consistently; we fell out with each other several times, sometimes spent years not talking over this or that perceived slight."

She licks her lips, trying to find the words to express a truth she may only now be learning herself. "But more often than not, we traveled together, just the two of us. Both of us inhuman, unfamiliar with humankind, running roughshod over every sensibility. I would get us into trouble, and Yves would get us out. There was this one time, we ran a con on a—" The joy in her voice strangles to a stop. "Well. We knew each other for a time, and now we do not."

I have had plenty of experience teasing intelligence out of people, like you would tease morsels of fish loose from its skeleton—you can find the soft, yielding places in a person and puncture them; you can seduce them with words and gestures until they burst like a brook after the spring thaw. Give me an hour or two at dinner, and I'll be able to learn most of a person's history, even the parts they'd rather not talk about, the murk and quagmire of shame. People reveal so much about themselves without meaning to. Inference can be like a scalpel, and you can cut apart your business associate, your ally, your enemy so that they'll better serve your ends.

But Dallas is not my enemy, and she is more than an ally. She is—it is too soon to think that way, isn't it? And yet when you've discovered a heart that beats in time with yours, you must recognize it for what it is, or else let it slip through your grasp.

"You had a difficult parting from her," I say at last. A frank push, so that she can push back or pull away as she wishes: every card laid on the table, face-up, no manipulation and maneuvers.

Again my tiger turns rigid. The line of her mouth pulls toward bitterness. It does not become her—her expression usually tends toward lightness, at least in my company. "I… wronged her. I wronged her badly." She jerks, as if flinching from her own confession. "She would be justified never wanting me in her sight again. She probably doesn't, truth be told."

Yet she went to Yves for me. "I love you," I say, simple and unplanned. It's true, too. She makes me earnest; she simplifies the running calculations that always, always turn and wheel in my head. With her, I do not have to posture or pretend.

Dallas blinks, startled. "I—well. I'm glad." She rocks her chair backward, making it teeter, precarious. I can read her—a thought has snagged in the brambles of her mind: has she ever said these specific words, *I love you*, to Yves?

"And you don't have to say it back to me." I make my voice gentle. "If that is not what you feel."

"No. No, it's not that. I cherish you, and I will honor you in all ways, I'm just terrible at actually voicing it. I do mean to fix that."

She stands, consumed with emotion. Her hand twists at the back of her chair; with effort, she lets it stand properly again. "But I have hurt everything I have ever professed to love, been reckless where I ought to have shown care." A shuddering sigh. "I am trying to avoid past wrongs."

"Dallas," I ask, "I willingly let you sup on my blood. What could you possibly do that would hurt me?"

"I could, I don't know, sleep with your sister."

It is my turn to stop breathing, to be cut to the bone by fear. How quickly this beast has placed teeth and talon on my pulse. How easily she would break the skin and leave me to hemorrhage.

And then we are both laughing, shocked by the audacity of it—her at what she's dared to verbalize as the worst-case hypothetical, me at the ridiculousness of the prospect. It lances the tension that has been building, our mirth loud enough that Chang'er begins to shout something at us from fifty meters away. Then she starts to march back toward us, grumpy as ever, and we only laugh the more.

Dallas is right, of course; I don't expect us to be exclusive, but the love I have for my sister is complicated, and the tiger bedding her would feel like betrayal. It is the bullet that would pierce what we have together; it would be the lethal strike. But love is trust, faith in the face of ten thousand painful eventualities. I think it's something we're figuring out—me so young to romance, and Dallas so old.

But we are figuring it out together, piece by piece.

I'm on the rooftop of our old home in Mount Nicholson, Hong Kong. The sun is shining bright, almost too bright, which is how I know this is not the nightmare about vampires. That one places us indoors, besieged and huddled together, the windowpanes fogged crimson. *This* nightmare is a perfect day, sky unclouded, summer's breath on my skin.

But it is silent, too. Unnaturally so. I hear a bird cry out, loud, and then watch its body fall and dash on the roof's concrete: the sharp crack, the wet slap. Those fragile bones shattered as it struggles within a pool of its own entrails. I try to make out the species: pigeon? Dove? But it's too big, and the size means there's more gore, more red. For a time I stare at the fragments of its hollow skeleton, once instrumental to flight, now reduced to so much kindling and pulp. Everything that flies can plummet.

I'm waiting for someone, and when the rooftop remains empty I realize I have to look for her. My sister and I have begun a game of hide-and-seek, and Viveca is nowhere to be found. I squint against the harsh noon, my skin prickling against the heat. Salt in my mouth: the wind has brought in some of the sea.

My search is halting, and the rooftop is immense. Potted plants form little labyrinths, rising too tall for me—at ten, at twelve?—to see past, even on my tiptoes. Colorful ferns and frothing flowers, palm fronds and fruiting bushes. The smells are cloying, so sweet and so thick that it's hard to breathe. The silence is comprehensive: even the wind moves without sound, and so do I. As if I am a ghost in this world, a shadow only, powerless to affect this space.

Viveca must be found. My certainty, and urgency, grows. It becomes bitter and sour in my mouth. I think, *Where is Mother?* Except my adult cognition, my awake-self, catches up and remembers that Mother is long gone. She cannot help us. I am the only one who can come to Viveca's aid.

I walk faster. I try to break into a run, but the ground—previously smooth—is suddenly pocked and pitted, every step threatening my balance. I stumble once and fall face-first into hydrangeas, and they pull at me, fill my nose and mouth. I fight and wrench away, choking and spitting, the world spinning around me. But I get back on my feet. I need to find my sister. I need to protect her.

Another bird corpse in my way, blue-feathered, decaying. Its guts are crawling with ants: bright black, bright red. My hands are bleeding.

And then, at the end of the hedge maze, I find *something*. It's not my sister. It's an enormous sunflower, the stem bowing. Petals are falling off or curling on in themselves in accelerated rot, spotted with disease. The soil in the pot is thick with centipedes, crawling slow and languorous up the stem; spiders are making webs across the flower itself, filling the plant with poison. My ears fill with insect buzz. Loud. Louder. Louder—

I wake in the middle of the night to find Dallas' side of the bed empty. That's not unusual; she occasionally rises very early, or spends the entire night outside, patrolling the garden on four legs. But my mouth is dry and foul-tasting, the nightmare like ash on my tongue; sleep does not return.

Bleary eyed, I start a pot of coffee brewing, mulling on what I dreamt. Dallas must see the kitchen light, because she steps in a moment later. Her skin is wet with the night dew, and the muscles of her back are corded taut, all of her held in tension. It surprises me that she's in her human form—the wildness in her eyes makes me think of the other—but there is an urgent set to her mouth, and she can no more enunciate human language with the great toothed maw than I can emulate tiger-tongue with my inadequate lungs.

"Bad dreams?" she asks, and the tone tells me she, too, has slept poorly.

I look into the depths of my coffee mug. Very sugary, lightly creamy. Rarely informative. Then again, most readers of tea leaves and so forth are charlatans. "I'm not naturally prescient. But there are certain bonds between me and my sister, built up for us by our mother, so that we would know when the other is in danger. Something, or someone, is coming for her soon. I don't think what you saw was Viveca, though, was it?"

She is silent. I cross the kitchen, plucking out of the refrigerator marinaded pork, tender and veined with fat. Over time I have come to learn her tastes. She appreciates tea, coffee, the usual things of the morning; she appreciates meat more, and better if they're flavored well—spices and fish sauce, palm sugar and coconut milk. I sear the slabs lightly, more to heat than to cook them, and plate them for her.

Dallas eats, and as she does she calms down centimeter by centimeter. The act of consumption soothes her, and it makes me think that once—a long time past, in the murk of her history—she went hungry often, approached the cusp of starvation. Even tigers can have lean seasons.

"Yves," she says, licking blood from her fork. "When we traveled together, when we were companions, I'd have these flashes of foresight when she was in peril. Those stopped a long time ago. I didn't expect them to come back."

She recounts a vision far more atavistic than what came to me. A shadow of the demon in the distance, sinking—being consumed—by an embodiment of sickness. Not something that would make sense in the light of the day; what pathology of the flesh could possibly touch a being of hell? But Dallas describes things crawling under her flesh, and how she woke in my garden screaming.

My tiger clutches, now, at her wrist. But she's not wearing anything; her fingers close in on emptiness, on her own flesh. "Danger to Yves," she says slowly, "means danger to your sister, does it not?"

"I think I know exactly what you saw, and why you saw it. There's a mage by the name of Cecilie Kristiansen." Not many thaumaturges specialize in her specific brand of grotesquerie. A Kristiansen ancestor must have learned to tame and communicate with, and control, certain insects: bees and wasps, the hiveminds. She has innovated a great deal on her family's magic, so much so that she has been able to stretch her lifespan far beyond even what is normal for mages. The spy networks and information brokers I work with are extensive, but even they don't know how old Cecilie really is.

"My version is a little more vague," I continue, sipping my coffee. I close my eyes. "We were in this garden on the rooftop of our childhood home. Playing hide and seek, only I couldn't find Viveca anywhere. In her place there was a giant potted sunflower, and it was rotting. Being eaten by bugs."

"Sinister. This thaumaturge threatens your sister—does she threaten you too?"

Should an opportunity present itself, I would personally empty a cartridge into Kristiansen's face. "She felled our mother. She hates us both, and would see us come to ruin. The feeling is mutual."

"Then," my tiger offers, "I will tear her to pieces for you."

It makes me smile. Perhaps I'm a simple woman, but the feeling of being protected, of being defended—it makes me happy.

Then I frown. "There was a gala tonight—the one I mentioned in the Arctic. I secured my sister an invitation. I think—" I am interrupted when the jade bangle on my wrist hums, a warning from Chang'er. "It appears we have visitors. Stay out of their sight—with whatever is unfolding, it's best we keep you as a hidden ace, for now."

I receive my guests in what Chang'er jokes is my throne room—high-ceilinged, perfectly climate controlled, lined with statuary I crafted myself before my magic left me. The walls are paneled with windows that look out to a multitude of views; unlike Viveca's, they are not truly doors but are much more cosmetic—snow-dusted mountain peaks, tempestuous seas, calm lakes. The agarwood desk and plush chairs I have had arranged are mundane, if luxe; I'm not so delusional that I would have for myself a throne.

It is not the first time Sealing and Containment has visited me in my home. I have a reputation, and crimes large and small are often misattributed to me; in actuality, I practice my trade in the most legal of manners, in accordance with the laws of mage society. Contracts and geas, bounties and retaliation, overseen by the finest attorneys on this island. It does not do to go rogue. One performs within the strictures of decorum, and assassination is as mundane as alchemy or transmutation. In fact, I once joked with Viveca that my work was a form of both—an ounce or two of lead, and I can make any living matter revert to its base elements.

The first officer introduces herself as Inspector Yuwada Thammarangkul. She has the aspect of a snake about her, cunning and venomous. She's younger than I am, too, fresh out of whatever academy turns out such creatures as she; her eyes burn with the zealotry of a new convert. I can already tell, without any aptitude whatsoever at telepathy, that she sees in me an obstruction to justice.

The second officer needs no introduction. Fahriye Budak cuts the same heroic figure that she has for thirty years—graying at the temples, now, and with a few more scars, but just as handsome as the day she first saved my life. There was a time I thought I would grow up to work for Sealing and Containment, all because of Fahriye's charm and skill; the angriest Mother ever was with me was when she found the pin-up calendar I was hiding under my mattress—not because they were butches, but because they were *cops*.

During her time as an inspector for Sealing and Containment, Fahriye has been the very image of a righteous public servant—not an ally of the Hua family, per se, but an honest broker that has defended my family from unwarranted censure and opprobrium just as frequently as she has held us accountable for wrongs we very probably committed. And though we have not seen each other face-to-face in years, we—Fahriye and I—have kept up something like a private correspondence, anonymous and deniable, quietly assisting each other in ways both small and large.

So it does come as something of a shock that Fahriye nearly recoils when I come into her line of sight. It's a subtle reaction, but visible to me—I've gotten adept at observing and deciphering body language—and I hold onto it, something to chew over later. I control my reaction far better, smile pleasantly and warmly gesture for the inspectors to take a seat.

Fahriye sits in one of the chairs. Its hydraulics hiss at her weight—she is a densely made woman. Broad, and I imagine with a trained physique.

Inspector Thammarangkul remains standing. Her gaze filets the contents of my decor, vivisecting, searching for signs of guilt and evidence of unlawful association. "Where were you last night?" she hisses, without tact or preamble.

"Ms. Olesya Hua," Fahriye says, shooting a cold glance at her partner. "Apologies for calling on you so early. We just need to ask a few questions."

Impersonal, all professionalism. "Please," I say, "I always stand ready to assist Sealing and Containment. The law is what keeps our society standing, after all."

The younger woman cuts me a sharp look, as though she expects that I'm being sarcastic. What I know of her is that she is fanatical in her pursuit of crime, of extinguishing every unlawful element from the face of earth. A caricature, almost.

"In Hong Kong—" Fahriye begins.

"Ms. Olesya Hua," snaps Inspector Thammarangkul, "three dozen mages were murdered yesterday evening, in cold blood and in violation of neutral ground. The traces left behind make it blatant that a demon was responsible, and every scrap of evidence points to a *specific* demon that serves Viveca Hua."

"Ah, and now you want to know whether I perhaps harbor my sister." I smile up at the girl. "Would you like to search my estate, Inspector? I have nothing to hide."

Yuwada twitches. She is, I think, about to get in my face and threaten me when Fahriye smoothly interrupts. "Inspector, do me a favor and talk to the alchemist. Ms. Chang'er should be able to give you a tour of the place. I'm authorizing the use of a truth-geas."

Thammarangkul's eyes nearly glitter at the thought. She must take genuine, borderline sexual pleasure in interrogations. A pervert, and not in the fun way. I'm never going to hear the end of it from Chang'er.

Once the younger woman has disappeared to harangue my alchemist, Fahriye shifts in her seat. She still isn't looking directly at me, as if something about me continues to unsettle her; always her gaze slides off. I'm trying to divine what it is: guilt? Revulsion?

"Inspector Budak," I say. "It's good to see you again. Must have been years since you last visited." She has disappeared from my sight ever since Mother died.

"I suppose that it has." Her head inclines. "You've been helpful to me."

She means the occasional bullet I have arranged to appear in her mailbox, when I hear that she is facing an especially challenging target in her work; my part of our secret correspondence. Everyone could always use ammo that will pierce and destroy anything, and I don't sell: it's an exclusive gift to her. I fold my hands. I rest my chin atop their knitted structure. "I don't imagine Sealing and Containment has mellowed out about my family." Viveca having become nearly as powerful as Mother—she has both refined and improved

Hua summoning rituals and techniques—likely doesn't help.

"I'm here in an official capacity, Olesya." Fahriye's expression smooths out, settling into remoteness. "My goal is to prevent unnecessary loss, to limit damage. Here are the facts of the case. The Hong Kong gala—hosted by the alchemist Ariadne Torres—was attended by thirty-six mages in total, at a banquet hall designated as neutral ground. You are aware of how those rules work; I was there to ensure they were upheld. An altercation started between Viveca Hua and Cecilie Kristiansen—"

My blood runs cold. "*Fuck*."

"Yes. I very much failed at my job. Blood was spilt, and I have thirty-three dead mages on my hands. Forty-six non-practitioners, too, including the wait staff."

It's an impossible number, unbelievable; a well-trained mage is worth a hundred armed men at least, and to hear that near three dozen mages died to sudden violence beggars belief. And now that I know what I am looking for, it's obvious: the bags under Fahriye's eyes, the slight crumple to her otherwise immaculate suit. She must have gone from the slaughter straight into the investigation, has spent the past night sleeplessly coordinating a manhunt that has brought her to my door.

And of anyone in Sealing and Containment, I think I am speaking to the one person who would care to include civilian casualties among the death toll. That is Fahriye Budak for you: always trying to save everyone.

"Among the remains," she is saying, "three bodies are missing—Viveca, Kristiansen, and Kristiansen's apprentice Maria Ying. Surveillance and scrying records were destroyed, but from forensic traces, it was obvious that there was an expending of infernal power. Your sister was the only warlock present."

"It's not a popular field," I say blandly, "not least because Sealing and Containment likes it so little. I hear you've gotten the faculty banned in Shenzhen." Dealing with the infernal was a revered profession, once, like sibyls and prophets.

"Not my division." Her voice grows more distant by the minute. "We're looking for all three survivors so we can interview them, get an eyewitness account."

"But *you* were there." My voice has a sharper point to it than I expect. "What more eyewitness account could you need?"

Fahriye looks, for the first time, directly at me. "Your sister summoned a slice of hell into the banquet hall, and demonic taint rests heavy on each body." Her answer is noncommittal, and she's not being fully forthcoming—she knows something that she is not sharing. "Is she a killer, your sister?"

I know what will happen to Viveca if she falls into the custody of Sealing and Containment. Mother instilled in us how much they hate the Huas, an uninterrupted line of warlocks—antithetical to all their organizational ideals, to the order and control they so crave. Viveca will expire in a gray, windowless box; the best she can hope for will be a painless execution, and most likely she will not get even that.

"All mages are raised to kill from a young age. This seems a silly question." To ask me this, of all people, the mage-killer par excellence. "Is Viveca the kind of person who might go on a rampage like this? Of course not. Surely you can't think my sister purposefully did this. We want Kristiansen dead for the murder of our mother, but what would be Viveca's motive for killing everyone else?"

Her eyebrow twitches, as if she means to say *I'm asking the questions here, Ms. Olesya.* But she does not indulge in such cliches. "The motive is beside the point, Ms. Olesya. The impact is what matters. Could she have lost control of the demon?"

"Being a warlock is about control, and she's very good at what she does. She could no more lose control of the demon than you could of your gun."

Fahriye nods once, as if only half-listening. All my fears are coming to pass; Sealing and Containment is satisfied that they know what happened, already certain my sister is responsible. The inspector is simply being polite, going through the motions of an investigation.

Does Fahriye remember what I was like as a child, I wonder. It's been some time. Does she remember Viveca as a little girl, and will that recollection soften her treatment of my sister? Or will all that be set aside in the face of Viveca's apparent guilt?

The inspector stands, our farce of an interrogation apparently concluded. "Officers in Hong Kong are searching for the survivors. You'll notify us, of course, if you hear from Ms. Viveca." She's renowned for her talent at finding that which is hidden or lost; she won't need my help to...

She's going through the motions, I think again. Methodically. *Slowly.* Dawning realization: whatever Fahriye Budak saw at the gala—whatever she is keeping to herself—she is pursuing this inquiry with the precise level of commitment necessary and no more; unable to voice professional dissent, save through implication and inaction.

"My utmost pleasure to assist, Inspector." I consider my next gambit carefully. "I have always admired your dedication to doing what's right rather than what follows the letter of the law."

Tension twitches in her jaw, as if she's been touched by a live wire. I wonder if Mother once said something like this to her, too. She nods once and turns to leave—then appears to think better of it and pivots back toward me. Incongruous, she frets with her sleeve cuff, working to undo a cufflink.

"Your mother gifted these to me, after that nasty business in Mount Nicholson." She extends her hand, offering me one of the cufflinks. "Citrine for Viveca—"

"And tourmaline for me," I finish, taking the jewel into my hand. So she does remember.

"These have been my good luck charms for years. I'd appreciate it if you hold on to this for me, if just for a time."

I am taken aback by the inspector's sudden forwardness, the unexpected familiarity. Then again, I am the one that has been shipping her illicit munitions coated in my own curse. I still find a chance to tease the inspector, levity in the face of this unfolding disaster. "Gifting a mage-killer jewelry, Inspector—whatever will that Thammarangkul girl think?"

Something flashes behind her eyes; Fahriye is deathly serious in her gift and in her fear. "There is darkness afoot, Ms. Olesya, a plot that is bigger than the both of us. Until we know more, let your mother's gift to me keep you safe."

And at that, she does take her leave, almost dragging her partner out with her. There is no love lost between them, it is easy to see, and now I wonder just how deep their professional animosity goes, and what it means for the investigation into Viveca's culpability in the Hong Kong massacre.

I find Chang'er fuming in her workshop—Thammarangkul has "accidentally" shattered a fair few vials, flasks, and pipettes. "I fucking *hate* cops," my alchemist mutters as she levitates the shards of glass and deposits them in a wastebasket. "Viveca didn't really do it, did she?"

"Kristiansen was there," I answer, and Chang'er sucks in a breath. Only now does the reality of our situation begin to sink in: Viveca implicated in the murder of dozens of our peers, on the run from the law. This could mean her death, mine, the destruction of everything and everyone I hold dear. My sister ought to have exercised restraint, I bitterly think, caution when the stakes are so high—

But I cannot believe Viveca is truly responsible. Even if Viveca came to public blows with Kristiansen—and *that*, I believe—she would have been exact, not scorch the entire earth. She loves power; loves, even, the awful structure of the world we inhabit. No matter her rage, there are lines she would never cross. She means to last so that Elizaveta Hua may be honored, our family name continued.

Not for the first time since I was cursed, I wish I had what I used to—my easy strength, my sorcery. Whatever peace I have made with my condition burns away before my wrath. Foolishly, I convinced myself we were safe, because it was the easiest way to cope with the crippling of my power; now, I am bitterly angry that I have been reduced to ensconcing in my mansion. Ruin like cancer in my bones, ruin like rot in the walls of our home, and me pretending neither existed.

Dallas is pacing my bedroom when I come upon her; she barely slows when I enter. Her eyes blaze—quite literally: were the room dark, they would be shining beacons. From her body language, I know she has heard everything.

"It is a perilous time for any who would call themselves friends of the house of Hua," I begin. She needs to be given a choice. "I can make arrangements to see you carried far away from here, covertly; you ought to save yourself from a battle that is not yours to fight."

"Of course not," she says quickly. "We'll need to—"

"You're not hearing me, Dallas. What is about to happen…" My voice cracks.

The tiger's frantic movements stop, and she fixes me with her unwavering green eyes. "In my youth," she finally says, "I would have told you that I loved you, that I would stay by your side in the battles to come. And then I would have slipped over the castle walls, guilt in my heart until I met the next woman I would love."

"This is about the demon, isn't it?" Under duress, resentment comes easy; I have known Dallas for so little time, I cannot hold a candle to those she has loved for so much longer.

"Yes. No." She shakes her head, as if trying to free herself from the cobwebs of the past. "Yves is caught up in this, and that complicates my feelings. And part of this is about *me*, selfishly wanting to prove to myself that I can be a better partner. But… I love you. I'm sorry I couldn't say it earlier. I will commit myself to this fight, against all who would raise their hand against you and your family. And I will be here when the dust clears, and we again know peace."

Her voice rings genuine, comforting in its sincerity. My throat closes and I want to cry into her shoulder, go back to sleep in her arms. Regain the serenity we knew, together, just a day ago. Relationships are tested by adversity, but I do not want tests.

"My sister will be going to ground," I reply, trying to focus past the tears in my eyes. "I will be obligated to stay here, but you can be our go-between. I will teleport you to her."

My tiger's features pinch. "You shouldn't be using any… can't Chang'er do it?"

"She's not adept in this art, or this individual spell—it's a Hua one. Don't worry. At most it'll eat a few months of my life, not fifteen years."

At this her expression falls. I am used to making light of my condition; I forget that she may never become accustomed to how little I have left.

"Speed is of the essence," my tiger replies, "but they are waiting for you to message your sister, teleport or no—this is *why* they visited, to spook you into revealing Viveca." A reasonable concern, even expected. What I do not expect: Dallas drops to one knee next, and with the courtesy of an age long gone, kisses the back of my hand. "I can call in favors, Olesya. I've lived a long time, made my own unsavory friends. It will take longer to reach the destination, yes. But better that than to lose months, even days, with you. Just point me at a map."

Few women have made me blush. She has joined a select company. The point of contact between her lips and my skin warms. I clasp my free hand over her jaw, her cheek. We have known each other for so short a time, and yet we have come fast and come far.

I have been practical, always; even in girlhood I did not dream of a love that would last, and once I understood the extent of the poison afflicting me, I dreamed of even less. And it was so simple when it was just Chang'er and me; our daily routines, our quiet estate—the pain excised for lack of desire to enflame it. Inertia ruled my days, and I told myself I was content.

Now, for the first time in my life, in the face of my family's destruction, I feel love. I feel truly seen—known, in my entirety, by this jungle beast who has as easily taken my heart into her maw as she has taken a place in my bed. Dallas makes me feel alive; Dallas makes me fear death. She makes me furious I have so few years left, because I need more with her; more decades, another century.

But even if I will not have long, I will have her the entire time. That's more than most will ever get. A great and gorgeous beast does not walk into every woman's life and pledge devotion. We will devour our foes, and then live out the rest of our allotted days free of every shackle and constraint.

"It's an old childhood haunt, a spot along the coastline of Scotland; Viveca will flee to it as a last resort, or leave a message for me there." I bend to kiss her. "Come back to me safely, and soon."

Interlude: Sealed with an Oath

Hong Kong. Thirty years ago.

The area is infested when Fahriye arrives. It is not what she would expect to happen in Mount Nicholson, a neighborhood so expensive that even to breathe in it feels like a risk to her financial health. But sometimes—very sometimes—the predators that hide in the world's bowels don't respect class. Or they are desperate, or hungry; almost certainly they have been intentionally lured here by someone with a bone to pick with the residents. She even has an idea of who the target is. Everyone onsite does. Famous or infamous, depending on who you ask.

Containment wards glimmer nearly every other centimeter: nothing unauthorized will get in or out. They press against her skin like a gentle buzz, warm. To any of the vermin attempting to pass through, they would be much less pleasant. The problem is that the wards also keep fleeing civilians *in*.

"What's the situation?"

The ranking inspector onsite—Stafford? Spumoni? if she is going to go anywhere in this organization, she really needs to get better with names—looks her over, putting in only the most perfunctory effort to hide his disdain. "Well, we're out here," comes the drawled reply, "and the vamps are in there."

Fahriye checks her sidearm—five rounds, infused bullets that glow like daylight in the revolver's cylinder—then grabs a handful of speedloaders from the arsenal that is being unpacked. "There's two kids in there, too. I'm going in."

True to their name, maintaining the cordon is the foremost priority of Sealing and Containment. Standard operating procedure states the dragnet will close slowly and methodically, no vampires allowed to escape; *civilians*, the protocols read, *should be considered casualties and are not to factor into planning or practice.*

A hoarse laugh from the man. *"Those* kids? They're devil spawn. Fuck, they probably caused this shit in the first place." When he realizes Fahriye is serious, his eyes narrow and his humor dissipates. "Who the hell do you think you are, rookie? I sure as shit am not backing you up."

And for that, Fahriye decides she won't ever learn the man's name, the pettiest revenge she can think of. She still flips him off as she steps through the wards.

The rumor is that the vampire incursion only happened because the presiding warlock is not home: an unavoidable function on the other side of the world demanded her presence, and Elizaveta Hua entrusted the safety of her children to the protection of wards, homunculi, and possibly a few demons. Whatever the case, those measures have clearly failed, and the elder Hua's presence or absence is not relevant to Sealing and Containment. At the moment, is not relevant to Fahriye either; she is bent to her objective.

In her right hand, Fahriye holds her pistol, the standard issue of her office. Forged from purified silver, inlaid with wards of recall, of aim, and of durability, it bears only a superficial resemblance to the sidearms of regular police.

In her left, the inspector has palmed two stones, slightly aglow with magic. Tricolored tourmaline for the older one, citrine for the younger—stones chosen at random, though Fahriye does not believe that fate is ever ruled by such vagaries. True, she knows little of the Hua siblings, and her knowledge does not extend to the esoteric nature of their births and the stars that govern their fates. But Fahriye is a superlative tracker by trade; signs, portents, the hidden connections that underlie all things—the stuff of intuition and unreality is her craft, and she has no equal. She chose these stones, the stones chose her—what does it matter? The children are alive, she knows, and with a little luck, these glowing jewels will be the lodestar that guides her to them.

Under the noon sun, it seems improbable that there could be vampires in the area, that each complex could hide an entire nest. By Fahriye's judgment, the Hua children would have been holed up in some warded chamber for at least ten hours. Terrified, no doubt; probably borne witness to what the vampires did to the rest of the residents. Not something she'd wish on any child, despite violence coming easily and early to the scions of mage houses. The Huas are the equivalent of aristocracy. Fahriye herself came from a much humbler background, a family of few practitioners, little inherited puissance.

But in her thinking, even the children of the powerful don't deserve to be massacred by vampires. Under ten both, typically not old enough to have done anything to warrant it yet. She is not here to judge and jury their future.

Finding the right building isn't difficult: from the outside it appears wreathed in opaque smoke, so black it blocks out the light. Made by one of the vermin, perhaps, or by a rival practitioner. Every prominent mage enjoys a bounty of enemies, any number of which would gladly stoop to consorting with vampires to see a foe's family felled.

She stands in the sun and gathers its light to her, until it clothes her in gold. She will not have long; she will need to make every minute count.

Through the door, across the foyer, quickly up the fire exit stairwell—a lift is a good way to plummet toward gravity's call; the vampires can cut the cables without ever coming near her—where each step echoes too loud, where the scent of blood is always near. Bodies, ripped up and drained dry. She doesn't stop to check. They're all lost causes, and will need to be incinerated later. An infestation is nasty business. Pyres for days after, the same as any site of plague.

It is not that Fahriye does not fear. She's as mortal as anyone, as tempting a morsel to the creatures. But a clear, tangible goal—that burns away the part that flinches, the part that cowers.

The vampires are silent when they fall upon her.

One burns instantly, scorched by the sunlight that cloaks Fahriye. The other takes a shot to the chest: a white-gold flash, a fall of cinders. The sun's gleam that armors her has dimmed. She climbs faster, steps two at a time.

The stones hum in her palm. This floor, down the corridor; when she comes to the correct door, she murmurs a charm of unraveling. The door opens.

She steps in and comes face to face—accounting for the vast disparity in height—with a child pointing a gun at her.

Two children: one small and in school uniform, the other very small and in a pastel frock. Neither looks like they've slept in the past day, though they aren't actively in tears. Fahriye's taken her turns babysitting nieces and nephews, and she would expect children to be less calm in the face of a vampire siege. More importantly, she doesn't expect them to have access to *firearms*.

The elder Hua sibling says, "If you so much as break my or my sister's nails, our mother's going to skin you alive and feed you to the hounds of hell."

Fahriye smiles, as disarming as she can be in the situation. "I've never met your mother, though I hear she is a very powerful lady."

"Then how did you find us?" the child replies, gun not moving from Fahriye's chest. She notices now that the young Hua has a knife in the other hand, not that it really matters. Armed to the teeth.

Fahriye wants to tell her, *Right now, that thing only works on the people trying to keep you alive,* but she doesn't; a little diplomacy never killed anyone, probably. So instead she opens her hand to show the two gemstones within, bright now with proximity. "I'm Inspector Budak with Sealing and Containment. I specialize in tracking. A little bit of magic into these here birthstones—"

"No one in Sealing and Containment wants to see a Hua alive," the child interrupts, unconvinced. "That's what Mother always says."

"Well, she's not wrong there," Fahriye replies, thinking of Inspector Struffoli. "But look. Maybe I'm here to kill you or kidnap you or something. But if you shoot me, the smell of blood will bring every last vampire down on *both* our heads. You can stamp your little eight-year-old feet once we are well and truly out of here, okay?"

"Finally," the child says, lowering the gun, "we are getting somewhere. My name is Olesya, and this is Viveca. Pleased to meet you, Ms. Budak."

"All my friends call me Fahriye," the inspector replies.

"That very well may be, Ms. Budak. Please lead the way."

She anticipates that at any second one of them, the younger in particular, might fall into a tantrum—exhausted, terrified, a meltdown. This doesn't happen as she shepherds them back down the fire exit. While they can hardly match her pace, they come along as best they can. Viveca looks at the gun in her sister's hand longingly. To Olesya's credit, she has evidently been trained in proper trigger discipline.

"Would you like to come to Viveca's birthday party, Ms. Budak?" Olesya asks, suddenly.

Fahriye sights down the next landing, then glances at her charges. Olesya looks just as precocious and severe as ever, but in the fading magical light that limns Fahriye, the inspector can tell the youngest one has turned white as a sheet. She curses under her breath; she forgot how many corpses have been left to litter the steps.

"I don't have birthday parties, of course," Olesya is continuing, rambling through her sentences, and Fahriye remembers that this isn't some skilled mage but an eight-year-old girl. "Mother says I must attend to my studies if I want to achieve my goals, and I want to be the most powerful sorceress ever. So I don't have time for birthday parties. But Viveca is very shy and also she has asked that her birthday party be Halloween themed and she would like to invite you."

The inspector realizes what Olesya is doing for her little sister, despite her youth. She stops and kneels, rests her hand gently on the young girl's shoulder. "I'll come to Viveca's, but only if I'm invited to yours, too."

"I just said I don't have birthday parties," Olesya complains. "Weren't you listening?"

Fahriye smiles and stands. The magic in the inspector's armor has extinguished, but Olesya's school jacket now glows with the dim light of a quarter moon. It is the smallest gesture she could muster, but Fahriye had to do something to dispel the lump in her throat.

They're back in the main foyer, only twenty yards from the door, when tiny Viveca stumbles. She doesn't make a sound, but the damage is done—she's skinned her knee badly, and crimson is already running down her shin.

Fahriye's ears pop as the pressure changes; the last of the vampires has smelled the fresh blood and is coming for them.

"Olesya," Fahriye says, again kneeling before the imperious little child. "May I have your knife?"

The girl nods, grave; she's smart enough to know what is about to happen.

"I need you," the inspector continues, beginning to roll up her sleeve, "to keep moving quietly toward the door. Can you do that for me?"

A second nod, and the slightly elder Hua grips her sister's hand tighter. "Yes, Ms. B—Fahriye. I can get us both there."

Fahriye turns back toward the darkened stairs and licks her lips. With a grunt, she cuts the back of her forearm—deep, deep enough that blood gushes from it, rich and red—and begins to sprint into the dark.

She doesn't have to go far; the shade is on her in a half dozen heartbeats, carrying her to the floor, then through a wall. The adrenaline dulls what must be broken bones, but the ghost pains of a thousand little splinter pricks delight the inspector. Good—more blood to mask the kid's.

The gun is in her hand still, and she gets a round off, a little burst of dawn that disintegrates the monster's shoulder. But this one is more powerful than its peers, smarter too; it has drunk deep of the dead of this place, and one round or a dozen will not end it.

The thing still squeals and grapples at her, returns pain for pain; Fahriye screams as her wrist shatters under its grip, and the gun tumbles away.

Well, she had a good run of it, all the three months she was on the job. Even with her limited tenure, she survived longer than some, saved more lives than most. If she had learned Inspector Spaghetti's real name, she realizes, she could curse him right now. Well, if that was the worst regret she has, then it has been a good, if short, life.

The hallway disintegrates. Everything disintegrates—the floor, the walls, the ceiling, the entire building is being furiously and angrily torn apart, as if wood and steel were no stronger than papier-mache.

The vampire keens, the horrifying noise of a predator that has finally learned terror, and tries to flee. A hand grabs it by the throat and holds the slithering beast in place as the building peels away and sunlight pours in.

The warlock of her age has arrived.

Fahriye Budak stands in a pleasant little library, warm woods and worn books on the walls. She wonders how the books are arranged and what sort of cataloging system they answer to—a passing fancy, not important, just a bit of distraction before speaking with the single most terrifying person she has ever met. No doubt many of the volumes are priceless, containers of vicious arcane secrets, the pages spelled to sear the eyes of a thief.

It is evening: the Hua children, she assumes, have been fed and put to bed. She tries to visualize the warlock of the house comforting them.

Elizaveta Hua is short, next to Fahriye; twenty centimeters shorter, even. But her presence is more than the physical space she occupies, with features that might be called arresting or forbidding, depending on who's looking—at the moment, Fahriye is inclined to the latter. No jewelry except for emeralds at the ears, tiny and inconspicuous. She has sustained no injuries, and she doesn't show the fatigue that accompanies the expending of power seen in lesser mages. Fahriye's still trying to figure out *what* exactly she saw, back in Mount Nicholson, the entity that Elizaveta brought to bear and which shredded the architecture like cardboard. Bestiaries taught at the academy only catalogue so much.

"I understand," the most powerful warlock in the world says, "that you are why my children survived the vampires."

"It wasn't all me, Ms. Hua." She conceals, as best she can, the evidence of her injuries. The medics are decent, but she still aches in more places than she would like, magic only slowly reknitting muscles and resealing bone fractures. Prescribed bedrest, but she considers that more of a suggestion; it's not as if avoiding this meeting would have been better for her health.

The woman's rouged mouth twists. "I'm pretty sure it was all you, as far as enforcers went. The rest was me. I also understand that your people have no intention of opening an investigation into why, quite conveniently, vampires happened to attack my home the very moment I was away. And are you the reason Olesya has decided she wants to join Sealing and Containment when she grows up?"

"I didn't exactly preach—"

Elizaveta cuts her off with a sharp slice of the hand. "If she applies to the enforcer academy when she comes of age, I'm going to track you down and kill you, Inspector Budak. No child of mine will be part of your organization." A pause for effect, a sigh. "But appreciation is due for what you did, an obligation owed. The other enforcers were not trying, in fact would have been happy to see Olesya and Viveca ripped to shreds. You put my children's life before your own. That is not easily repaid. Is there anything you want? A prize that can only be obtained through infernal pacts?"

Fahriye toys with the thought of asking for Inspector Scialatelli's death. But she is, for now, above such pettiness. "Nothing comes to mind, ma'am."

"I dislike standing debts, Inspector. They're like pebbles in my shoe." The woman studies Fahriye, expectant; "nothing" is not an answer Elizaveta Hua will accept this evening.

And in that moment, something occurs to Fahriye, a terrible and stupid idea that no sane member of Sealing and Containment should countenance. But she is young and she has lived through certain death, and in the right light, Elizaveta is far more arresting than she is forbidding.

So Fahriye cocks her head and flashes a wry smile; the worst that can happen next is that she is flayed alive—faster, at least, than dying to a vampire. "The last thing I want is to be an annoyance to the warlock of her age. Why don't we discuss your debt over dinner? For some reason, I've really been craving Italian."

Six: Inferno Orchid

VIVECA

For all my training, I have not been on the run before.

As warded as it is, we couldn't stay in my home: the location is too well-known, the building too easily breached. I took everything that matters, but that means I have to watch from a scrying lens as black-suited enforcers tear up the ferns that I've kept to honor my mother. They throw out the soil, upset and shatter the pots, even though it cannot possibly serve a purpose—they ransack and break for the sake of doing so, for the sake of declaring a petty victory over the warlock line they hate so much. The ferns lie in pieces. It bothers me more than I would like to admit.

One small blessing—my homunculus has escaped notice, abiding as it does in its hiding place behind walls. Just as well: it would otherwise have been studied or reverse-engineered, and High Command—the cabal to whom Sealing and Containment answers and ultimately serves—would see it auctioned off for lucre.

We are, for the moment, safe in a subway station that was built but never put to use, the tracks never connected to the rest of Hong Kong's vast underground network. It's been walled up, and I have layered the place with illusions; Yves has raised her own barriers of secrecy. My demon's protection means I'm not liable to die from some ancient pathogen, but it is not the most pleasant of accommodations. Dank old air, ventilated but only by the barest of technicality; the stink of sewage is, blessedly, distant. A muted note of the sea.

Yves hovers, half-corporeal, over the cracked, dust-laden bench I am resting on. "These are very rough conditions, for you."

"I've gone camping." To find rare components for my work, usually. Accompanying my mother, once. "But you can be my bed."

Even though she is more shadow than facial features, I can nearly feel her eyebrow shooting up. "Indeed?"

"I like waking up next to you, Yves."

The dark cloud of her stills. "Not the sanest thing to say to a demon." Then, "I've been meaning to ask. You have not chosen a human partner?"

"Long-term, you mean?" I've bedded all sorts of women, of course. But when my mother was at the height of her power, other families brought their daughters and sisters to my and Olesya's birthday parties, hoping to marry their relations into the house of Hua; it left a sour taste in my mouth. Have you *met* mages?"

An impression of a thin-lipped smile. "A time or two."

"Whoever I wedded would have drawn me into the obligations of *their* family—their rivalries, their alliances. Other mages are fun enough to sleep with, but a permanent tie is out of the question."

"And you would never have chosen a woman who's not a practitioner."

"What can one of those do for me? She would be a liability." Eventually I will need an heir or two, but you don't need a partner for that. When it came to us, Mother had none; both Olesya and I, like most children of our society, came out of artificial wombs. Some of the most intricate thaumaturgy goes into such arrangements, and Mother could afford the best.

Something glints within the roiling shadow of my demon. "Then all of this is a calculation for you."

"All of life is, Yves. Even stray animals calculate when and how their next meal's coming." I dismiss one of the shimmering circles of lights that gives me a view into my ravaged home. "I have engaged the service of a succubus to find Maria Ying."

"A succubus," she repeats. "Why that in particular?"

I widen my eyes at her, all maidenly innocence. "Why, are you concerned my chastity was at risk negotiating with one? The dossier my sister compiled on Maria indicates she has a weakness for demons. She'll be easier to find than her master, and from there…"

I trail off, then resume. "About Cecilie calling you her petri dish, and my sister…"

Through the connection we share, I can feel Yves *shrink*, pulling into herself, growing dense. She drags the shadows of this place with her; light flows like ink.

"You saw her fell three dozen mages this day. Have you perceived how she did it?" she says, her voice the smallest I have ever heard it.

I do my best to recall the death of the bystanders—the golden miasma that settled across the hall, the way the other mages clutched at themselves, as if consumed by internal flame.

"You see it now," Yves continues. "The curse she wielded was forged in shadow and unreality, obverse to the life and magic of this world. Your erstwhile colleagues attempted to call on their magic, and the contagion tore them apart from the inside, drawn like beasts of prey to carrion."

Diabolic, effective—a potent tool of assassination or mass death. And also a weapon previously unknown to mortal men. "You seem to know a great deal about this."

All light has fled this warren; I cannot even see my hand in front of my face. And in this absolute darkness, Yves says, "That is because the curse was made from me—is, in essence, composed of my body."

The empty station begins to brighten, and in the twilight I see Yves in her human guise, her back to me; her posture is one of hard lines, inflexible stone, so very opposite to her regular smoke and shadow. "You are aware that I was held in bondage by Cecilie Kristiansen," she continues, slow. "The mage inflicted horrors on me, used my body to test new weapons and spells. It would seem she succeeded in tearing away a part of me, without my knowledge, and now wields it to cut down her foes."

"And you were completely unaware of this? You cannot command her curse as your own?"

A scoff. "No more than you could lose an arm, and then manipulate your amputated hand. As for what I knew… I rested uneasy, in the span between when Kristiansen dispelled me and when you resummoned me. I thought it a byproduct of the mage's treatment of me, but now it seems clear that part of me was still anchored to this realm, leaching life from it. You have been more than falsely accused, you have been framed; demonic energy tore those mages apart, and you were the only warlock there."

"I knew you hated her, but I didn't not know how deep she had hurt you. We'll—"

"That's not the sum of it, warlock," Yves uncharacteristically interrupts. "The tiger approached me, several weeks back. She asked a favor of me, then begged me to keep it in confidence from you. I intended to, but after the events of the past day, you ought to know: your sister has been afflicted with a wasting disease that eats at her magic. Dallas asked that I try to remove it. I did not succeed, and it is now clear why—your sister is infected with the same curse that wiped out that gala. She appears to have tamed it somehow, so is not in immediate danger, but it is killing her slowly." Before I can process what I am hearing, Yves continues: "I pledge to you that I will help resolve it to the best of my ability."

That surprises me: demons don't usually offer extras. They perform within the precise, legalistic terms of their pact and not a single centimeter more. But Yves, I have established, is little like the rest of her kind.

"What does the curse *do*? To Olesya." I saw what it did to the other attendees. That my sister has been struck with it, and yet has kept it from me all this time—has endured it alone in the shadowed chambers of her mansion—is a thought that cannot be borne.

A flash of gold and red within the hadopelagic cloud of Yves. "I have not precisely studied its parameters. Dallas indicated it was a curse. I would expect it interferes with the use of sorcery—all kinds. You will, perhaps, not have seen your sister cast any spell for some time."

And I have not. But to think that she *can't* has not been anywhere near my list of conclusions. It's our birthright. To be barred from it is unthinkable, unbelievable. How long has it been for her? When did this begin? Seven years, at least, since she began to avoid meeting me in person. All this time I thought... all kinds of things, really: that she's come to feel acrimonious that I have Mother's mantle and not she, that I have offended her in some way, that a wedge has been driven into our relationship by means unknown and unknowable to me. It has kept me up at night trying to puzzle out what could have caused this, what could have stolen from us the closeness of our childhood. I would even work up the courage to directly ask her, *What is wrong, sister?* only to be told, oh, of course nothing is wrong. That nothing can ever shatter our bond.

Instead, it's because she has hidden this from me. Perhaps to not worry me, perhaps to not distract me from our quest to see Kristiansen destroyed. And she is right, because I would have prioritized my living kin: I would have done everything in my power to cure her, at the expense of our hunt for Cecilie.

The thought closes my throat—I have *never* wanted Olesya to sacrifice herself, not for any reason—and then it fills me with fury.

I will flense Kristiansen's soul. I will visit upon her every agony and indignity she's visited upon us, and then I will make it tenfold. It is a shame she loves no one and nothing, because that's where I would have started, to break her spirit by breaking those she treasures.

For the moment, we can't stay put and hope Sealing and Containment gets bored and goes away. They have scryers and seers of the most honed sort, enforcers talented with sight potent enough to pierce Yves' barrier. I take stock of what I brought, weapons and reagents, the tokens to which all my significant pacts are bound: a few necromantic ones, as my reach exceeds most warlocks'. What I couldn't grab on the way out, I destroyed—an unhappy occasion, to burn up my own work of years, but I'm not sentimental. Mostly. The homunculus I deactivated and concealed; the magical pathways to my personal libraries, collapsed. We have to travel light, going forward, unable to call on the full resources of the House of Hua.

According to the scraps of news I caught after the gala, surveillance devices present were destroyed; there is, as it were, no footage that points to Cecilie as the true perpetrator. Fahriye Budak may have attempted to delay the inevitable, but if she has testified on my behalf, it has fallen on deaf ears—I have been declared a fugitive. The death toll is nearly forty, considered one of the worst mage massacres in recent memory; silence on the number of civilian deaths, if anyone even counted them. For violating the neutral ground, I'll be wanted anywhere, so fleeing Hong Kong is not a permanent option. In a single night, I have been brought low.

Capture Cecilie, then, and hand her over to Sealing and Containment. There is no other choice. They'll make her admit her guilt—about the only thing they are good for. And if they do not, well, *I* will myself extract from her a confession.

"We're going to have visitors," says Yves.

So soon. "Then we best get on the move."

Without needing to be told, she flows over me, shaping herself into an angular jacket, a crimson blouse, black trousers. I wonder how she would react if I let her know that donning her feels like having a fortress between myself and the world, that I feel more protected than I have ever been in my life. An aegis equal to any slings and arrows, one that'll stand firm for eternity. Too much to admit, perhaps.

She carries me out through the cracks in the wall, making me as incorporeal as she is, a thing of dark smoke and red haze. It's not like anything I have tried before, and she does it so effortlessly. That she is powerful, I knew when I called her into my circle; that she is this exceptional has been a learning experience. My sight turns to the preserved demon eyes I've scattered throughout the area in place of conventional cameras, and soon I realize the ones coming for us aren't Sealing and Containment enforcers at all—none of the signature black, none of the signature arrogance, none of their G-man black suits.

"Cecilie's men," I say, or rather communicate—my vocal cords are not exactly solid.

Yves' reply comes as whispers against my nape. "Then we can butcher them as much as we like."

I grin, in spirit if not in actuality. "I knew I chose the right demon."

Cecilie's soldiers are searching the area in pairs. They wear wards against demonic influence, but those are shoddy and cheap, the work of lesser warlocks. It takes a sliver of my will to puncture them, tease them apart. And then nothing more stands between us and these intruders. I feel something like glee; anything that belongs to Kristiansen, I will crush underfoot. The hopes of these underlings, their dreams, their loves, reduced to dross before us—all that matters is that they have allied themselves to my enemy.

My first time ending a human life was at the age of fourteen—late by the standards of mage society—and I took from it an important lesson: killing is an event. The first occasion determines whether you have what it takes to do it again, and the visceral reality of it is sanded off with each subsequent success. Your technique grows even as the shock dwindles. Out of necessity, you arrive at a point where it is no longer aberrational to reduce a container of sapience into a collapse of meat, or you collapse into a pile of meat yourself.

For all my bluster, I've always felt ill at ease in the act of violence; I have thought this due to a secret squeamishness I've not addressed, one I needed to purge and move past. But with Yves, there's none of that, and no early experiences of killing could have prepared me for the experience of fighting with this demon. I intend, and she executes: she turns what would have been clumsy into surgical strikes, allows me to move at preternatural speeds. She is my armor; she is my weapon too, and in this union we are capable of anything. I will not break my hand on unyielding stone, I will not be bruised by steel. Instead, the world shall bend and submit. Combat becomes the most luxuriant, smoothest sport.

I wring a neck. Yves adjusts my grip, subtle, her hand on mine to guide and improve. My fist goes through a stomach clad in an ensorceled vest as though it is paper, and Yves drinks up the blood. I shatter an eye socket, pulverize a nose, crack a skull until the brain matter spills out; each step and motion is better for Yves' addition, for the finesse she has honed over eras uncounted. Ribs snap as easily as matches in my fists. Arteries give up their essential fluid. She has lent me the grace of a warrior, a mighty field general. With her, I am an engine of devastation. I could cut through twenty, fifty, a hundred bodies and not tire.

Cecilie has sent eight women and two men. None survive. I crush the spying larvae each of them carried—she will still have seen how we cut down her little unit, but not beyond that. But some are less... human; under my

101

hands is the texture of honeycomb, the writhing of maggots. There is no time to analyze the remains, consider the implications.

We leave carcasses, human and not, in states of dismemberment and desiccation. I feel like a flower basking in the sun, brought to sudden bloom. By the time we're done, back in our warded compartment, I'm breathing hard, even though no exertion presses on me and no exhaustion weighs me down. Yves' mass writhes around me, greater than ever, well-fed from the slaughter: a tide of void, the edges of her corroding the old, stained cement. Both of us have exulted.

I don't quite realize her intention until I feel the fabric of her grazing against my breasts, the pressure a little like fingernails and silk. My senses, already sharp from adrenaline, respond. I put a hand on my blouse. Already the trousers have become something else, black cilia caressing my calves. "Here?"

Yves slows, considering; her sight, half-shared with mine, takes in the cobwebs and the filth as if for the first time. "My apologies. For most of my existence, reality—your reality—has been an undifferentiated mass to me, just... matter." I can feel her focus turns back toward me, her tendrils holding me imperceptibly tighter. "It's only recently that I have begun to appreciate the variety of this world. That some places are cold and hard, and others"—the shadow moves across me, and I bite my lips to hold in a traitorous noise—"are soft and warm. So I apologize again, Ms. Hua, for my neglect. Where should I take us?"

"There's a little house I own."

She grasps the location, the image, from my mind.

We arrive. The place is as I remember it, small, cozy—meant for a mother and her two young daughters. I can hear the sea, the crash of the Scottish coastline (how different from what I hear in Hong Kong, as though the physics of tides have separate rules between there and here), but do not have long to appreciate it. Yves bears me to the bed. It's deadly frigid here, but I do not feel the fact. Her presence effortlessly warms, so much so it's hard to believe I may ever feel cold again.

She is both the dress, all shadow-appendages, and the hard human-seeming body that holds me. Darker than the lightless room: clouds have blotted out the moon on this side of the world. I take hold of one shadow. "I've been wondering if demons have a libido," I say, stroking what is both corporeal and not in my hand, feeling it tauten under my fingertips. "Since you don't have a nervous system."

"Is this the time to pursue academic inquiries, warlock?" A tendril grazes my inner thigh, more supple than any finger. I wonder if she's going to manifest those mouths again.

I find a solid wrist, bring it to my mouth. Press my teeth to where the pulse point would be, if she had cardiovascular organs. "You must think me a completely selfish lover."

One of the shadows, shaped a little like my ferns, has curled around my ankle. "And I'm far from selfless. Rest assured that I have every intention of sating myself inside you. I will give, Ms. Hua, and I will take."

If our first time together was otherworldly, she seems determined to outdo herself for the encore. The mouths return, more numerous than before, more attentive if that is possible. This time I give in to my curiosity; I kiss the mouths, discovering that each has its own set of wolf-sharp teeth. I taste their points. I allow their tongues into me. Thin, some bifurcated and some not.

And I probe her mouths with my fingers until I find one that opens to me like a flesh-flower, pliant and cool—like the insides of a snake, I imagine. My fingers sink fast past the knuckles, until my entire hand is inside Yves. What I find there is peculiar, soft cartilage that hums under my touch, harder bone that bristles with small protrusions. As I caress them, I can feel my demon shiver. My finger presses. I prick my skin open on one of the barbs, let her have the blood.

"Ms. Hua," she says, voice low and harsh, "my control is considerable; it is not limitless."

"Oh?" My thumb runs over a membrane of cartilage.

She moves abruptly, pinning me down. But my hand is still inside her, and through the bond that anchors her to this reality and to my flesh, I can taste the periphery of her reactions. I grab tight to what I have found within, my palm sheering across the thorns, and am rewarded with a surge of eldritch need as she enters me, malleable tendrils grown stiff with desire; her outline pulses when I clench down on those parts, too. Inside me, she thickens. An education in her desires, I think, and then I'm past thinking altogether.

Being taken by her is like being devoured; it is like being rent apart, put back together, reconstituted piece by piece. She leaves no part of me untouched, unpleasured. I grasp at her, find something solid, sink my teeth into it as I come. She bleeds and I swallow—the sweetness of blood, the fragrance of star anise.

Her shadow seems sheened, after, not in the way of sweat-bright flesh but in the way of burnished metal. My hand withdraws from her fluttering insides. When I touch the lines of her muscles—knowing they are not that technically—I find them dewed too, and it is a little easier to believe that she got as much from this as I did.

"Every time a human woman takes me to bed," she says, "I can reach out and close my fingers around the thread of her fear. Always, there is a sourness hiding behind her libido. She knows I can wring the life out of her, end her where she lies beneath me, right as she finds release."

I want to say, *I shall be the harbor for your tenderness.* "I'm not afraid of you, Yves. Our pact protects me thoroughly."

"Despite being hastily made." Her voice is dry. "In all the worlds, does nothing make you afraid?"

My choices: give her a real answer or give her bravado. I choose the truth. "Not anymore."

The pantry has been enspelled in stasis against pests and decay, and so when I come to it in the morning I find the stored pastas, meats, and eggs in good shape. The worst that's settled on them is dust. I clean plates, cutlery, a single pan. The stove functions and spares me the need to conjure otherworldly heat. About all you can ask for.

It's been more than a year since I last saw this anonymous house. I have been busy with my long war against Cecilie; it's not left me much time to visit my childhood haunts. Mother bought this cottage on an odd whim, a construction of fortified stone she had to renovate and furnish both conventionally and thaumaturgically. I loved it as a little girl—compared to living in Hong Kong, it seemed exotic and remote. Miserable climate, but always comfortable inside the house; no neighbor to bother us. There are goats to watch, on occasion, and birds we don't see in Asia.

Over my shoulder I ask Yves, "What do you prefer for breakfast? There's bacon and sausage."

A considerable delay. Then, "I don't eat, Ms. Hua."

It says something about a person—an entity—that she's fucked me well and thoroughly twice, and still insists on calling me *Ms. Hua*. "But you *can* eat?"

The shadow shimmers. It resolves into the tall, broad-shouldered woman as she enters the kitchen. "Not this kind of food. And I don't really taste—"

"I'll season the bacon with my blood," I say, not seriously. "Give it a try. Considering everything, you might well be sharing my palate."

Rain patters the roof and the window as I cook. Not much visibility, but both of us would know if anyone comes within a radius of seven kilometers. Sealing and Containment may reach us eventually. Still, this wouldn't be their first—or fifth—choice for pursuing a Hua. We can collect ourselves, prepare for what comes next.

And I must contact Olesya. Already I'm composing what I should say to her, in as compact a manner as possible, that would express my—how I feel about her having hidden her illness from me, how I can make it clear I'm not furious at *her* but at the confluence of circumstances that has necessitated her eliding the truth. When we met in the Arctic, was she suffering? Was she in pain while she pretended to enjoy her bicicletta?

Such things must wait, though. I plate the eggs and bacon—normally I prefer congee and lap cheong, but the pantry is stocked with local ingredients—and bring them to the table. Carved oak furniture, embroidered little placemats, a table meant for three. Yves has performed the courtesy of seating herself, and now she studies the food. "I didn't know you could cook," she says.

"Survival skill." I pour us both water. The pantry ran out of tea or coffee long ago, the wages of neglect.

The way she eats makes it evident that even the mechanisms of it are foreign to her, the motions of chewing and swallowing. She does know her way around a fork and a knife; perhaps she's had to pretend at human tables in the past. "It *would* be improved if you'd flavored it with your blood," she says, after a few bites. "But it's interesting. It's... corporeal."

"That's not much in terms of feedback. Anything else?"

"It's..." She puts down her fork, so carefully it is silent against the ceramic. "I've never had anyone cook for me before."

I recognize the tone: the caution, the distant bewilderment—the knowledge that you are exposing your raw, trembling nerves to another. I spoke to her the same when I told her that I hate sleeping alone. To her, expressing this enjoyment, this *appreciation*, is more vulnerable than admitting what Cecilie did to her.

"There's this one steamed cake I like to make," I offer. The kind that Mother liked to make, the kind I have never had occasion to make since. "I should bake that for you some other time."

"You're the warlock, Ms. Hua." Then her tone softens, as though she's catching herself; as though she is making a conscious effort to be less brusque. "I would, of course, be honored to taste your cake."

It's so incongruous that I cough out something like a laugh. "A demon with a sweet tooth."

"No, I said I don't taste human food as you... ah, you're having fun at my expense."

"I'm not mocking you, Yves. I just think you're being adorable."

She stares at me as though I've gone mad. Then, perhaps to have something to do, she tries another forkful of egg and says, "What do you intend to do when all this is over, and you have—inevitably—emerged triumphant against your enemies?"

"Advance the warlock arts, naturally." It's not an answer. "You?"

"Visit family." There's a touch of humor to her voice.

"Naturally, naturally." I smile at the image of her supping with other demons in some realm mirror to ours, mundane conversation and family gossip in eldritch halls. The joke dissipates into seriousness. "It's a loaded question," I admit.

"But one that is pertinent to me. I'm often summoned into a time of war—a tool of last resort, once a practitioner is driven into a corner, and thus needs a potent weapon. I am… curious what it would be like to be drawn into a time of peace."

It shocks me when I realize that I, too, have come to know only war, at least in my adulthood; the last time I was expecting to grow up in peace, to have aspirations beyond might and vengeance, was before Mother died. And now the world threatens to take away another of my family. It demands and demands until I would have nothing remaining.

Yves notices the shift in my expression. "My pardon. I seem to have ruined your mood."

"It's not that. I'm worried about my sister. But I am determined to survive this, and to win, too. Everyone will live; no one will die. As for what I will want to do then…"

Yves' head twitches. "Someone is coming. I ask that you not harm her."

"I don't sense—is it an enforcer?"

"No." Her mouth is thin. "It is an envoy from your sister."

Seven: Flowers for a Siren

YVES

Dallas Seidel stands at the door of the cabin, waterlogged and miserable. Shivering: she is a creature of the tropics, and for all her gifts she cannot lose her inherent nature, a skin that longs most for shadowed heat, for humid warmth. In this gray place, she does not belong; she is rejected in almost the same way that this reality attempts to reject me.

She's wearing a different face than the one I have become accustomed to—a Rajput prince, I recall, one of the first she took during our travels together. Not seen in years, either, such grandeur now reduced to a disguise, a face previously unseen to the surveillance of the modern world or the scrying of Sealing and Containment.

But I will always know her by her eyes—and despite our mutual failings, our bitter antagonism and now fresh blood, I swear I see her expression soften, a momentary flash of relief; she has heard nothing of me since before the disaster at the gala.

"You're my sister's companion," Viveca says from behind me, less with recognition—the face is not the one she saw in the Arctic—and more with the confidence that I have not led her wrong. "Come in. It's warmer inside, if nothing else."

I have been preempted; after this, I cannot keep Dallas waiting at the threshold. Grudgingly, I step aside and let her through.

For several moments, warlock and weretiger regard each other. Viveca's attention is like an incision, her second time meeting her elder sibling's chosen. Whatever face Dallas' wears, I do not need to hear Viveca's thoughts to know she is evaluating one of Olesya's potential consorts. "You are here on my sister's behalf?" she asks politely, a well of complicated emotions just under her pleasant tone.

Dallas' response is much simpler: it's outright hostile. "Yes." Her mouth is the hard line of a battle trench. "Ms. Viveca, your demon's been running amok."

"*Master* Viveca," comes the correction, precise and clipped. "That's the warlock title, Ms. Seidel."

She marches to the blazing fire, yanking off drenched clothes as she does, oblivious to the mess she is creating the way only a cat can. A moment later, and she *is* that cat—a tiger of lush fur and striking colors, a queen larger and more august than the pretenders of this less enchanted time. She shakes herself next, spray and stench filling this peaceful retreat. With an ill-repressed snarl, I will away the wet Dallas has brought with her, casting it into a sea somewhere far, far away.

"I did not—" I begin, and never quite finish.

She is herself again. That's unfair of me to say; her truest nature is a beast of claw and fang. But the flash of recognition is instinctive, unavoidable; she stands now in the glow of the fire, naked, returned to the shape I most associate with her—tall, wiry, a mane of untamed hair and a strength that lies coiled under scarred skin and calloused hands.

The original owner of this face had been a nobody, a woman who died in the Appalachians, that most ancient and storied of graveyards, fighting against the grasping covetousness of man; I think Dallas found a kindred spirit in that struggle, in that warrior's sharp chin and furrowed brow. Whatever the reason, she once confided to me that of any form she took, this was the one that most felt like home, found only after we had known each other for the better part of the century. And for all its newness, this shape is unmistakably *right*.

So I cannot resent her for this, even if she spoke to me with this very face when she ended our relationship, even if she used these lips to ask me to heal her new partner. Perhaps my face flashes a similar relief as she showed at the door, a passing joy that an old and unforgiven once-friend is still safe.

With the shift to this long-backed, small-breasted form, Viveca's scrutiny changes in nature: I can feel the beat of her blood, the growing warmth, an interest that surprises me because she's never struck me as quite *this* capricious. She's a woman of quick passions, yes, but—

She's taken a few steps closer to the fireplace—and to Dallas. I put my hand on the small of her back and she startles, as if jolted out of a trance. My warlock blinks up at me, her lips red and slightly parted. I repress the urge to run my thumb across, to feel them soften and yield.

Dallas has not failed to notice. She wrings the rain from her hair, to little avail; her voice drips with similar scorn. "I'm aware of the effect I have on women, but—pardon the language—the two of you are acting like you're in heat. Didn't think that happened to demons and humans."

Viveca stiffens against my hand. She shakes her head, hard. "Well," she says, "I suppose there *are* some disadvantages to binding a demon to my flesh."

I say nothing. It'd reveal too much: that the surge of desire Viveca felt—still feels, brimming in her chest—is in sympathy to my own, a reflection of this unique compact. It is very probable that Viveca was only acting out my own ambivalence toward Dallas: my old feelings for the beast resonating into my warlock, whose lust fed back into my own. Perhaps it is for this reason that this type of covenant is so rare.

And Dallas responds to this revelation with the shock it deserves. "You bound her to a *what?*" She bristles, and I relish the surprise in the tiger's voice. "Aren't demons usually anchored to..."

"Objects can be lost or stolen, Ms. Seidel." My warlock's tone is dry, but there is a sharp point to her words; I wonder if she knows the details of my old arrangement with Dallas and its fallout. "I won't get into the advantages of this binding, or the level of skill necessary. But put something on, unless you're one of those women with a fetish for bedding sisters."

Even after Dallas has thrown on a thick, wooly robe, Viveca's eyes remain riveted, as if she can still see the lines of wiry muscles, the way Dallas' spine bends and rises. I pull Viveca onto my lap and hold her there; amusement ripples from her, and I can nearly hear her whispering *Possessive, Yves?* into the crook of my neck. The thought is certainly there, inhabiting the interstices between her body and mine.

"Well," begins Viveca, "what news from Olesya?"

"Sealing and Containment came to your sister. They believe they have evidence you are responsible for murdering dozens of mages. They'd have arrested Olesya as your accomplice if Inspector Budak had not stepped in. Do you understand the seriousness of this?"

"Ms. Seidel, I very much grasp the threat. *I* have been entrenched in mage politics and have been since I was, oh, ten? And the inspector—" Viveca's expression shutters. "I'm glad she was there, absolutely. But more importantly, I know who turned the gala into a bloodbath, and the same party is responsible for the curse on Olesya."

At this, Dallas grows even more surly—she wears her emotion and her stress on her sleeve, and she reacts poorly when she discerns that I have not kept her confidence as she asked. She still turns the realization into a barb: "So you are aware, *Master* Viveca, that she's dying, and have done nothing?"

"The very second I learned of her illness, I have been bending everything I have toward her restoration. She is my only kin on this earth; I happen to have known her for more than a few months." Viveca is bending the truth, and she is unnecessarily confrontational in more than just words; she shifts on top of me until she has practically draped herself on my body, making herself both comfortable and dangerous to look at. She flaunts her beauty as a weapon. "Anything else?"

I worry for a moment that this reaction, too, is an artifact of our pact—that her antagonism of Dallas is in response to my own deep-seated feelings. I feel a reassuring pulse back, and the texture of the warlock's thoughts opens to me—she's annoyed that her sister trusted the tiger before anyone else, obviously, but there is also a thread of righteous fury: she wants the old ex to know that I am now in far better hands. It's almost... sweet.

And if she meant to rile Dallas up, she more than succeeded; the tiger looks as if she is in a cage, all but gnawing at the bars. And then, to my surprise, she bites back her anger. "I'm here to liaise between the sisters. I've updated you on the situation with Olesya; what message should I carry back to her?"

"You can do one better than that." Viveca takes on a slightly more conciliatory tone. "A succubus in my employ has found Cecilie Kristiansen's apprentice. Because you have no attachment to any family and no formal ties to Olesya, I think you'd make the perfect messenger. And you'll get to the root of the curse, too. How about you speak to Maria Ying on my—our—behalf?"

"I can't believe you do what the younger Hua tells you to."

I don't look at her, or at least not with my human-seeming eyes. My vision is comprehensive, parallax and composite, my line of sight far exceeding any mortal's. Flesh and blood count light in the visible spectrum; I count it in somewhat greater ranges. "She is my warlock. I'm contracted. That is the definitional nature of this business relationship, tiger."

We are on a train. Not the ordinary sort, very magical: this cuts through the depths of Earth's oceans as though they are nothing more than prairie and soil, a landscape of smooth and paved ease. It is not much of a view, to the human gaze. Both Dallas and I can see better than most mages here, but I can view more still. I like the deep—bathypelagic here, by human estimate, but I prefer what they call the hadopelagic zone, where the inhabitants are closer kin to the beasts of my home realm than anything else in the mortal world. Sheer accident, the result of evolution's complex braiding. Mages have not yet delved into the trenches. The ancient things there have not yet been touched by sorcerous regard.

"And here you were," Dallas says, needling on, "commenting on *my* collar."

A sudden recall of Viveca's hand deep inside me. I've not let mortals touch me that way before, but then again most don't have the courage. I turn, now, to the tiger and hold her bright gaze.

"Dallas," I say, voice even, "didn't you want me to move on."

Her gaze slides over the length of our carriage. Cobalt-painted oak, lacquered. Smooth flooring. Each compartment is finely paneled, private; here we are anonymous—the train doesn't answer to Sealing and Containment, or much of any authority. It will carry us to where Maria Ying has gone into hiding.

Finally, she replies, "Are you moving on, or is the younger Hua *convenient?*"

I could say many things. That Viveca Hua is like few other warlocks: the rejoinder of a besotted fool. That she is uniquely alluring: the rejoinder of a jilted lover, protesting too much, implying that Dallas cannot compare.

Or I could turn it back on her; rarely have I known someone well enough to precisely disassemble them with a word. How like a warlock, to undo with a phrase. *Olesya Hua is the sort of commitment that you always make: short-lived,* and I would be free of the tiger for another decade at least.

Finally I settle on, "Viveca Hua does not fear me. When I asked her what she is afraid of, she said simply that she no longer is. You should decipher that for me; you seem to know human women so well."

Dallas tilts her head to the side, thinking—she has opted to take my request at face value. "As you might be aware," she opens, in the tone of an attentive but put-upon schoolteacher, "mortals are defined by *loss*. A mother, a child, a relationship, all of it turns to dust. The one constant of life is that it eventually ends. Every living thing fears the coming dark."

I wonder how this applies to Dallas—how much she is talking in generalities and how much from experience. Every woman she has ever loved has died, many years past. And the jungle that she called home, that she spoke of so often on our travels, was destroyed so easily, so thoughtlessly. By the time I bore witness to its state, there was barely a single standing tree.

I felt that loss for her, then, and I rained ruin upon those that had taken her jungle from her. But how could I ever know what that loss *truly* felt like? I, who used to have no interest at all in mortal landscapes, until this tiger taught me the distinction between the green of a pond next to the bluer depths of a lake; until she picked out the gold in the glint of a leaf that looked otherwise red. It was only from her that I learned what it meant to lose a home.

So I hold what passes for my tongue and listen. The truth is, I don't understand humanity; all these years, and it is still a foreign shore that I watch from a distance, one that I occasionally sail to, only to find everything I once knew has changed. For decades, Dallas was my lodestar on those expeditions, the one unmoving referent, the guide who would explain to me the customs of the strange land she called home. She isn't actually human, of course, and her soliloquies could grow grating and pretentious. But... I have missed them, I think.

"The most powerful mortals believe they are special," Dallas continues, "that their wealth or magic will save them. But in truth, they wear their fear worse than peasants and ants; all their thoughts turn to prolonging their lives. When they finally realize they cannot buy or command Death, they fall into the blackest fear of all."

"And Viveca?"

"It strikes me that she's trying to tell you she's suffered loss, has come to intimately understand death, and that she no longer fears it." Dallas shrugs. "You've always had a type."

I chuckle, and something in the dark water beyond shifts. "I think you compliment yourself too readily. You run harder and faster from death than anyone I have ever known."

She growls, instinctive, the noise of a cat that is suddenly and dramatically done playing. "This Maria Ying girl, what's she like?"

Diverting away from personal affairs, the better to armor herself against injury. "Possibly descended from something aquatic."

"Like what? A shark?"

"I have not examined her genome." My affinity with the deep sea is personal rather than taxonomic. "Siren, sea nymph, mermaid. The usual candidates to spawn with humans. It would have been many generations back; she looks and feels nearly completely human, even if one of her forebears hatched out of an egg and had a larval stage."

Dallas frowns. Pauses. "Did *you* hatch out of an egg?"

"I don't ask *you* about tiger biology, Dallas."

"That's because there's not much to it; we have litters and go through all the usual mammalian things. Estrus cycles, if you really want to—"

I spread my senses across the carriage. By my estimate, we're half an hour from our destination. "Maria," I say pointedly, "is young and invested in establishing herself, independent from Kristiansen. It is this trait that my warlock wishes to exploit—that she's not necessarily loyal to her master. The weakest link, so to speak. Perhaps we could present Kristiansen's demise as an event from which she may benefit."

"Mages. They do nothing but sell each other out." The tiger snorts. "Do you always call her 'your warlock'?"

Throughout our meeting in the cabin, I have been patient. "And what do you call your sorcerer, tiger? Is she your mistress?"

Dallas shrugs. "My mate."

Did she ever call me that? No. I close my teeth on the answer I want to make. "We'll reach Maria Ying's hideout soon. Let me do the talking."

By virtue of its location, the undersea complex is private, strongly built and shielded against the ocean's rot, warded against its killing pressure. Breathable air as humans account it, saturated with brine—the illumination is warm, and there are efforts to drown out the inevitable smell, most of them futile. The place must have been intended to be palatial, a hidden city for the most prestigious of thaumaturges.

"I can't stand the stink," Dallas mutters behind me as we ascend a barnacle-encrusted path toward one of the residences.

She is pale. To her essential nature, this is even more antithetical than Scotland. "You're one of the least adaptive creatures I've ever met."

"My bad for not having been born a mass of shadow and smoke."

Maria's place is dingy. It must have been exceptionally unglamorous for the succubus to find her here. One lone slit of a window. Plenty of wards, none against demons. I slip in, solidify on the other side—the furniture is surprisingly well-made, though like everything here it is perpetually damp. Mold congeals and blooms in the corners. I listen for Maria. A footstep, unshod. She is aware someone is here.

I follow in time to see her creep out the door, whereupon Dallas pounces and pins her to the wall.

Maria freezes. I approach. "Ms. Ying. It's understandable that you have come here, to hide close to your element, but this entire area is shielded

115

against the sea. Makes it *tricky* for you to deploy your specialty, does it not?"

She scrabbles at Dallas' wrist. The tiger does not budge. "You're Viveca Hua's familiar," she says, glaring daggers at me.

"I am her business partner." Familiar is what you call imps and hounds. "Where is Cecilie Kristiansen?"

"God, I *knew* I shouldn't have fucked that succubus." She sighs, then lifts her chin, imperious. "Well, let's get on with it. Neither of you is a necromancer, so you're not going to get the answer out of my corpse. Let go of me and we'll talk like civilized... neither of you are human. Civilized *beings* then."

Dallas glances at me—not deference, but an old habit from decades of fighting together, a confirmation that we are on the same page before committing. I nod, and the tiger releases her grip.

We follow her back into the house. The moment we cross the threshold, the dilapidated parlor changes. Brighter, more whole, the decor done in gold and greens—what this place must have looked like once, before the sea corroded all. This is not the same sort of magic Viveca used to summon a slice of hell to Earth, but it is similar; Maria Ying is not as novice as I estimated.

"This way we'll have total privacy." She drops into one of the gilded, thickly upholstered chairs. "No refreshments, but I get the impression neither of you wants any. And not to be rude, but now I remember where I heard of you before, demon. You were the one Cecilie kept imprisoned for years, weren't you?"

All of me goes rigid. Dallas makes a very small, guttural noise.

"You must underestimate me a great deal," I say, making the temperature drop several degrees. Literally.

She holds up her hands. "I'm trying to say that I've severed ties with her. She's my master no longer. Why else do you think I'm in hiding? And you don't have to make it so cold. I'm just human."

"One of your forebears was a siren." If she would provoke me, this seems only fair. "Why have you parted ways with Kristiansen?"

"Come to find out, I really don't like bugs." Maria plucks a folded shawl off one of the cushions, draping herself. "Specifically I don't like them in *me*. The real reason she took me on as an apprentice was that she wanted to consume my line of sorcery; she's quite the collector. I'd rather not be hollowed out and have my insides replaced with her worms."

"That a new discovery?" says Dallas.

Maria fixes her with a look. "My moral compass isn't the topic at hand, shapeshifter, unless you'd like to spend the next hour berating me for signing up with Cecilie to begin with. I have an idea of how to find her, and how to take her down for good. Interested?"

I don't bother approaching to loom over her. I can do much better; I turn the inside of this space—this pocket dimension—the color of the Mariana Trench. Making this girl uncomfortable is both petty and simple. "You're very assured that I will not simply kill you after you've given me the information."

This time, she doesn't try to make a show of how deftly she can respond to my control of the environment; in our contest of wills, it's an acknowledgement of sorts. Instead she speaks into the darkness, as if alone. "I was there when she bragged about taking apart pieces of you, cultivating them into her most potent curse. She takes so much pleasure in *power*, in the control she has over others." And then she takes a risk: "Cecilie cut me open sometimes, too, looking for something. Took things out, put things back in."

A ruffle of clothing, as she closes off that part of herself. "*Victim* is such a... thorny word, when used to describe creatures such as us. I want to think you have a certain sense of honor, demon, and that in the matter of Cecilie Kristiansen, we are of one mind."

In the dark, Dallas tenses, subtle movements of repressed aggression. She is angry.

I keep my focus on the descendant of sirens. Little by little I thin out the black until it is merely the dim. "How can Kristiansen be undone? Permanently."

"She has decoy bodies. Actually, all her bodies are decoys. There are..." Maria bites her lip, remembered revulsion flickering across her expression. "She's achieved something quite close to immortality, if very grotesque. Her consciousness is spread across her hive, and she can absorb the abilities and memories of those she consumes. But her soul is stored inside one of her bugs, a phylactery of a sort; where that specific worm might be is another matter, but I can show you what it looks like."

"And what do you intend to do, hide here until we conclude our business with your former master?"

Dallas interrupts before she can answer, words grinding out through a clenched jaw. "What do you mean, 'cultivating them into her most potent curse'?"

Maria looks at the tiger, then at me. She doesn't answer, I'll give her that much. Instead she says, "When the time comes, I'm going to help you kill Cecilie."

"What the fuck did Kristiansen do to you, Yves?"

We have barely left Maria's room, are just out of earshot on the encrusted street, under the gloaming light tinted by the sea's shades. I keep walking. "Does it matter? My warlock and I will resolve the matter. She hates Kristiansen as much as I do. You do not share this animus."

"Like hell I don't. I want to help Olesya. And now I've learned Cecilie hurt you, too. Why the fuck didn't you tell me?"

I snort. "Tell you when? You've shown no interest in me for decades; you called on me only when it suited your new belle."

"That's—" she starts. "That's not fair. I *did*—"

"Go home to your rani, tiger. I'll get this sorted soon enough, and you can..."

I trail off. She's stopped dead in the street, staring at me. In the twilight of this undersea retreat, her eyes flash with nightshine, unreadable. I think I have mortally offended her with my comment, but it doesn't seem to have registered. When she does speak, her voice is low and dangerous. "What aren't you telling me?"

"I have told you I cannot remove the curse. I have not lied to you."

We traveled the world for decades, fought a thousand battles side by side, speak languages only known to the two of us. I read her face like it is my own, watch as she sifts through the facts that she knows: that the disease that is killing Olesya was manufactured by Cecilie, that I spent our years apart in the orbit of Cecilie, that I am unable to—or disinterested in—a cure. I wait for her to figure it out.

"You made this fucking thing, didn't you?" The venom in her voice is great, so at odds with what truly happened, the conclusion so unexpected, that I can only laugh. From a certain perspective—an uncharitable perspective, one that assumes every action I take is opposed to her well-being and happiness—it is even true.

Dallas leaps at me.

We barrel into a tenement. Architecture cracks and crumbles. I seize her shoulders, shifting for the leverage to pin her down. She does not oblige; her hand, gone to claws, rakes me open. I reknit my substance. Her mouth opens wide and her fangs sink into my throat.

I grip her skull and slam her into the pavement. She groans into the fractured rock while I step back, trying to physically disengage. My tongue, I control less well. "Do you think so little of me that you immediately assume, what? That this was intentional? That I anticipated you falling for yet another human trollop and poisoned *that* specific one a decade ago?"

Dallas pulls herself to her feet, wiping blood from her mouth. "I don't put anything past you, Yves. Everything you do is with intent."

She lunges again, and I turn myself into shadow, allowing her to pass harmlessly through.

Except that isn't what happens. Her claws find purchase—she knows me as well as I know her, and under her hands I am made solid, as surely as if she had uttered my True Name. She sinks deep and hits something hard, something that wasn't meant to be touched, and I shriek at the sharp and unexpected pain. On instinct, I run her back into a wall. This has the unintended consequence of driving us into each other; my body, still flesh, feels her hot breath against me.

"Did you not listen to a damn thing that girl said?" I growl at the pinned tiger, brick and salt-thick mortar cracking around us. "Cecilie tortured me, Dallas. She—"

She headbutts me, a distraction from her real attack. For all I call her tiger, I've forgotten that her feet are claws, too; smoke spills past exposed bone as she virtually disembowels me with a deft kick upward.

I am trapped at an odd place in the fight. I could end it instantly at any point—could crush every organ within Dallas simultaneously, strike her completely blind, undo her at my leisure. But I don't want to do that, even as her hate and her knowledge of me render me more mortal than I would like; she can't kill me, not in any meaningful way, but it still hurts.

So I stumble back, less from being overwhelmed by the pain and more to keep from being overcome by my instinct to murder any threat that hurts me so.

Dallas takes the opportunity to glower down at me. "You have never done *anything* that you did not want to do. Every goddamn decade we spent together was an object lesson in your thoughts, your wishes, your choices for me. You control everything, and no one can make you do a damn thing unless you wanted to do it. You spent years away from me because you *wanted* to. And now you've helped make—"

The unreflective cruelty in her words, the willful ignorance, tears at me; I am losing whatever restraint I still have. The shadows begin to creep like fog, curl like snakes, and still she goes on, blaming me for not being there when she needed it these past years, blaming me for the new evils Cecilie has wrought.

I'm suddenly on top of her, lashing her in place with cords of living night, pinning her limbs and wrapping around her neck. "I spent a decade as Cecilie Kristiansen's lab rat." My voice is terrible in the way of dark depths, and the rubble under us trembles at the touch of my words. "She found the silver bracelet you threw away, then chained me to this world with far stronger manacles. And *then* she cut away at me, amputated parts of me, used them to breed pestilence." The shadows twist tighter, bending her head back, exposing the long line of her neck. "You think I left you? You think I chose to ignore you? Dallas, there were some days that were so painful, the only way I survived was lying to myself that you were out there looking for me."

Some reaction rattles through the tiger, some emotion that tastes like death. But her look is defiant. "I searched, gods damn you. I spent years retracing my steps trying to find you. I called out, and you never answered."

"And whose fault is it that I…" I gather myself; there is still a deep pain in my voice, a pit that took years to excavate, but at least the anger has begun to crest. The shadows flow back to their corners, and my hold on Dallas loosens. "And once I escaped—once I was bound to Viveca and free again—when I finally did hear you call my name again, it was for your *mate*. This woman you've only just met. You did not even ask what had happened to me."

She snarls at me. In her human mouth gleam the incisors of her nativity. "You're one to fucking talk, ███ ██ ██." Despite everything, she uses my True Name for emphasis, not control. "You let a *warlock* bind you to her flesh. The demon I knew would never stoop so low as—"

My grip again tightens on her throat. "You'll not speak of her again."

Dallas wrests one of her hands free—in a human it'd have involved dislocation—and grabs my lapel. Her head slams into my nose. This does less than most would expect; my human-looking form is primarily cosmetic, and all my cartilage is inside. Nothing breaks. I grow my mass, try to pinion her again, when she bites my mouth. Vicious, as though she means to devour me, as though that is possible or this is a sensible way to go about it. What passes for my blood seeps onto her tongue.

She slows down. Her lips part. "Fuck," she says. "I forgot what you tasted like."

I could make her drunk, she used to joke, the only substance in the world that could meaningfully intoxicate her. "Are you satisfied, or are you going to keep up your temper tantrum?"

The tiger stares up at me. She reaches for me and I prepare for another bout, except this time she pulls herself *up* and then kisses me.

Her desire lances through, echoing into me, finding purchase. It is both like and not like my own, the sort of sensation that can only come from a being of flesh and blood, the libido of a beating heart and cardiovascular concert. I remember Viveca's flush, the heat humming through her arteries.

This is different. Seizing her face, I kiss her back, pouring into it not just lust but fury—that the decades have passed and they have left us this way, that we parted in the first place and in the most acrimonious manner possible, that Cecilie Kristiansen was able to bring me low.

This time she grasps not at my flesh but my clothes, raking apart the thin layer of smoke-fabric. Her claw-tips graze against my flank, forcing it into solidity, keeping it there. Anchoring me to the world of flesh. Just like old times.

What happens is more rutting than love-making, a union between beasts, the blood and the near-kill heavy on our breaths. I take her into myself, mounting her, stroking her from the inside as no human could. This is not unfamiliar to us, not the first time we've fucked after a fight, after a bitter but temporary parting. To damage and bruise and cut and then to end it all with this act. We break each other open, hold onto each other, close each other's wounds—two seismic forces in synchrony.

She bucks and arches. She gouges out my flesh as she comes.

We don't hold each other in the ruin of what we've made of this street: such gentleness would seem, now, wrong—conciliatory when we are anything but. I'm thinking of the years I spent under Kristiansen's tender mercy. I'm thinking of the image of Dallas that I held on to, back then. So we sit, each panting, on opposite sides of the crater we have made of our lives.

"I want," Dallas begins. "I want to—never have thrown that bracelet away."

"That's the wish of a child, tiger."

"Well." Her voice is thick. "I miss my mother sometimes, too."

It's not often she talks of her life from before she seized her first human form, of her life from when she was truly no more than any other tiger, a mind awake in its own way but not as complex as it'd eventually become. I knew, once, how lonely she must have been—and then forgot it somewhere along the way. A willful act, perhaps, a choice to assume that I had made her complete and so she must now be happy. Arrogant of me.

"We really do come from eggs," I volunteer. Dallas stares at me like I have lost my mind. "Earlier, on the train—you asked if I hatched from an egg."

Her eyes narrow, distrustful. "You're shitting me."

"I mean, the shells that hold us are spun from the Stygian black that lies silent between the stars, and the albumen we devour howls and keens like a sea in storm. But it's an egg. Broodmates, too. I had to feast on them to grow; each clutch only ever births the one survivor."

Dallas looks at me with a mixture of horror and revulsion. "All this time," she whispers, "I've been fucking a *reptile?*"

I feel a sharp comment coming on, an annoyance loosening my tongue. But then her face splits into its characteristic, toothy grin, and I flush with a heady mix of emotions. The old comfort. The ease we shared, the way her humor could deescalate nearly any situation when my first inclination was always to use force. Yes. I have missed her, despite everything.

"This is not forgiveness, Dallas. But…" I extend a hand to help her out of the debris. "When Kristiansen is gone from this world, so should the curse on your—on the elder Hua. Are we united in this cause?"

She takes my hand. "Yeah." Her fingers lace into mine. "We are."

Whatever touching moment we have, it is lost the next when she puts her weight on a sprained ankle. "For fuck's sake, Yves, did you have to be so rough?" she complains as we hobble toward the train station.

"You got me good, too," I bicker back; I am stiffer and more bruised than I would like. "Now we'll have to explain to both our women how we—"

I am distracted; it's Dallas who sees them first and pulls me into cover. A dozen Sealing and Containment personnel are disembarking from the train—not inspectors, but heavily armed and armored shock troops, expurgatory units fanning out to secure the platform.

"Do you smell that?" Dallas asks next. And she's right: rot is in the air, a poison that hums like chitin under the skin.

The realization lands like a blow: "Cecilie Kristiansen is working with Sealing and Containment, and they're here for us." The implications are horrifying; I am already reaching out to Viveca, warning her of impending doom, and she will alert Olesya.

But before I can pull Dallas in to teleport, she's twisted away—is galloping back the way we came in tiger form, rushing to warn or rescue the siren, sprained ankle forgotten. The tiger, off to save a beautiful face: the more things change, the more they stay the same.

Eight: The Life and Death of Fahriye Budak

The Scottish cabin is burning, despite the driving rain; magic pyres will do that. Not that it required much to flame out and blacken. The place is mostly wood, after all, not seamless armor against the world.

"Well, that's one less place those bastards can run," Yuwada says beside Fahriye, eyes almost manic with the reflected fire.

By the time they arrived, the cottage's inhabitants were long gone, forewarned or foresighted. A warlock of incredible puissance, a demon of the same: in absolute terms, if they had remained, she and Yuwada would be overmatched. Viveca has chosen to avoid conflict. One way or another, she'll have found shelter elsewhere. A Hua does not survive the world without a hundred contingencies over.

Good for them.

"Tell me, Yuwada," Fahriye says, masking her voice with affected disinterest. "Why did you sign up with S&C?"

The younger inspector gives her a sharp look. "Many things shouldn't be in this world, Inspector Budak. Someone has to make sure they don't gain a foothold."

The world's constant is that knowledge cannot be contained—this is not a threat, but a truth. A line from an old report she read, unbidden. Fahriye pushes the thought aside. "Is it personal or ideological, for you?"

"That's a tiresome question. And I should be the one asking." Yuwada cants her head, and then keeps canting it, a little too far. "What did you say to Olesya Hua in her estate? We did not advance our investigation there."

"I like to think," Fahriye says, tasting now the danger in the air, "that I have seniority over you."

Her partner looks at her. "Inspector Budak, I receive my orders from High Command itself. Your obfuscation is no matter; one of our quick-strike teams is descending on Olesya Hua's estate even as we speak, doing what we should have done days—hell, *years*, ago."

A deep cold coils in her gut that has nothing to do with the frigid, miserable rain. "The elder Hua hasn't done—"

"She's a *Hua*."

"I am beginning to think," Fahriye says slowly, dangerously, "that as it comes to the gala, High Command has a very *specific* version of events decided upon, and that my survival was neither intended nor welcome."

The gun is in Yuwada's hand, almost materializing from thin air. She has always been quick on the draw—eager to put a bullet in flesh, eager to see a body burst apart, what is inside it pour out in a lymphatic rush. Gloating at the world: this is power, and it is hers.

"That sounds like a confession to me," Yuwada declares, and her gun makes it so.

Fahriye wants to sigh at this excess, this pretentious display. A normal bullet won't penetrate her wards, of course, but at least the threat clarifies. "I never did like you, Thammarangkul."

"And your commitment to this case has always been in doubt, Budak." Her smile is vicious. "I'm going to bring you back to HQ for an interview. By all means, *please* resist. I've never liked your attitude—your lack of dedication to the law, your hesitation in carrying out justice as it should be carried. Someone like you doesn't *deserve* to be an inspector. You're a stain on your own fucking badge."

A part of Fahriye has always expected this: that someone would see through her, locate within her soul the secret, judge it the reason she is not so quick to shoot or destroy.

No matter. She learned, long ago, what she had to do to live with herself—the things she believed, the things she would do for those beliefs.

Acceptance, too, that death is the end of all mortal flesh, and that to die for something good and true is the best anyone can hope for.

This day was always going to come, one way or another, and Fahriye Budak meets it without fear.

And so she holds Yuwada's gaze, even as her fingers surreptitiously curl up and back, probing for the one cufflink that still remains. "My first dedication, Yuwada, is to what is *right*."

There must be some tell, at the end; Yuwada shouts, a second before the flash.

But Fahriye has no ear for it. She thinks of tourmaline, and then she is no longer there.

"They're cufflinks. A matched pair."

Fahriye picks the open jewelry box up, looking them over—master crafted and humming with impossibly intricate wards; identical, save that one is inlaid with citrine, and the other tourmaline.

"Oh, don't fret—you're not a bodyguard, I don't expect you to need to track my children ever again. Consider it more a reference to your skill. This is about me being able to know where you are, so that someday I might return the favor."

Between them rests the remains of the greatest meal the inspector has ever eaten; when Fahriye joked to the warlock that they should go out for Italian, Elizaveta called her bluff and invited her to a family restaurant nestled in the Tuscan countryside. It was the young inspector's first time teleporting; for as long as she lives, she will remember Hong Kong one instant, a flash, rolling hills and ripe vineyards the next.

Now, over tiramisu and dessert wine, sun sinking low, the conversation again turns to what is owed; it has, awkwardly, never really moved past that point.

"That's—that's really not necessary, Ms. Hua. I did what I did because it was the right thing to do, not because—" She has the intelligence to stop herself before casting aspersions on the pact-making and obligation-seeking that warlockery delights in. "The warlock of her age, owing a favor to a rookie inspector, is an unhealthy professional precedent. It isn't appropriate, and I can't—"

126

"They're bound to each other, Inspector. Grasp one in your hand while thinking of the other, and you will be brought to its location."

The inspector holds one up to the light, as if she is some simpleton yokel trying to measure the coin value of something priceless; maybe next, she chides herself, she will bite it to see if the jewels are real. "Teleportation?" she manages, still fumbling for how to politely decline.

If Elizaveta is put out, she doesn't show it; in fact, there is a slight eagerness to her voice—a desire to share, hidden under her affected distance. "A cousin to teleportation, more like—different metaphysical concepts. I've forged a leyline between the two stones; you'll be sent right along it, negating any wards or barriers between them."

Fahriye almost drops the stone in shock. Teleportation is already a closely guarded mage secret, but what Elizaveta is casually describing goes far beyond that: the warlock has performed a minor miracle, a feat of magical engineering that ought not be possible.

And now the warlock of her age is handing it off to a nobody in Sealing and Containment like it is some old, worthless bauble. "I can't—" Fahriye tries to insist.

In the evening light, she sees Elizaveta's confidence, her easy expectation that this gift will be accepted. But Fahriye reads portents for a living; she can just as readily discern the warlock's discomfort, the need with which this gift must be accepted.

"Thank you," the inspector concedes. "I will wear them in the spirit they are offered." After a moment, she adds, "Do you know anything about krasue? Floating head and organs?"

The warlock laces her fingers together, faint distaste staining her lips. "I didn't bring you here to talk about work."

"On the contrary, that is precisely *why we are here." Fahriye plunges onward, before the warlock's withering gaze drives off the madness that has seized her. "I saved your children and your heirs, Ms. Hua. I can tell that, to you, a piece of jewelry—even something as extraordinary and impossible as what you have gifted me—will never be enough to make that right. So I'm giving you a chance to help me with something mundane." She flashes her trademark smirk. "Let's take the shine off that guilt and replace it with some casual annoyance."*

Elizaveta rolls her eyes and sighs; she hates this already, which is the point. "Fine,

I accept. I will help you this one time, and then we are even."

Fahriye almost sighs with relief. "That's all I ask."

But the warlock keeps staring, hard and probing. "This matter between us... why do you care how I feel?"

And, foolishly, Fahriye speaks the truth: "You're a beautiful and powerful woman, Ms. Hua. I think I'd like to get to know you, when you are not laboring under the weight of obligation."

Elizaveta Hua laughs, cold. "I am a warlock, Inspector. All I know are debts and obligations."

"Well, that doesn't suit you at all, Ms. Hua. It's about time someone told you that."

And in the evening light, Fahriye swears she can see the older woman flush, a tad more red than the wine can explain.

A flash of light, and Fahriye is standing somewhere else. It's evidently the right place: for the second time in their lives, Olesya Hua is pointing a gun at Fahriye's chest.

They are in what must be the panic room, thickly walled, heavily warded. Well-furnished too, in case of a long siege, and windowless. It is more utilitarian than the rest of the estate—no paintings, no wood trims, no figurines of ivory and whalebone.

"Inspector Budak," the sorceress says, voice tight but controlled. "Where exactly did you learn *this* trick?"

Fahriye raises her hands. "Your mother." Not a lie; she can explain the cufflinks another time.

They are not alone; Chang'er stands behind Olesya, a sphere of burning light gathered in her palm. "I find that impossible to believe, Inspector," the alchemist interjects. "Sealing and Containment has attacked us, warded the entire estate against teleporting in and out, so that they can leisurely destroy my—*our*—life's work. Why would—"

"No one in Sealing and Containment wants to see a Hua alive," Fahriye interrupts. "And I'm no longer with them."

Chang'er puts a reassuring hand on Olesya's shoulder, and the sorceress lowers the gun. "So what is the plan, Inspector?" she asks.

"Well, I..." Fahriye has no plan; she's puddling the floor with water from half a world away. "We need—"

"You need to get Olesya out of the estate," Chang'er says, taking charge. "And I will trigger the estate's self-destruct."

Olesya whips around in protest, just in time for Chang'er to gently close her hand around the Hua's throat. Magic glows, and Fahriye recognizes it for what it is: a geas, the blackest of compulsion magics, made all the more potent by intimacy and knowledge.

"I'm sorry," Chang'er says, flinching from what she's just done. "But it's the only way. You have been my truest companion, through... everything. I owe you. *Save yourself. Lead Fahriye Budak out of the estate.*"

Olesya stumbles back, a look of betrayal on her face as she grips the glowing band around her neck, mouthing silent protest. But they have no time to plan, no time to second-guess; Chang'er is already lowering the wards that hide the panic room from augurs.

"Good luck, you two," the alchemist says, and then she is sprinting down the hallway toward certain doom.

"What the fuck have you gotten yourself into, Budak?"

Fahriye almost screams in surprise, only doesn't because Elizaveta has slipped a hand over her mouth and pulled her back into cover. When she can speak, she does so in a sharp hiss to the new arrival: "What are you doing here?! Did you teleport?"

"I warned you, the cufflinks let me know where you are," the warlock replies, blase. "But where are we?"

It's a flat plain of barren shrubland, dried mesquite as far as the eye can see; more immediate, the desiccated husks of dying industry. "West Texas oilfield," Fahriye replies, which explains the massive, grinding pumpjack they are crouched behind. "Some sort of snake cult among the roughnecks."

Elizaveta looks at the inspector and in complete deadpan says, "We're literally up against American snake oil salesmen."

The inspector stares back, trying to parse the reality of Elizaveta Hua cracking a joke. After a delay, Fahriye's face splits with a grand smile, and it hurts—the underused facial muscles first, the wound to her side next.

The warlock sees the grimace, and with it comes the realization that Fahriye is in worse shape than she looks, that at least some of the blood covering Fahriye should be inside the good inspector. "Where is your backup?" *she asks, stern.* "Where is your team?"

Somewhere beyond the pumpjack, a sibilant song is rising, the noise of scales and the blackened blood of dead things.

"Pah, that. I have a reputation to maintain—handsome, fearless, a lone defender of the weak. But people are depending on me, you know."

"Really? People *are depending on you."* The warlock gestures wide, sweeping the dead landscape, the cruel, cloudless blue sky. "Like who?"

Fahriye finally feels the stab of loneliness. There have been consequences—not for her interactions with the thirteenth Hua; those, Fahriye is certain, are completely unknown to her superiors—but for what she does, how she does it. She cares, and to the other members of Sealing and Containment, that makes her dangerous. A maverick that might get someone killed a week before retirement, a firebrand that won't play nice with a mage that needs to grease some palms; she's getting a reputation, and one way or another, reputations mean you die alone in a puddle of your own blood.

Elizaveta sighs, stands, snaps her fingers—there is a sound of brutality, wet with gore and dry with cracking bone, for too short a time. And then silence, save the rusting pumpjack slowly rising and falling.

"Now that that is taken care of... I'm in need of an escort for a formal function tomorrow night. I don't trust anyone else, and maybe in the idle dinner chatter you'll uncover a clue that's relevant to one of your quixotic quests for justice."

"Ms. Hua—" *the inspector starts.*

"Elizaveta, if you will. And it's a masquerade; your chastity will be preserved." *The warlock looks the battered inspector over.* "Don't bother dressing up; I'll have a suit made for you. We can be a matched pair."

They make their way slowly through the estate, Fahriye and Olesya, carefully avoiding the prowling members of Sealing and Containment. Olesya is sullen and silent; she has, as best Fahriye can tell, been forced to leave behind a boon companion.

Between them and escape lies the collected might of Sealing and Containment, here to bring the Huas to justice. Except—

—except in the silent halls of the estate is a sibilant hum, a stridulation just at the edge of hearing. That the walls are filling with the dark things of the earth, Fahriye is certain; she does not know what gives her this confidence, but she does not doubt her atavistic intuition. Some evil is here, something foul.

They're passing through a long hall when she hears approaching feet; she grabs at Olesya and pulls her to the safety of a side room. It's barely enough; someone passes by, and Fahriye's flesh crawls. She almost retches at the corruption that claws at her nose, taints her eyes, despoils reality around her.

The oppressive wrongness lessens as the figure retreats, and through the tears and the bile Fahriye can hear a conversation.

"I had to walk through the teleportation wards to get here." It is a cold voice, commanding, but there is an alien hum of locusts underneath it; Fahriye has the impression of ten thousand insects rubbing their wings in unison, emulating human speech. "And yet Inspector Budak can come and go as she sees fit?"

"She ran to her true masters at the first sign of trouble, exactly as we hoped. Her and Olesya Hua—they're both here. However she evaded the wards, we'll find them soon enough. And once we do, you'll know what she knows, and then you will be able to come and go as you see fit, too."

A laugh that makes Fahriye want to tear out her ears. "Within the legion that is me, you have been allowed to persist, because you are useful and because your hunger amuses me. I leave the rest of this to you—but mind that you do not disappoint me here."

Fahriye claws her way up to peek down the hallway—a blonde woman of imperious bearing, beautiful in the way a scarab's wings may glisten like jewels. Cecilie Kristiansen. Kneeling at the warlock's feet is the obsequious conversation partner, face obscured. Around them stand inspectors from Sealing and Containment.

Or what remains of the inspectors, at least. They look as if they are animated corpses, bugs of every shade and size crawling over their suits; underneath, limbs that are swollen, flesh that is melting. Thirty years of hard-won experience is all that keeps Fahriye from crying out; it takes every ounce of her self-control to reach down and take Olesya's wrist, and together they make a quiet retreat.

The hum of insects is louder now, but there are no pickets, no conventional guards; with time and effort, the two of them methodically work their way toward an exit, and out into the clean light. Fahriye can barely perceive the wards preventing teleportation, hanging in the air like gossamer—one sprint and they are free.

But before they can, Olesya throws herself into the shade of the building, wraps both hands around the halo of light around her neck. Blood flows as she tears at the binding, her palms cutting open as surely as if she were handling blades. Still she struggles, and with a silent scream, a titanic effort, the band breaks.

And then it isn't Olesya Hua standing before Fahriye, but Chang'er.

"It was an illusion," the alchemist gasps, tears streaming down her face. "She threw it up before you arrived, to confuse whoever found us. I couldn't say anything—she compelled me to lead you out. I'm sorry, I'm sorry."

Fahriye feels a flash of disappointment, which she tries to bite back; she has saved one soul today, and that is a victory, even if not the victory she anticipated. Realization follows: but if Olesya is the one still inside the estate, she will have with her the cufflink. Leylines do not care about the wards; Fahriye can simply teleport to Olesya, and then they can fight their way out together. Except...

"Chang'er, I will save Olesya. I swear it. But I need you to do something." She throws off her black suit jacket, rolls one sleeve up—a scar there, light against her dark skin—then unclips the citrine cufflink on the other sleeve. "Saving Olesya depends on you putting this stone in your pocket and getting as far away from here as possible."

The alchemist looks at her in anger and disbelief; for the second time today, someone is lying to her, sacrificing their life for hers.

"My cufflinks are, uh, linked," Fahriye explains. "Olesya has one with her, I have the other; it's how I teleported in. And if I can get to her and explain the mechanism, it'll be how she can teleport out, to wherever that stone is. But it depends on you—"

"The self-destruct mechanisms are buried in the foundation of the estate, activated at close proximity. The passphrase to slip through the first set of wards is 'through a mirror darkly.' If she's already activated the other defenses, Olesya will have to let you through the rest. Otherwise—blow all to hell." The alchemist uses her own blood, dripping from her torn palms, to draw out a map of the estate. "But I know Olesya's alive. This is where you'll find her. Get her out or—she means the world to me, Ms. Budak."

And then Chang'er breaks into a sprint; like a fox, she blazes across the lawn, no further words of parting. She's to the treeline without any issue, and then out of sight. A survivor, committed to the cause of saving another.

Fahriye will just have to trust and hope one part of this day goes right. She rolls up her other sleeve and steps back inside.

"You're doing it wrong," Elizaveta complains. A moment later, and she's wrapped her arms around Fahriye, long and elegant fingers finding the inspector's rougher digits, guiding arm and hand to a new position. "There—can you feel the difference?"

And she can, Fahriye is shocked to realize: for a moment, the magic in the wards resonate, the etched lines glowing with promise and purpose. They have worked for weeks at this, struggling while Elizaveta acculturated Fahriye to a different, more formal kind of magic than the younger woman was used to. A very simple ward of unknown style and provenance, and Fahriye has pulled at it like fingers against an iron lock, rubbing her mental digits raw trying to pop it open.

And now she has done it. The glow fades a moment later, but the joy does not. With a whoop, Fahriye sweeps the smaller woman off her feet and spins her around; only after she has carefully set Elizaveta down does Fahriye realize what she has done.

They stare at each other for a moment, breathing hard. Practicing magic is hard work, as demanding of the body and endurance as any physical training. These past weeks, Fahriye has never been more sore, and Elizaveta is little better; the older woman is also winded, skin limned in a sheen of sweat.

"Oh, I'm sorry," Fahriye starts. "I got—"

Elizaveta charges her in the same moment, hand cupping jaw and lips on lips. The inspector is taken by surprise; it takes a conscious effort to not instinctively and immediately step back, to disentangle, to throw up the barriers that have always kept her safe.

And then she leans in, as she always does with Elizaveta; relaxes, trying to live in this moment, to remember that life is more than—

And like life, it is over too soon. Elizaveta pirouettes away and begins packing away the equipment they have practiced with today.

Fahriye is suddenly gripped by confusion. Mages are envious of their power; they are not known to willingly teach those outside their families, much less outsiders whose day job is to hunt and imprison their kind. Fahriye knows she has good instincts, a deftness for tracking—but real magical tutelage is something she has always stood outside of until now. "Why are you teaching me this?"

"Because you have a bodyguard's instinct," Elizaveta says, then plows through the thanks that Fahriye offers. "That is not a compliment. You too easily and too readily put yourself in harm's way to protect others. And"—she pauses for a moment—"I can't stop you doing that. I don't need to be a soothsayer to know that some heroic death is written inside your bones. But what I can do is help you keep yourself alive a bit longer, buy you the time to save one more life."

There it is again, the old debt that Elizaveta can never quite forget. But for the first time, Fahriye believes that it is more than that—believes it truly, feels it as something like love.

She doesn't know how to respond to this generosity. So instead, she responds to the stated goal: "And this small spell you've been teaching me—what does it do? How will it keep me alive?"

"It's a simple shield spell, though of unnatural resistance, fortified by my family's knowledge—should you ever have the misfortune of being pulled into hell, it will

even preserve you for a moment or two. Perfectly suited to your sensibilities, methinks." The warlock frowns, reaching her point. "Too perfectly suited—if left unexamined, it is a safe cul-de-sac for your skills. But shields are versatile things, Fahriye, and I want you to see that; they can be about so much more than protection, if the caster puts her mind to creative pursuits."

In no time at all, the transformation of both Olesya's home and Sealing and Containment is complete.

Venturing back into the estate, Fahriye carefully navigates the hallways, her ears pricked to the omnipresent susurrus. The hum of wings, the clicking of countless mandibles, the scrabbling of too many legs—all these signs of corruption combine into a single muted roar. Occasionally, there is the wetter noise of fluid sacs bursting.

It's like walking into a nest of vampires all over again, except this time the monsters wear the skins and faces of her colleagues. The implications are troubling: if this is any indication of how deep Cecilie's corruption has spread within Sealing and Containment, then it is very likely that many of Fahriye's colleagues have been turned for some time; that she has spent an unknown time walking unknowing amongst catspaws and collaborators. With gallows humor, she acknowledges that this probably changes little: she's always been an outsider, and there has been a target painted on her back for years.

Very briefly she wonders whether there have been attempts to infiltrate her body, too.

She emerges into a parlor: once an airy place, well-lit by the floor-to-ceiling windows, now covered in filth—seeping perivitelline fluids, burst eggs, the oddments of larvae that have been devoured by their batch-mates. Everything twitches and wriggles. It seems that Cecilie Kristiansen means to use the entire estate as a new breeding ground. Out of spite and in triumph, Fahriye thinks. With effort, all that is cherished and loved may be despoiled.

Her footfalls are precise and soft. Most likely the worms are blind, but step on one and the rest of the hivemind would likely realize. In one corner, she spies an officer's remains, collapsed and husked out. One wet eyeball lolls on the floor; wetter offal collects in coils and puddles. The insects must have eaten some of those for sustenance. Even the man's skeleton looks more like jelly than bone, and there is less gore than one would expect—converted already to insect matter. She has a sudden vision of these things covering this entire island, burrowing through, darkening the waters; covering the world, and changing everything to more of themselves. She shakes it off. This is not the time to be distracted.

The estate's self-destruct mechanism—something that no home should ever need, Fahriye muses, but the usefulness of it in this specific situation is self-evident—is located not far from here. Through the parlor, through the library, every nook and cranny crawling with millipedes and nymphs and things for which she has no immediate taxonomy; slow progress through this waking nightmare of teaming death.

Fahriye runs her hand along one wall, and under her breath mutters the passphrase Chang'er gave her. And then she is *through* the wall, not a door but an act of phasing into the architecture itself.

Here, she finds steps leading down. Mercifully free of the crawling and creeping things—they have not penetrated this far. She is able to quicken her steps, then she's racing down, hurling herself toward her objective. And there, at the end of the stairs, is a small chamber, thickly warded. Through the magical distortion, Fahriye sees Olesya Hua—the real Olesya Hua, illusion of Chang'er dispersed—standing with one hand on a stone plinth.

When she hears Fahriye's approach, Olesya jerks her head up. "Inspector? Why on earth are you here—is Chang'er...?"

"Safe, I made sure of it. Let me in, please."

The sorceress straightens, her expression taut and dimly lit by the wards and the mechanism on which her hand rests. "When you came to the estate a few days ago, asking questions about Viveca—you couldn't look at me straight on. Why?"

"You—you are the same age that Elizaveta Hua was, when I first met her," Fahriye admits, "and very near her splitting image. Well, you're taller, but... it is selfish of me, but looking at you reminds me of the friend I lost."

Olesya nods once and then lowers the wards, seemingly satisfied that the inspector is who she says she is. "What a fine pair we make, Fahriye," she says, flashing a sad smile. "Did my mother ever tell you I wanted to join Sealing and Containment because of you?"

"She mentioned it, once or twice. Threatened to have me flayed if you went through with it. Threatened to strip my soul from my body when she found that pin-up calendar of yours, too." Olesya blushes like a school girl, and Fahriye laughs, genuine. "And yet here you are, running head-long into trouble, sacrificing yourself for others."

"What can I say, I had a terrible role model." The humor fades. "If you stay, we'll both die. But I assume you are here because you have a plan."

"That I do." After a fashion. "Olesya, do you still have that cufflink I gave you?"

The mage gives a dry laugh, takes her hand from the plinth to dig in a pocket. "Your lucky tourmaline, right here." She holds the jewel in her palm, iridescent. "Though it doesn't seem to have brought either of us much good fortune. Listen, we don't have much time. I'm going to prick my finger and bleed on this, and that's going to trigger the mechanism—everyone in this estate is going to be incinerated. You've come a long way to a very sad end, Inspector."

Fahriye merely nods at the tourmaline. "Say, do you remember what Viveca's jewel was?"

"You're getting old, woman. We just talked about this. It's citrine—"

And Olesya is gone, teleported to wherever Chang'er has escaped to.

"I told you it was lucky," Fahriye says to an empty room, the moment before she's shot in the back.

The evening is deep: sunset comes fast in this part of the world, nightfall rapid, the cold absolute. But within the cabin they are warm, insulated from the land's intent, muffled from the ocean's power. Each time Fahriye comes here, she feels it is a world apart, a sanctum just for the two of them. Ridiculous, yes. A comforting thought all the same.

"I know what you did for me," Elizaveta says, a murmur so soft that Fahriye can only hear it because the warlock is wrapped around her. Occasionally it strikes her how slight Elizaveta is, even though in combat she is so imposing, a warrior without equal.

"Hmm?" the inspector asks, stalling for time while she tries to intuit what Elizaveta is referring to. They're meticulous in keeping their lives apart, minimal professional overlap; anything more would be inappropriate.

Well, she did bring Elizaveta's favorite coffee out to these god-forsaken highlands; they keep running out. Maybe that's—

Her thoughts are interrupted by Elizaveta taking her hand, then gently pulling the arm to her lips and kissing the scar she finds on the forearm, long and deep despite the intervening decades. "You never told me the details, but I can trace the general outlines. And Olesya talked..."

Ah. Fahriye blushes, as she always does when this shared piece of history comes back up. "It has been years, Liz. And I did what anyone should have done," she insists, as she has every time before.

"You used your own blood to protect them. You were going to die, to save them." Elizaveta rolls on top of Fahriye, her small hands on the inspector's broad shoulders. The light of the crackling fire beyond halos her in soft focus; the sight takes Fahriye's breath way.

"Every day, I look at them and I see what you did for me. Do you know what kind of joy you've brought me, Fahriye?" She sinks down, resting her ear against Fahriye's chest, listening to the beat of this powerful heart. "Of all the debts I carry, this is the heaviest, and the one that makes me the happiest. Thank you."

For a moment, Fahriye has a flash of fear and doubt—that maybe this thing between them is just Elizaveta trying to thank Fahriye, again and again. That Elizaveta feels compelled to perform, as surely as if the inspector were a demon she had pacted. That maybe—

"You are a very silly woman, Fahriye Budak." Elizaveta chuckles; she has watched Fahriye's expression the whole time, and with experience can now read that face like one of her grimoires. "I share my bed with you for many, many reasons, and trust you for even more. And independent from that, I owe you." The warlock's sclerae darken, as often happens when she feels emotion deeply. "It's a debt that

would take two lifetimes to repay, and before I die I will find a way to make it right."

The wound is mortal, Fahriye knows immediately, large caliber through her back and out her chest—her own personal protections pierced by one of Olesya's rounds, or something very much like it. She slumps against the wall as she turns, a stripe of blood following her down to the floor.

Towering above her, smoking gun in hand, stands Inspector Yuwada. She smirks, and as she does something crawls under the flesh of her face, up her cheek and then across the surface of an eye: a long coiling body and innumerable legs, an arthropod of unnatural hue and dark portent.

"You're not looking good, Yuwada," Fahriye jokes, blood dribbling from her mouth. "Something eating you up?"

"Your last breaths, and you're going to waste them on that?" The insect buzz is softer than it was upstairs, but unmistakable; Yuwada's body thrums with verminous life. How did Fahriye miss this before? The younger woman shakes her head; a worm wriggles against her jawline. Half a wing, growing directly out of her skin, flutters.

"What do you want me to do? Ask why you sold us out? Ask why you're working with Cecilie Kristiansen?" A wheezing gasp. "I already know the answer to that: you're a piece of shit, Yuwada."

"You still don't get it, Budak. There's no *selling out*. Sealing and Containment, High Command—they welcomed Cecilie. *We* accepted her. She's the future, not whatever this lone wolf bullshit you have going on."

Yuwada kneels in front of Fahriye. Something dark and shiny scuttles quickly from her ear to the neckline of her jacket. "Nothing you have done here today will matter. Nothing you have ever done will matter. This? I should thank you for this—you led us right to the heart of this estate. Olesya Hua dropped the wards for you; how *pathetic*." When Yuwada sees emotion darken Fahriye's face, she preens. "Cecilie knows about your burgeoning band of misfit heroes—the warlock, the demon, the tiger, the siren. She'll make them her, in time. And you will make it possible, of course; all the knowledge of Sealing and Containment's paragon for her to call upon. It won't even be fair, how easily she'll take them apart; she'll wear your face as she does."

Fahriye knows she doesn't have long; she's confident there's now more of her blood outside her body than in it. "One question, before I go—the wards are keeping you from teleporting out, right?"

A flicker of hatred behind Yuwada's eyes. "A minor inconvenience. Whatever method you used to circumvent the wards, we'll know soon enough." Yuwada puts one hand under her shirt, then keeps going, not up but straight back, her arm sinking into her own chest cavity, halfway up the forearm. She doesn't react as she does this, doesn't even seem to notice the anatomical grotesquerie. After a moment, there is a sick, wet pop, like a bone being twisted out of its socket, and the younger woman's eyes roll white; whether in pain or pleasure or some other, less human sensation, Fahriye cannot guess and does not wish to know. Yuwada withdraws her hand: now soaked in ichor blacker and thicker than blood. In her palm, a slate-blue worm, squirming and thrashing.

"Welcome to the new you," Yuwada sneers.

Fahriye wishes she had a final quip to make; she wishes that here, at the end of it all, she wasn't alone.

But it can't end, not quite yet; one last act of heroism, before she gives up the ghost. Her fingers suddenly move with masterful precision, hours and hours of training with Elizaveta helping her stay alive a few seconds longer—all of her remaining vitality, thrown into a spell that is like a shield but is not, crafted not to protect but to contain.

She clenches her fist and the spell contracts around Yuwada's hand, crushing bug and bone alike. Yuwada begins to snarl something profane, and an insect tide rises with the words; mandible and stinger will reduce this tiresome foe to gore in the flash of an eye.

But Fahriye moves faster, lunging through the swarm; her bloody palm finds the stele.

There must be some tell, at the end; Yuwada shouts, a second before the flash.

But Fahriye has no ear for it. She thinks of tourmaline, and citrine, and for one final, infinite second, she thinks of Elizaveta—and then she is no longer there.

Nine: We Fall Together

VIVECA

The room smells of gunpowder and dried blood, clinging to our clothes and our hair. My demon has labored hard over the last few hours, bringing us here—returning to me with a report of the meeting with Maria Ying, then immediately teleporting us away as Sealing and Containment massed their forces to assault the cabin; has just returned from saving my sister and Chang'er from a similar fate. Sealing and Containment must have staged their attacks against us simultaneously.

Dallas understood immediately the scale of the disaster and suggested that we use one of her safehouses to regroup—a place unaffiliated with the Huas, deed buried somewhere in the tiger's long life. So we find ourselves in Ayutthaya, in a pleasant flat with a clear view of the river. The tiger looks much worse for wear than when I saw her last; her suit is torn and she's walking with a limp as she paces, counting the *minutes* Yves has been gone.

There is also Maria, who has stayed silent through this unfolding ordeal. She is technically our prisoner, but Yves arrived with her unbound, and she seems grateful enough to be with us and not left behind.

And then in a burst of smoke, Yves returns; Olesya and Chang'er step out of the shadows. As soon as she sees me, my sister holds me tight. Then she says, her voice tight, "Inspector Budak is dead."

That stops me short. I don't have much of a personal connection with the woman, but I remember well her presence in our childhood, and she did rescue us from vampires. "How?"

"She saved us." My sister gathers her alchemist close—Chang'er rests heavily against her, hands wrapped in bloody rags—and tells me what happened at the family estate. "She saved us, *again*."

Olesya makes the accounting of it quick, the way you might rip the bandage off a wound. But I can hear in her tone the acrimony that, once more, she was not able to save the day, drive off the invaders on her own. Now that I know what I am looking for, I can see the shadow of what her affliction has done to her—the undercurrent that, were she in her prime, Inspector Budak wouldn't have needed to die and the Hua estate would not lie in scorched ruins.

Maria sits at the window, staring out longingly at the river beyond. Her domain is the sea, but any body of water lends her a certain advantage; perhaps she wishes she were on some far shore, and not here on the land with us.

"It's not over," she says, to no one in particular. As one, we turn to look at the interloper.

"Listen here, you little shit—" my sister snarls, her pent-up rage turned to deadly venom.

"I've thrown my lot in with your ragtag band," the sea witch continues. "The sooner you realize that I am your ally—that I have never lifted my hand against the Huas—the more likely it is we will succeed. If you can calm down long enough to listen…" She trails off, surprised by our incredulity. "What? The chicken is invested in breakfast, but the egg is *committed*."

True to her word, Maria ends up giving us what amounts to a blueprint of Cecilie's consciousness. The woman—though how much of her humanity remains is truly debatable—has spread herself across a dozen bodies, at least.

"Not every bug is the same," her former apprentice explains. "There's the dross, ten trillion magically imbued bugs she can summon and manipulate at will. Then there's a main phylactery that holds her soul, which we absolutely must destroy. And between them is something like an intermediate vessel, a fragment of her consciousness. Think of them as little outposts of herself that allow her to communicate and travel over great distances. They're versatile backups and decoys; we start by killing them and giving her no place to run."

"Why can't we just find and kill the main phylactery?" Dallas asks, ever the predator.

Yves nods in agreement. "Kill the head and the body will die."

Maria sighs. "I *just* said that her secondary bugs serve as backup for her consciousness—she would be reduced but still herself, still bent on killing all of us. And do any of you know where she actually is? Can you scry through the wards and magic chaff she has thrown up to protect her location? No?"

Everyone in the room bristles at the whelp's impertinent tone. Maria just rolls her eyes. "Cecilie's absolutely ensconced herself in some magical redoubt, and her phylactery must be with her. And I have a plan to find the location, but it also requires killing the decoys first. So we can either sit here and stare at each other until the ramen runs out, or I can help you kill Cecilie. When it comes to her fragmented consciousness, I'll show you what to look for."

The difference between searching blindly for something and actually knowing what to look for, as it turns out, is decisive; Maria's cooperation is, frustratingly, the key. A hellhound brings me a scrap of cloth. A succubus returns with a photo. Lesser spirits that belong neither to the mortal nor the infernal realm fetch me street addresses.

Some of Cecilie's vessels are non-practitioners, ignorant entirely to the matter of mages; others are minor makers of cantrips, those without either the spark or the discipline to pursue true might. Our foe has chosen people who will either never realize what's happening to them, and have no cause to see the sort of doctors who would notice and diagnose, or those who lack the means to resist.

I mark the map as we work through the clues and the data. Dallas did not mean this safehouse to contain so many, and it's a wonder we can all fit in, even if one of us is incorporeal half the time. Olesya occupies the other bedroom with her tiger and alchemist; our quasi-prisoner Maria sleeps in the bathtub she keeps half-filled (I try not to ask). It's a crowded arrangement—all of us are used to having our own spaces.

The seething resentment Dallas and Yves have felt for each other has been resolved, it seems, only to be replaced with a more awkward status quo, somehow simultaneously too formal and too familiar. They will talk in esoteric trivia from their lives, and one will laugh; the next moment, curt nods.

When we have a moment alone on the patio, I tell my demon that I know how Dallas sprained her ankle. Yves' eyes go wide, like golden saucers. She recovers quickly. "Ah, our bond."

"Because you very clearly hate-fucked out the problems the two of you were having, and good riddance."

"I—" She looks everywhere but me for the right word to express her contrition.

I cut the demon off. "Yves, you've been in a torrid affair with Dallas since the Industrial Revolution, and she's seen more facets of you than I could in three of my natural lifetimes. I can't be jealous. In fact, I'm the opposite of jealous: if it weren't for my sister, I'd invite the tiger to a little tryst myself."

Yves glances back through the patio door. "Olesya does seem a tad more possessive than even I."

"And," I slyly add, "if you ever want to throw me through a wall and then pin me down—"

"There's a lead I need to follow up on," Yves hurriedly says, and vanishes.

It is, ironically, my sister and I that are the most uncomfortable around each other, even more than the demon and the tiger. We step uneasy, for all that we're glad our kin has survived; we have each been wrenched from our successful, powerful lives and thrown into the deluge. Me fleeing my skyscraper, then the Scottish cottage; her leaving her estate in ruins—it's quite a lot more vulnerability and tumult, *weakness*, than we are accustomed.

And I still haven't spoken to her about the fact she hid her affliction from me, that she felt she had to protect me in that regard. There hasn't been an opportunity, I tell myself; we need to keep it private from her retainers, I think… and then realize everyone in this flat—even Maria—must have known before I did.

I find my sister and her women in the kitchen, drinking coffee. They have been subdued since they arrived, laboring under the weight of what they experienced; it sounds as if escaping Cecilie's corruption was a horror show, and Olesya is particularly impacted by Ms. Budak's death.

But Chang'er now puts on a brave face, brightening when she sees me. "Ms. Viveca. Would you like some coffee? Perhaps you could give me a kiss?"

I raise an eyebrow and then blow the alchemist a kiss. "That'll be all for today, pending good behavior. These are what I have so far." I put down the tablet I have brought with me, sliding it over for them to peruse.

Olesya zooms in, then out, of the map. "Chennai, Paris, Vladivostok, Vatican City… Haiphong? They're very scattered. Probably the point, but this is going to be a challenge."

I lean against the counter. "I want to strike them all down simultaneously. If we pick them off one by one, Cecilie will send the survivors into hiding."

My sister does not ask me how I mean to accomplish that. Instead she says, "What will it cost you?"

"What does it matter? This is the endgame, one way or another."

"Smoke 'em if you got 'em," Dallas calls out, muffled from fruitlessly checking the fridge again, as if food will just magically appear.

"I mean," Olesya continues, annoyed, "how much will it cost you, versus how much of your resources can we keep in reserve?"

"A few pacts will be concluded for good," I admit. "No matter. I can forge more. The denizens of hell and elsewhere are quite infinite."

"We're not *all* interchangeable." Yves has half-materialized, solid enough to pour me tea. "In the time it takes one of your retainers to execute a vessel of Kristiansen's, I'll be able to take out three. How much will that cover?"

I eye the pins on the map. "Nearly completely. I want you to bring me to this spot in Paris, then leave to do your part. We aren't going to hit them in perfect sync, but it should be close enough and quick enough Cecilie doesn't have time to move them."

"I'll keep the apartment clean," Olesya says blandly.

More than ever she is furious that she, alone of us, cannot actively *do* anything. In this, she is a Hua: power is our birthright, and peace merely the mask.

"I think this is very much an 'all hands on deck' scenario, sister. You're a trained marksman—some of these can be taken out a range—"

"It'll need to be large caliber, destroy as much of the chest as you can in one shot," Maria chimes in; she's eating the last instant ramen packet raw.

Olesya relaxes, almost imperceptibly. She can help; she has purpose. I take her hand and give it an affirming squeeze. We are made a certain way: as siblings, we must look unaffectionate to most, a pair of unloving sisters who live far apart. But we are most together when we are united in a common cause, and we'll defend each other at any cost.

I ready our forces, such as they are. Assassinating a few humans of limited or no power is trivial to my retainers, and they'll be glad to be liberated from our contracts. Most of these creatures are fickle, always in search of the next master, the next games of mayhem and novelty. More than that, the Hua star is at its nadir. But that is why I have implemented a clause that, for the entirety of my lifespan, they cannot go negotiate with Cecilie. A pity she never put in place a similar contingency when she held Yves, but refinement of contractual obligations is what separates a true warlock from someone who merely thieves and harvests sorceries.

Yves takes me to a Metro station in Paris. I wait for the local vessel to come into view: an older Caucasian man, fifty or so, of no distinguishing characteristics or features. He's coming down the escalator, eyes riveted to the phone in his hand. There will be a considerable audience, but I have no time to waste. Through the lines of communication that join me to Yves and my retainers, I begin the countdown.

I take the ascending escalator. Ambient music and the cacophony of commute around us, mingling with the smells of any city, the body odors that ventilation cannot disperse, the foulness absorbed into the architecture. Paris is a graveyard, burials layered many times over, the asphalt and steel and stone brimming with grudges. Even its glamor and wealth are stolen. A suitable place for a piece of Cecilie.

In a moment, we line up. The concentration of force I direct with my hand tears through the man, its fire rapidly spreading through him. I reach into the dissolving flesh and seize the worm hiding there, forcing it to stay within the conflagration.

The phone and the body tumble down the toothed steps. My gloved hand is wet with worm fluids.

In the ensuing chaos, I calmly get through the exit, then out onto a busy Parisian street. The filthy glove I peel off, and that too I set on fire.

"Back to Ayutthaya," I command, and Yves envelopes me for transport.

"This isn't Ayutthaya," I say. "Where the hell are we?"

We are standing in a glade of red spider lilies, long stems and thin umbels gently shifting in a faint and pleasant breeze; above, a gentle sun warms us. But it is not trees that enclose this bucolic scene, but a howling inferno, ghastly shapes bending and twisting just beyond some impenetrable barrier.

"Precisely there," Yves replies with a self-satisfied chuckle. "Your ability to pull a fragment of my world into yours inspired me to try the opposite—a garden of earth, in a kingdom of hell. And do not worry about the time, Ms. Hua," she adds, anticipating my concern. "It flows a little differently here—we can spend an afternoon lying amongst the flowers, and a second will have elapsed elsewhere."

"I—" My heart still beats with the adrenaline of my recent kill, and my mind is focused on planning the battle ahead. "I didn't pack for a vacation like this."

"Of course, of course," Yves says. "But this is also a type of preparation."

She sits, inky black spilling out under her to form a checkered picnic blanket. I smile at the absurdity of the gesture, and some of my tension eases; I join her.

"You know I was in a relationship with Dallas." A memory of the tiger's naked back comes to me, and I flush. Yves side-eyes me with a smirk, but I can feel the flicker of my lust echo within her, too.

"Yes," I answer dryly. "This may have come up once or twice."

"When we traveled the world together, the tiger and her shadow, I made certain assumptions. About what a relationship was like, about how to express care and affection. With the benefit of hindsight, I can see I was not a good partner for her, and I left many words unspoken because I thought they were obvious. Ironic that I learned this lesson, only to share a near-psychic connection with my next partner."

And it is because of this connection that I feel how tense she is, how she roils with emotion. "I'm listening," I assure her.

"When I stay too long—" She corrects herself, eliding the assumption that there's such a thing as too long: "In your world, if I stay for an extended period of time in one place, reality begins to deform; nature, abhorring anathema, tries to find a way to cohabit. It was only when I was with you that I realized the reciprocal might also be true." She motions at the field of flowers around us. "The fruit of my labor."

"Our connection—it bleeds both ways?" It stands to reason that it must, but I haven't thought of it as such. And then I think of bits of earth and rock and grass popping into Yves' home reality, and giggle.

"It's not as if every step I take here bursts into greenery, and the real analogy would be you staying here and bringing order to the realm. But what I am trying to say is that I drew on your strength and your example to make this place. It is… it is the first thing I have ever made outside the duress of a contract. I wanted to thank you for that."

"It's beautiful, Yves. It matches you."

"You flatterer," she snorts, then sighs. "Against my better judgment, Viveca Hua, I think I might love you."

And then she kisses me.

We've been rough with each other in the fever-pitch of new lovers, but she's gentle now, her lips meeting mine in pavane—stately, chivalrous. She means to savor this, to savor me in this dilation of time where we may pretend we can capture a piece of forever.

I snake my hand under her jacket. "Disrobe me, Yves."

She is clothing me in any case, but she takes her time unbuttoning my blouse, unzipping my skirt. My stockings she peels off as though it is delicate ricepaper, and each patch of newly exposed skin she anoints with her mouth.

On the picnic blanket, I push her down. Her hand slides from my flank to my hip, down my thigh; her golden eyes gleam under the warm noon, under the idyll of this impossible place. "You're the heart of this glade," she whispers. "And sometimes—sometimes I suspect you may also be the heart of me."

Straddling her, I cup her face between my hands. The embers-on-black luxury of her hair is silken against my fingers; her long lashes tickle the pad of my thumb. "Hell has never birthed a creature as silver-tongued as you." I kiss her nose. "As a warlock, I'm exceptionally fortunate." Then I kiss her mouth, and from there her throat.

It's the slowest we have ever paced ourselves. Both of us want it to last, to have an excuse to linger here, to prolong this flawless afternoon. To never have to think of anything but each other's skin, to breathe nothing but each other's scent. She cups between my thighs, opening me finger by finger; I tend to each of her mouths, stroking where I know will make her arch and twitch under me.

By the time we are exhausted, twilight has fallen over our little glade, and something approximating stars burn overhead. "Technically, I'm just as naked now as when we came here," I purr against my demon. "Among your many attributes, you make an impressive wardrobe. If our arrangement lasts much longer, I'm really contemplating throwing out the rest of my clothes."

Beneath us, the flowers susurrate; a far more pleasant bed of blood red than the one I lay on when I first met Yves, dying in the Antarctic.

"Cecilie Kristiansen knows my True Name," Yves replies, a grim non-sequitur. From her tone, it is clear this thought has preoccupied her for a while.

"Of course she must." I sound more nonchalant than I am; the demon would not be bringing this up without cause. "But my pact with you supersedes any authority she had over you, and she was clearly not wise enough to forbid you from working with me."

150

"She can still thwart me—halt me for a critical moment, or craft a bullet that pierces through my body to reach you; she has already found a way to tear off a part of me and subvert it to her commands. And don't forget that she knows your True Name, too—I learned it from her, after all."

"You're really concerned about this."

"I swore that I would be your armor. I am particularly motivated to keep a certain warlock alive, but even if I weren't, this very much falls within my remit. So, a solution of sorts."

She reaches over and plucks a red spider lily from the field, then gently puts it into my hair. Power pours from it a moment later; I pull away from Yves and stand in time to see black onyx flow over my body, then harden into body armor.

Yves is polite enough to summon a standing mirror. "Soil and material from your earth," she explains, "exposed to the unreality of my plane and imbued with demonic emanation. I used this garden to craft more than one thing, you see."

It is beautiful—shiny black with highlights of red, Yves' colors with a touch of the spider lily's hue. Laminate plates protect every joint, but flexibility is completely unhindered. It is perfect to the point of superfluous.

"It will respond to your thoughts and no other, draws its strength from this patch of reality and nowhere else. Without using a drop of your power, you could punch a hole through the front armor of a main battle tank, and will be shielded from any magics, even those imbued with your True Name. It will never know rust, and with a word you can hand it down to your heir."

"You—" The smile on my face freezes, my good humor turned to sudden foreboding. "You don't plan to come back from this."

"Viveca," Yves replies, after a moment. "If it were just a function of planning, then I would chart the path of every star and every atom and make of our perfect future an inevitability. And if it were a matter of will or desire alone, then Cecilie would be dead a dozen times over from boiling sea and blackened sky. But it isn't."

"Then promise me that we'll both survive, at least. Promise me we'll come back here."

"I can't. You know I can't. But my pact with you is inviolable, for as long as I exist, in your world or any other: to stand by your side in battle, to protect you from harm, and to guard what is yours."

I swallow my fear, crush it into nothing with thought and will and anger. It is, finally, courage enough.

"I love you, ███ ██," I reply.

It is the first time I ever say it.

OLESYA

In the apartment's confines, I lay out my equipment, transported here from one of my caches in the region: I follow best practice for arms-dealers. It's ironic that, a long time ago, I found firearms beneath me: convenient, yes, but not of any particular interest. In the times since, I've become intimately familiar, an expert at the matter of chamber and muzzle, ammunition and trigger discipline. Gunmetal has become dear to me, almost dearer than silks and satins. There is a smith I have commissioned custom pieces from, and the crafting of any one firearm they perform is an act that approaches love. They lavish such attention on the process, treat every new pistol or rifle as its own unique work of art. Not far from the truth either.

"Preparing for war," Dallas remarks as she comes in, putting down her purchases—sticky rice and mango, milky Thai tea. For me; she doesn't have much of a sweet tooth. "Like a field-general of old."

"My sister is the general." I keep my voice dry, devoid of feeling. For the moment the others are out, and we have some privacy. "I could flatter myself that I'm second-in-command, I suppose. More realistically I'm the quartermaster."

"You're far more than that." She plates the sticky rice for me, sets it on the kitchen table. "It must have been... difficult."

I could deflect. It's so easy to: I do it all the time, so much so that it's become instinctive. If I never speak of my hurts, then they are not real. If I pretend then I am whole, then I must be. "Preparing to take the fight to our enemy isn't the occasion for you to attempt to give me therapy, Dallas."

"You're being prickly on purpose." She is smiling as she says it, scooping up a spoonful of rice and mango. "Luckily I have a thick hide. Here, have some of this."

It's a sweet treat and, I must admit, quite good. Topped by the right amount of coconut cream, garnished in white sesame. Perhaps this is what I needed all along, a bit of sugar to lift the mood. I lick the spoon, and then I lick Dallas' finger. She meets my eyes: there is an unspoken accord between us that, within the atavistic recesses of our respective brains, there abides a predator-prey impulse. To devour; to be devoured—and sometimes it is not as simple as the tiger eating the sorceress; I am capable of hunger, too. I have thought, as I bury my face in her golden neck or her white belly, about what it'd be like if I had a carnivore's teeth of my own. How she would taste as I sink my fangs past the silk of her fur, all that savory brilliance hiding beneath fibrous muscle. My incisors graze her skin.

"From the start," she says, "I've recognized in you a kindred spirit. I saw in you a deep courage and strength. You don't live in your sister's shadow. You are a great beacon, and nothing less."

"I'm rational, Dallas. Even if I felt... anything about that, this battle is too crucial for—"

"For your feelings to matter?"

My mouth hardens into a thin line.

"Your feelings and you," says my tiger, "are everything. And—I don't think of you as weak. As fragile."

"If in battle, I have to act to protect *you*, then what?"

And here, she falters; of course she'd falter. It is then that I know she would rather I stay here, out of harm's way, that deep down she believes I'm a thing of fragile ceramic and—

Dallas seizes my hand. Grips it tight. "Whatever you decide is right and correct, Olesya. I, of all people... I'd never put you in a cage. Not even under the pretense that it's for your own good. I will be at your side, and I will guard you—we will protect each other, as two mates should. To me it is that simple."

Little by little I untense. Little by little, I relax into her touch. "Then that is how it will be. I pledge to defend you, my tiger, as you will defend me."

Rifles are so much more impersonal than knives, I used to think. With a knife, you feel the arterial spray, the cooling warmth of dying flesh. You look your foe in the eye, their great plans of conquest naught before a keen edge and a steady hand. You can *win*.

When this curse fell upon me, the magics that let me knit flesh and bone with the ease of breathing are now strained to their limit merely to keep my heart beating. In turn, I gained a reputation as a ruthless killer of other mages, the coldest comfort. And though most of those assassination were at the hands of the cadre of snipers I employ, I still found it prudent to train, relentlessly, with long rifles.

I remember, vaguely, my mother doing the same—for sport, on the lawn of our estate; in this small way, in this perhaps-false memory, I still feel like I am her daughter.

And you might believe a gun more detached from the act of killing, physical distance mirrored in the metaphysical. But it's so much worse. With a knife, melee is joined; strength is pitted against strength. But through the scope of a rifle, the person is so normal, so *pathetic*. Your foe is reduced to a target; they have no chance to rise to the occasion, no chance to grit their teeth, take the blow, return blood for blood. You see them, not as they are in battle, but as they are alone, the way we all are when we are alone: they eat, they shit, they read the newspaper.

I once asked my sister if she thought us worse than the normal person—perhaps, I argued, the inability to take life easily is a virtue in itself; that effortless death was a power man ought not know, and we mages were made less for possessing it. And my sister, content in her own way, said that within us is also the capacity for goodness, for restraint. What if, she said, we mages have an opportunity to be kinder, because we do not have to be cruel?

And I would like to believe her. But if she is right, we certainly have a funny way of showing our love.

I am on a rooftop in Rome, above the Via della Conciliazione, looking down the thoroughfare toward its terminus in St. Peter's Square. Tourists, vendors, an occasional holy man for flavor; among the latter, my sights are trained on a young, shaggy-haired priest with a winning smile, eating soup in a corner cafe on the edge of Vatican City. Perhaps this one took the poison into himself willingly; Chang'er reported that she overheard members of S&C colluding with Cecilie, so it isn't a stretch of the imagination to think that other powers have done the same.

I lie prone, curled against an anti-materiel rifle. I would normally need a spotter for this sort of precision work, someone to call targets and watch my back. I have something a bit better, if less human: a minor demon that Viveca has seconded to me, freedom promised in exchange for aid in this kill. It floats above Rome as a hawk of finest jade, eyes of ruby seeing all, feeding me data more true than telemetry and wind speed.

Thanks to her demon, Viveca is in all our ears, counting down to the kill; no need to synchronize our watches or use jammable comms when my sister can provide otherwise. I bite back my resentment and focus. It is good that my family has an ally in Yves; it is good that my sister is so strong.

"Five," Viveca announces, at the precise moment a bus obscures my line of sight.

"Four." No matter; with the demon's aid, I have perfect knowledge of the target, clarity of all that is and will be of the atoms that make up this priest and the worm inside his chest.

"Three." A modicum of correction, anticipating steel and viscera altering my projectile's traj—

"Two." It's a *school* bus. They're children on a tour of St. Peter's Square.

Mencius once argued that man must be innately good—for if a man saw a child about to topple into a well, would he not, on instinct, reach out to save the youth? The fool; it was Xunzi's cynicism that influenced the Legalists and formed the backbone of Han thought. How else does one build an empire, if not by understanding that man is flawed, instinctively drawn to low things, driven by the basest of self-interest? Only the naive and the young believe in restraint, in kindness.

I don't hear the rest of the countdown. I have stood, focused, and reached out with my true power. For a moment, the world is right; for a moment, I am cloaked in the gold of the sun, and as radiant. I feel within my target his heart, and then his truer heart, the slug that has burrowed into his soul. It sees me, in that last second, and it knows fear.

I furl my fingers into a fist, and every organ and bone within the priest's chest is liquified at two hundred meters. He slumps backward, smile still on his stilled face; I don't think he felt even a second of pain. The children happily march pass, none the wiser, ignorant of the corpse beside them.

I don't see what happens after that. Our target is slain, and the terms of the demon's covenant are fulfilled; it departs, and my perception shrinks back to just the rooftop. Further even than that: I collapse to my knees, heaving, acid spilling from my mouth, blood from eyes. Debilitating pain seizes me, and I feel regret; I ought to have chosen the path of least resistance, shot through the school bus. Instead, I've done this and forfeited years of my life. I can feel how I have again been reduced, sanded away, hours bled out in seconds.

Stupid, naive. No way to build an empire.

I cry, I laugh, I'm not certain which. Blackest nihilism? Acceptance? Relief? The pain is cathartic; I have not used this much magic in years, flinching from the torment of this curse.

A hand takes mine, made of silk and smoke, and gently pulls me to my feet.

"Oh, it's *you*," I groan, wiping snot and vomit from my face; already, I can feel the clarity passing, the tide of resentment and anger rolling back in. "Back from fucking my tiger?"

The demon Yves stands in the midday sun, as dark and deep as the void of space. She watches me with her citrine eyes, and then pulls a handkerchief from her breast pocket to offer me. "My apologies, Ms. Olesya. I believe this is the first time we've ever interacted, alone."

I take the luminous gold handkerchief, delighting in the idea of staining this gift with bile. "No? My sister, then."

"You are a remarkably angry woman, Ms. Olesya."

I snort. "You are from hell, and you want to lecture me about being angry.

That's almost funny."

She looks at me, the gleam of her eyes dimmed within the shadow of her substance. I wonder what the priests below would think if they knew a demon stands mere meters above them. "We are more kindred than you might like. My body has been subverted against me; I seethe with resentment at a woman who I also love." She sighs, almost too human, deep in contemplation. "Dallas has told you of the source of your affliction, no doubt."

"An empathetic demon. How very novel." I make my tone one of poisoned honey; malice and cruelty come easily, no demonhood needed. "And *yes*, I am aware of your hand in my malady."

She nods, impervious to my barbs. "I am sorry that such a curse was made of my body; were it within my power to reverse, it would have been done the first moment Dallas asked." At this, I expect her to reach for me and whisk me back to Ayutthaya without ceremony. Instead she remains where she is; I catch a glimpse of her golden eyes roving over her body, taking in the excellent view of St. Peter's Square. "You are an important person—arguably the most important person—to the two women I hold above all others. Whatever the cost, I will see you cured."

The handkerchief, infuriatingly, seems to absorb the grossness from my body; I can only imagine where it disappears to. I hold it out, offering it back to her; she nonchalantly tucks it back into her pocket without the least sign of disgust. "It's likely you will test your limits with your affliction in this battle," she goes on. "And if you must do it, then you must. I shall not stop you. I only ask that you stay alive until the end. Because then, I promise that your curse will be removed."

"With Kristiansen's death?"

"That first of all. But by any means possible."

Intuition scrabbles at me. "You know something my sister doesn't."

Yves' expression is placid. "What would that be? She is my warlock, and I am deeply bound. We share in all things. Shall we return to Ayutthaya, so we might proceed with the rest of our preparations?"

We step out of the shadows to find Viveca screaming in fury. She pivots to fix me with a half-crazed stare. "She's nesting in *my* tower!"

According to Maria, every decoy we killed sent the faintest magic pulse back to parts unknown—a fraction of soul, returning to the phylactery. We have, apparently, triangulated these telltale signs to a certain skyscraper in Tsim Sha Tsui, Hong Kong.

The sea witch is looking particularly nervous. "We're dealing with some really esoteric magics here. Maybe Cecilie is spoofing the signal—I don't even know if that's possible." She glances around. "Look, I don't want us to show up in Hong Kong and no Cecilie. You'd be thinking I've betrayed you all, and then my neck would be wrung on the spot. And she *could* still run."

"Oh, she's there," Viveca snarls. "That's *my* building. She's desecrating it to prove a point." To show that she can; that she will take everything from us.

"In the days of old," Yves says, a touch of admiration in her voice, "the Ottoman sultans would name imperial gardens in Istanbul after newly conquered provinces, as a way of showing mastery over their enemies' former holdings." When every eye in the room turns to glare at her, she shrugs. "Pride and power go hand-in-hand, but there is artistry to both. Recognizing your enemies' achievements makes your victory over them that much sweeter."

"We could mine the foundation, bring it down on her head," Chang'er suggests; since our arrival in Ayutthaya, the alchemist has proven herself to be a steely-eyed explosives expert, and more than one of Cecilie's bodies died to a well-placed car bomb.

"I mined it when I moved in," Viveca says, etheric sigils beginning to glow in front of her. "I can activate it from a distance, take out the whole goddamn city block."

Maria whoops in excitement; Dallas looks on in horror. "Do all you mages booby-trap your homes!?"

I take my sister's hands and gently pull them down. "You know Cecilie will have disabled those first. And she'll be scrying about, keeping an eye on attempts to remotely access those measures."

Viveca begins to deflate, just a little. "Well, my homunculus is still stored there! I could—"

I take her head in my hands and gently kiss her forehead. When I pull back, I realize that I am smiling and that her anger has frozen in the shock of intimacy. I laugh at the sight, genuine. In that moment, I again see her for who she is—my younger sister, so brash but so young, the person I cherish most in all the world.

I'm not the Hua heir. I don't *have* to be the Hua heir. But I do *need* to be a good sister. I need to keep her safe, for as long as I draw breath; I need to shield her from harm, so that she might endure.

Whatever empires are made of, it isn't me. So be it. I can sell my life dearly, see my mother's killer slain, preserve my sister. That will be *enough*.

Ten: And Then the Plummet

VIVECA

Tsim Sha Tsui, Hong Kong. Where it began—or, at least, where I began with Yves, forging that crucial pact.

From the outside, little about the building looks different. The facade appears as immaculate as ever, black glass gleaming where it catches the sun's rays. A tower that has been family property for years, after Mother sold the house in Mount Nicholson; she wanted each of her daughters to have a place of their own, once she was gone. I have thought myself unsentimental—what warlock can afford to be so?—but this building, like so many others, is part of my inheritance, the same way the Singapore estate was for Olesya. We carry our lines of ancestry on our back; we carry our mother's wishes in our bones.

And now Cecilie Kristiansen has defiled yet another one of Elizaveta Hua's legacies. *Our* legacies.

There are several channels into the building: aerial, ground, basement. As we observe it from a nearby skyscraper, I draw on the etheric controls that link to the tower's self-destruct mechanisms. The actual detonation is disabled, as we suspected, but the controls still exist. The magical wards and circuits that would have facilitated the explosions can be repurposed into something like a binding circle, when the time comes. The ground entrance is manicured; the telescope—we're sticking to mundane means of surveillance for now—shows nothing untoward, no bubbling froth of insects, no black tides of roaches. Nobody is going in or out, either. From the air, there would be multiple potential points of breach...

Dallas is, as always, direct. "Why don't we just walk through the front door?"

"That's an absurd idea," I retort. "There is no way we're doing something so simple."

"We're going to walk through the front door," I announce.

Olesya looks at me like I've lost all sanity, and Maria is elated; neither reaction fills me with confidence. I press on. "Cecilie knows we are coming and will have arranged traps and defenses for every type of ingress, magical and mundane. Simple is best: we go in the front door and work our way up the building until we reach Cecilie. She'll be in my old office."

Now, Maria looks unconvinced. "How can you be certain?"

"I do not know what Cecilie shared with you in her time as your master," Yves answers in my place, "but in the years she spent torturing me, I came to know facets of her well. She despises all mages, but has for the Hua lineage a special, almost unfathomable hatred. I believe that she has wished ruin upon the Huas for centuries, and that everything else—her suborning of Sealing and Containment, her open war against other mages—is merely the fallout of her overarching ambition." The demon nods thoughtfully. "She will be there, because she intends to end the Hua line with her own hands."

"If she is so old, and her hatred so deep, why only go about her revenge now?" Olesya asks.

"The tyranny of geometric growth—big things may have small, slow beginnings," Dallas replies, revealing a greater appreciation for human mathematics than any of us suspected. Her tone darkens: "And because she needed the right growth medium to perfect her mage-killing toxin in. I doubt lesser demons proved strong enough to breed the pestilence with the yield and virulence she needed to fell a dozen mages at a time, and acquiring the right demon would have taken time and—"

"What has happened has happened," Yves says quickly. "We work with the reality we inhabit." She turns to me and, with a glance, asks that I steer us from this unpleasant topic.

I oblige. "We'll divide into two teams. Dallas and Olesya, you'll go in the front and fight your way up. Yves and I will hold back until you've either drawn out so many enemies you can't make forward progress, or you make contact with Cecilie."

Olesya and Dallas listen to the instructions with stoic resolution, but Maria immediately raises an objection. "Yves is our most potent weapon. Why isn't she the tip of the spear?"

The tiger's hands ball in clenched fists; all her sins have chosen this moment to roost.

"Cecilie is aware of both my True Name and Viveca's," Yves says quietly. "Our pact offers certain protections, but without care we will be more of a liability than an asset. We'll commit when and where we can, but not without understanding the situation first."

Yves is overstating the case a little, but I make no move to correct her. We have agreed to keep my suit of armor a secret for now; Cecilie is waiting for us, and it's prudent to expect her to glean intelligence through our True Names.

"I'm going, too," Maria interjects. "I've thrown in with you sorry lot, and it'll be stupid if you get yourselves killed while I stay home playing videogames. And on a more serious note—I don't know why, but Cecilie didn't eat me at the gala, and she sent her men to take me alive from my home. Whatever is staying her hand, let's use it to our advantage."

Chang'er, under protest, will stay in Ayutthaya, where she will hold one of the cuff links Mother evidently forged for Inspector Budak; it will provide us—mostly Olesya—a path of egress if worse comes to worst. Still, she readies herself for war, all her alchemical knowledge turned to violent ends: enruned ballistic armor, a drum-fed automatic shotgun that bleeds shadow, a bandolier of grenades etched with eldritch sigils. "The teleport stones work both ways," she points out. "Send for me, and I will be by your side in but a moment, Ms. Olesya."

I swear, I think I see my sister blush.

DALLAS

Olesya was right: I don't want her to come.

But I understand, too, the feeling of being caged—the knowledge that you *cannot*—and spoke true when I assured her: her life is hers, and as her partner I must, at minimum, respect that. She has, at least, promised me she will mostly use her guns and knives. And who am I to object? All of us: each formidable in her own way, each branded by Cecilie Kristiansen's schemes, each motivated by causes most dark and personal.

We make our goodbyes. Viveca and Olesya embrace again, long. Yves and I stoically duck our heads at each other; in our centuries together, we've said all but three words to the other, and now is not the time to give that sentiment voice.

But rather than turn away, she fixes me with her golden eyes. "Watch yourself, tiger. The Crown Prince has a gun of foreign make, and he will shoot you dead."

I start at the memory—one of the first things we ever said to each other, so long ago. "Watch my back," I reply, "and I'll help you with your feet of stone."

She smiles—the way she once did, as she watched me when she thought I was asleep—and offers her hand. It is the closest she can come to say that she forgives me, and I take it; it is more than I deserve.

In contrast to me and Yves play-acting our ancient past, Maria is noisily using a straw to suck down the last bit of a lemonade she managed to get *somewhere*, eyes behind dark sunglasses and head shaded by a massive sun hat. She could be walking to the beach, not a life-and-death fight.

"Does nothing concern you?" Olesya grouses.

Chang'er is worried, and she hates to be the one tasked with sitting out of this fight. But she puts on a brave face and commits to doing what she can. To me, she hands a satchel of ensorcelled breaching charges that hum like piano chords. "They're skeleton keys," she says. "They'll open any door."

To Olesya, she gives a hand-crafted ring, emerald mounted on white gold. "It's a small token of my—oh, *fuck it.*" She seizes Olesya's face and stretches on tiptoes, kissing her hard, in a manner that widens Maria's eyes and almost makes even me look away. When she lets go, both her mouth and Olesya's are swollen. "You're the only woman I have ever loved. I belong at your side alone. Promise me that you'll come back whole, Ms. Olesya."

I resist the urge to clear my throat. But I do say, "Congratulations."

The alchemist glares at me as she slides the ring onto Olesya's finger. "We'll settle this someday, Seidel."

"What is there to settle? You have excellent taste in women."

"Of course—I love her and loathe you." She hesitates. "I'll never forgive you if something happens to her."

"I'll bring her back to you in one piece, I swear." My life for Olesya's. I've already decided that.

Chang'er gives a curt nod. "Then she's all yours. Remember: keep her safe, or I'm getting a new tiger rug."

Yves swoops us up in a sea of shadow, then deposits us carefully a block away from the building. And then the demon and warlock are away themselves, off to loiter who knows where, waiting for their opening.

As we approach the tower, I ask Maria, "What is the point of all this? Why does Cecilie Kristiansen want so much? And why does she hate the Huas so badly?"

Maria cuts me a look. "Maybe an earlier Hua warlock offended her. Her true age is a mystery. As for the rest, being power-hungry is the *norm* for mages, Dallas, haven't you noticed? She just takes it to extremes."

I could say Olesya is not like that, but I'm a biased observer. "But what does she want exactly? To do with all she's stolen."

"To become a perfect being." Maria's shoulders twitch. "I vaguely remember her muttering about the bending of possibilities, the rearrangement of time itself. She believes that if she has this—command every sort of sorcery conceivable, pilfered from the mind of everyone she has consumed—she'll be able to find the origins of all things, look for another world in which she may thrive. She doesn't *like* this one, you see, but then not many mages do. We're always looking for something more, a place over which we can appoint ourselves the monarch."

"It doesn't really matter." Olesya's voice is flat. "What matters is that she dies today, for good."

Until now, I believed Olesya had accepted her fate, quietly and terribly. To see her hardened with fury makes me glad, even if she is about to walk into mortal peril.

We pass into the enemy perimeter—my skin itches at the moment of contact with Kristiansen's wards—and then into the lobby. Dark, quiet, and frigid. Potted palms and succulents gather in one corner, in a miniature garden of black pebbles and blue glass statuettes.

The space is completely quiet, devoid of all human life. And then the lift arrives, as though summoned by our presence—it dings and opens into a well-lit, mirrored little chamber. Warm gold, innocuous as anything.

None of us makes a move toward it.

And then the lift *unravels*: ribbons of steel and copper burst forth, bearing with them reflections of golden illumination. Black cables and shards of glass roar through the air. I take hold of Olesya, shielding her with myself.

In the next breath, we're in a chamber much vaster than the deserted lobby. Still empty, but the material of the walls is impossibly warped—obsidian shot through with bioluminescence, pulsing as though with its own breath.

"How very polite of our host—spatially, it looks like we've been pulled to the fifth floor." Olesya's voice is dry. "Viveca's office is on the twenty-eighth. We're lucky she didn't put it at the very top, or it'd be what, the fortieth?"

We take care as we traverse the sloping, spiraling ground; every straight line has been distorted, as if all that is solid has begun to melt. The lift is gone, though most likely we're moving through some sort of illusion and the real thing must still be there. I keep my ears peeled for the hum of any worm or insect. For a time we meet no resistance: I don't know if Viveca ever staffed this building or rented out any of its floors—probably not. But anyone who lived or worked here has been devoured since.

It is not until we reach what might have been the seventh floor that we hear the locust begin to swarm.

Maria cracks her knuckles and extends a hand. I've read of sea witches before, but never seen one in action—in a moment, she's summoned before her the depths of the ocean, and the floor is awash in a tide that flows and swells, pulling the locusts into its embrace. Bodies puppeteered by Cecilie join battle next: not mindlessly either, each still sapient enough to utilize the magic of their origins. Olesya sights and shoots them down, her bullets undoing their bonds to Cecilie in an instant. But this is all dilatory combat, not the stuff of life or death; our foe is testing us, probing the edges of our defenses. We take the opportunity to continue our ascent.

Several more floors up, and the architecture around us begins to shift. It's subtle enough that we don't even notice at first: the floor opens, and Olesya nearly stumbles into darkness. I grab at her and pull her back, only for the tiles under both our feet to vanish. We yelp and begin to fall. A splash of ocean spray saves us, buffeting us back to solid ground.

"What, no thanks?" Maria mocks. "Cat got your—" The wall shifts to surround her. It happens so fast that we barely have time to react before her scream fades, swallowed up by stone.

Cecilie is apparently done testing us. More architecture flows and rises around us, as fluid as Maria's conjured sea—bricks spiraling, closing on us like a coiling serpent.

Olesya pulls from her dress a charge crafted by Chang'er and tosses it out in front of us, into the writhing mass of smooth bricks and rough concrete. A detonation follows, but none like I have ever seen—a flare, and then the architecture is frozen in place.

"Sometimes you need to knock a building down, and sometimes you need a building to stay in one piece," Olesya says; I am beginning to realize Chang'er has skill sets I cannot fathom.

We hurry forward, through the stilled, silent hall. Quickly, we batter through an emergency exit—

—only to find ourselves stumbling into another alien floor. This one stretches toward infinity in all directions—not obsidian black this time, but blinding white desolation, as lifeless as scoured desert bones.

"This is beginning to get old," Olesya calls out. "Just fucking *fight* us, Cecilie."

A voice chuckles from the light, everywhere. "Now why would I do that? I want to savor your deaths for as long as possible. Next on the docket: let's reacquaint you with some old friends, Olesya—you left them behind when you fled your estate, and they're just *dying* to meet you."

I have felt the bead of a rifle on me before, in the jungles of my youth; I feel it again now. There are hunters out there, of singular skill—some of Olesya's vaunted snipers, perverted to Cecilie's ends. The air currents electrify with anticipation, but I am already moving to shield Olesya: a roar of gunfire, the crack of a sniper round, and I roar back.

But the bullet—an ugly thing of warped geometries, a mathematics that hurts the soul to look upon—stops short, a centimeter over my heart. Olesya has thrown up a barrier; at her gesture, the bullet ricochets back, tearing through space and time, and then into whoever fired it. A cry; a stench of something much more vile than blood. A figure cloaked in white stumbles in the distance, perfect camouflage ruined by black ichor spreading from a gaping wound.

Olesya reaches out a hand, palm up, and lifts; I can *feel* more than see light cloak both of us, armor and concealment both. With a nod, I take her rifle and advance, beginning my own hunt.

Sight is useless here, in this wasteland of white. I close my eyes and instead rely on my centuries of instinct, on my senses of hearing and smell. Olesya's snipers were good, and now they are enhanced by a hivemind of chittering intelligence. But the hunt is my domain, and here I am queen.

And soon, I have them—not a breath among them, but their limbs still move through muscle and sinew, and behind it all is a *hum* of wings and writhing things, Cecilie's signature magic always true to form. A shot fells one, two; there's return fire, but it bounces off the armor Olesya has clad me with, ablative radiance undoing deadly lead. The third and final, I find close; I tear into the husk with flashing claws, and see up close the corruption Olesya and Chang'er described from their destroyed estate—chitin and black gore, a tide like tar.

I rush back to Olesya's side to find her resolute, if bloodied—untouched by the enemy salvos, but teeth and chin red from the effects of her ailment, red splashing across the too-white floor. How many days, how many weeks has she burned up, to protect me?

She cuts me a withering glare, furious not at me but at *everything*. "I am your armor, as you are mine," she says, brooking no argument. "I am not so weak that I cannot lift my hand in our defense. And once Cecilie's dead, I'll be free of this curse, yes?"

All the same, I can see sweat bead on her brow. I pass no remark; after this, I tell myself, she will be just fine. We will have decades together. She'll live to be over a hundred.

"All the same—" I start, and then there is the cracking of rebar and reinforced concrete, and the illusion of infinite distance dissipates as the far wall collapses under tremendous force.

Across the white floor spill broken bodies, desiccated by Cecilie's touch. Among the husks is a new foe, covered in putrid gore and not-quite-human viscera—a homunculus of stone. Except... except the stone beast is tearing into its own faction, limb ripped from limb as it screams out a challenge, the sound of an avalanche.

No enemy rises to the occasion; the stone stands triumphant, heaving with the affectation of human breathing.

"My mother built for us a guardian, hewn from ancient basalt," Olesya says, voice low. "My sister was forced to leave it behind when she fled, but it seems it may have some sort of defense protocols built in to it—"

The homunculus whips around when it hears us, its emerald eyes glowing with an anger and intelligence that is most certainly not automated. It strides toward us, one heavy step at a time; I pull Olesya behind me, readying my claws.

It draws up short, then extends a hand, palm up. "Olesya, may I have your knife?"

Olesya hesitates, then unsheathes the blade she keeps at her hip, more tool than weapon—a mage never knows when she might need to spill ritualistic blood—and reaches between us to hand it over. The homunculus takes it in one hand, rolls her opposite limb to expose the back of her forearm, and then draws a long, deep cut across it. The blade is ensorcelled, and slices deep into the stone; when the light fades, a scar like a gold vein remains, kintsugi reknitting basalt.

Whatever ritual the construct has performed, it convinces Olesya completely. "Fahriye?" she cries, and throws her arms around the stone figure.

"Inspector Fahriye Budak, in the flesh." The granite mouth curves at the joke.

"What the hell happened to you?!" Olesya is weeping now. "You—I thought you died when the estate self-destructed."

"Between that and the mortal gunshot wound to my back—yes, I very much did. But…" She stares down at her hand, spreading gray fingers. "It would appear that at the moment of death, my soul was instead transferred to this vessel. Remarkable work; impossible. I suspect Elizaveta Hua's hand in this."

The construct captures her human mannerisms with unreal fidelity; I can hear the little white lie in her statement, the obfuscation—she does not believe but *knows* the late Elizaveta Hua is responsible. I think I like Fahriye Budak.

"It has taken a bit to realize what had happened and where I was," she continues. "I've spent the past day or two in a fugue state, uh, working through some stuff." A glance through the broken wall reveals a fractured loft, destroyed furniture and dashed ferns; every surface is covered in twisted corpses. "It's been something like hell? *Am* I in hell? Are you real?"

"We're in Viveca's skyscraper, somewhere near the twenty-fourth floor, it would seem. I think you have been contained in my sister's personal apartments. We're working our way up to the twenty-eighth. Cecilie has encamped there, we think, waiting for us to commit to a final battle."

A dry chuckle, a weary sigh. "Ah, so I am to be one of the einherjar, transported to the final reckoning of Ragnarok. Well, now that I know where I have been trapped—let me carry us the rest of the way. I was once taught a trick by your mother, Ms. Olesya. Allow me to show you."

The homunculus—the woman—instructs us to draw within a certain radius of her, and then a barrier of force shimmers into being. For a second this is confusing; there's nothing to be shielding from, unless she means to maintain this until we reach the very top—

The barrier ascends. And then it ascends very fast, going *through* the ceiling.

Olesya clings to me for dear life. The homunculus alone stands steady and stoic, controlling our rise with expertise, and I wonder if she's done this before and how often—the storied life of a Sealing and Containment officer, perhaps the only one among them dedicated to good or something like it—the one uncorrupted knight. Even death has broken before her.

We slow down. We have reached the floor of Viveca's office, and it is frigid.

Inspector Budak brings us to a section of undamaged floor and carefully lowers her barrier. Before us, a single door awaits at the end of the corridor, black and unmarked. Unlike all the other floors, the architecture has been left untouched here: the walls are ordinary, paneled and painted, and the floor simple black marble.

"Someone should tell Viveca to opt for less sinister decor," I mutter, if only to break the tension.

"My sister does like black." Olesya's tone is not entirely even. She's rubbing her face, reorienting herself from our dizzying rise. "Her wardrobe, too."

There has been no communication from Viveca. But we are here, and we must trust that the warlock is doing her part. We march down the corridor's length, step through the door, alert at every second to a trap.

A single person sits behind the desk, where Viveca Hua normally would. A middle-aged woman, features slack and nondescript—a shock of auburn hair gone gray with deterioration; freckled skin turned leather by age and sun. She's long dead; I can tell from the smell—postponed decay.

And then the corpse distorts and twists. It gashes open, and from its rippling chrysalis of flesh emerges Cecilie Kristiansen in her imperious glory, scurrying bugs merging into a simulacrum of cold beauty, adorned in a white suit.

"Welcome to my new office." Her red grin splits her face, unseaming it. "I hope you like what I've done with the place."

Fahriye's fists glow blue as she augments them, a bludgeon even sturdier than rock. I feel Olesya's magic hum to life just under her flesh; for what is to come, she will not hold back, I know this of her. And I… raise my rifle in a threatening manner. Anticlimactic, beside a woman of stone and one of the world's most powerful sorceresses. But I am old, skilled in matters of death; together, we will find Cecilie's jugular.

"You won't, of course," the mage says, turning away from us to look at the cityscape beyond. "I've known your plans since before Maria suggested them, that ungrateful harlot. It was fun, watching you delight in your supposed cleverness. But you are here for no greater reason than because I wanted you to be here—because I wanted the House of Hua to have a final chance to muster all that they are and hurl it at me. Pool your might into this moment of defiance—and then, with no place to run, be confronted with the weight of your failure, watch as your pride breaks and all that you hold dear turns to ashes."

"For Olesya," I say.

"For Viveca," Olesya echoes.

"For Elizaveta," Fahriye concludes, and hurls herself forward.

With a flick of her hand, Cecilie slaps the homunculus back; the next moment, chains of black iron have wrapped around my neck, strangling fast. Olesya's power frees us both, but it is immediately evident what the dynamics of this battle will be.

"Did you think I would fight *politely*, girl?" Cecilie mocks. "You have brought with you people you love. I will tear at them, and you will protect them. Good. Call out your magic. Let the curse gnaw at you. I want your death to be agony. I want you to shield your loved ones with your body, and for it to not be enough. I want you to know how it feels—"

Cecilie is cut short when she explodes in a burst of glowing light; more insects begin to swarm, slipping from the cracks of reality to form up again. Fahriye sweeps them up with planes of etheric blue and smashes more against wall, floor, ceiling. And I—

—I hesitate. To fight on Cecilie's terms invites futility; it is a harrying action, meant to kill us by a thousand stings, all to draw out our deaths for Cecilie's amusement. It is the phylactery we must destroy, and that must be here somewhere near, no doubt protected and hidden. But when has that ever stopped a hunter of my skill?

I twist to look around, drawing out my senses, reaching beyond this fight. And in that moment of distraction, I am caught again—ice forming around an ankle, tumbling me down. I try to call out to Olesya, just a few feet away, who wields daggers that glow with the heart of a star. But the swarm is descending.

And then a second roar, of artillery. No: of an automatic shotgun, spent casings crashing around me. "I thought cats landed on their feet," Chang'er shouts as the insects pull away, repelled by whatever malediction the alchemist has imbued her cartridges with.

"You took your sweet time teleporting in!" I yell; the noise of this melee has risen to a crescendo.

"I fucking *knew* I'd have to save your life." But still she offers me her hand, pulling me up.

"We haven't found the phylactery," I tell Chang'er; even with my lips right to her ear, she can barely hear me. "It's—"

I am knocked across the room, a blow like a freight train. Cecilie manifests in front of me, her implacable grip pinning me to the wall; other proxies of herself are tangling with Olesya, Fahriye, even Chang'er now, drawing them away from each other and from me.

"You didn't think it would be that easy, did you?" Cecilie taunts. "A good showing, kept your eyes on the ball, just like Yves said you would. It was disgusting how fondly she always spoke of you, but it'll be my pleasure to break her all over again by killing you."

"I doubt," I gasp, buying time, "that Yves even mentioned me once."

"On the contrary. I know everything about your travels, Dallas Seidel. She was almost incoherent with pain, most days—she would tell herself stories of your time together, little memories to keep her sane through the torture." A cold sneer, the most hateful expression I have seen in all my years. "I just thought you should know that, before you die—nothing kills quite like guilt."

Behind us, unnoticed by Cecilie, the windows flicker, and the view changes—no longer the Hong Kong skyline, but an Antarctic landscape in tumult.

"I will spend the rest of my life answering for what I did to Yves. Nothing you say can damn me more than I've already damned myself." I smile through bloody teeth. "But guess what, Cecilie? The rest of my life is going to be long. Yours, I would wager on being *much* shorter."

Through the windows, I can see it now—across the pallid wastes, a wraith of shadow and bone, hurtling toward us at astronomical speeds.

"The death rattles of a dying animal," Cecilie gloats. "What could you know that I don't?"

In the next moment, glass shatters and ice thorns the air; the blizzard's roar overtakes the office.

From the shadows, Viveca Hua unfurls, cloaked in deepest night and armored in timeless infinities. The warlock of her age has arrived.

VIVECA

I don't have time to lose, no time to take note of what Kristiansen has done to my office. My fist goes through her, and the web of power I've strung around this building—newly made, rough work—draws taut.

The moment of penetration is visceral, almost as if it's my hand through her other bodies, through her puppets. Yves' puissance went into forming this web, and the seek-and-destroy formula woven into it has done its work. We haven't incinerated every single hive-corpse, but we've gotten rid of plenty.

Enough to make Cecilie's face twist into an enraged snarl as I tear her insides out. Guts and centipedes pulp in my hand and fall wetly to the marble. I have forced the sum of her to manifest here, and here she will be hurt.

Before we came I made sure to shore Yves up, feeding her power stored over the years in artifacts—giving freely of my blood, too, pouring into her such might that she could swallow up the sky.

Behind me, I seal the window off with shadow's breath and Stygian membrane. The mesh of power I've spread thrums, and the rest of the building is sealed too, every window and exit, even the little gaps fit for roaches and mice. The conduits of my disabled self-destruct mechanism, repurposed to a sealing ward. Only a fool would have chosen *my* tower as the site of battle, a place I know inside and out.

I have thought of simply collapsing the entire edifice onto Cecilie, crushing it down to nothing once my family and comrades have been teleported safely away. But the point of her is that she can inhabit tiny bodies capable of slipping between the cracks, in the most literal sense. What we do here must be final and absolute, and whatever happens, she must be trapped and contained before she can be killed.

Cecilie dissolves, only to reform at a distance. I step, my heels clacking on white marble, between my sister and my enemy. "Hello again, Cecilie. I see you've gotten no younger."

Our mother's killer glances at me, as if I matter to her no more than a speck of dust. "Very considerate of you to come. For a moment, I thought you the coward—I would have been devastated if I could end only your sister here, then have to waste time tracking you down. But here you are, ever the child—both of you, your mother's daughters."

The ground seethes. Dark fluids coalesce into wasps and locusts.

I respond immediately, searing the bugs with black fire. I twist space itself to crush them where they crawl, pulverizing worm-flesh and chitin. But another tide comes, flowing fast and high.

Yves intercepts. Cecilie snarls her True Name and my demon falters, staggered back by its enunciation. Another snarl and Yves is forced into a cloud of shadow. She tries to rematerialize, and for her trouble is struck by a javelin of force—one that is able to pin down demonic smoke.

I invoke the flower of Yves' glade. It blooms, rapid, sheathing me in the red of its nativity. It is both like and unlike wearing Yves: might courses through me, but it is without my demon's warmth and appetite.

My enemy screams my True Name, imbuing it with the command to *cease.* Though it lashes at me, it doesn't slow me down; the power of it washes past me, no chink in Yves' bespoke armor for it to find purchase. I reply, drawing into combat the demons I have bound to pacts made over the years; the work of decades, spent in an instant. Each of them takes a blow meant for me—an inversion of gravity here, an impaling spike there, all the things that would mangle bones and shred flesh, rendered as harmless as a breeze.

The building deforms. Walls pour over each other like ink; I attempt to counter it, but my hasty work in weaving power through the architecture does not hold up.

And then I am alone.

Not completely; a thought brings the demons to me, a hot tide roiling within my shadow. Only half the battalion—the rest I have instructed to defend my sister—but still a host of near fathomless power, matched in strength by my foe.

Silence. The space in which Cecilie has imprisoned me stretches forward into a long, spiraling corridor. A distant echo of laughter. It sounds exactly like my mother. And I know, too, what I will see when I turn the corner.

An image of the house in Mount Nicholson. Cecilie, wearing Mother's skin, tidying her books and files.

"This is a farce," I say, loud. Of course she'll have absorbed some illusionist or another. Nor is it well-crafted: I can still feel the carpet of my office under my feet. The skittering and chirring of insects; that too she has failed to hide. "But since you've decided we should have one-on-one time, I am going to ask: by what treacherous means did you kill my mother? Because it wasn't a fair fight. In a duel of sheer might, she'd have reduced you to chitin powder and maybe half a millipede."

She sneers at me with my mother's mouth. "Only children believe their mothers are immortal, Viveca."

"The demons she bound to her would have erased your existence, backward and forward." I advance into the room. "You come to me in this mirage, insinuate that within you is the stuff of Elizaveta Hua. I think you're lying, Cecilie."

Her head throws back—in that, nothing like Mother—and she brays. "And you know nothing about *your* family, your stained legacy. Why, you should feel such shame you'd want to bury your name. But a creature like you isn't capable of shame, are you?" She lifts and clenches her fist.

I move to counter the spell, too slow. My right arm bends, the muscles twisting, the bones crunching; the pain takes my breath away as the limb is torn free.

Blood hemorrhages. In the back of my mind, I hear Yves scream with echoed pain.

But the spider lily lives up to her promise. The process of regeneration, far more swift than my own protections, brings its own mentholated agony. In seconds, my arm is whole again.

That brings a flicker of surprise to the face that pretends to be my mother's, and then I'm close enough. I grab her head and twist, and tear.

Skull and spine have barely impacted the floor when the room bends again, trying to furl me into the architecture, drawing me down. I command one of my servitors to bear me away from the growing pit of lashing teeth and golden maws. Another pact burns up.

The spears of night I summon meet her shield and dissipate; the swarms she conjures meet my barrier, limbs and mandibles scrabbling against it as they turn to cinders. The next strike of destructive pressure closes in on my knee, begins to bite through flesh and tendon, before I banish it. Almost instantly the flower heals the damage.

Brilliance kaleidoscopes around us as we lash out, sear, riposte. We're more evenly matched than either of us would like, a blow to the ego.

Something *inverts*—the entire building turning upside down. It disorients me so much I don't react quite in time when a flower of rot closes in around me. For a moment I can't breathe; decay seeps into me, gnawing at my defenses. Old wounds are reopening, every scrape and bruise I've ever gotten, every fracture and break of bone. I claw at the ethereal cage around me, my lungs struggling to work, my every organ desperate for oxygen.

A technique Mother taught me, so long ago, that I perform now: a materialization of entropy, a brief force of flux.

Everything scrambles. Cecilie's flower becomes glass becomes sand. The spell of decay transmutes, filling the room with iridescent bubbles.

"You'll run out before I do," she hisses. "All you have is a single body, weak and mortal."

"We'll see about that, won't we?" I wipe my mouth, readying myself for another bout. "And now I know you never killed Mother, because throughout all this you haven't been able to manifest or replicate any of her powers. If you'd slain and stolen her might, I'd have been dead long ago. You're just a two-bit mage, like I thought all along."

A crash of marble and cement interrupts us—the crumbling of physical reality, breaking through Cecilie's illusion. A glimpse of golden fur: Dallas has evidently used one of the alchemist's breaching charges to blow a hole in the wall. From the far side Maria is clawing her way out of broken bricks and rebar, fingertips bleeding raw, all of her drenched in saltwater.

The sea witch grins, manic. "I figured it out, you bastard."

Cecilie swivels to look at her, staring hard at her former apprentice, no longer minding even me. "What do you think you're doing—"

"The vivisections, the grotesque surgeries. I was never your student—I was the goddamn *carrying case* for your phylactery." Maria takes a deep breath and sinks her hand into her chest. She gags, spits blood on the ground, shrieks when she touches what she's looking for… and then, with the most grotesque sound of flesh ripping, pulls her discovery out with her fingers.

"There you are, Cecilie." In her fist writhes a parasite the color of albumen, bigger than the rest we have killed, its tail a thin, trembling sliver and its eyes housefly-red.

"This isn't over," Cecilie screams, but now there is real fear in her voice. "I can't die here. I *won't*. I'll be back, and you'll—"

I take advantage of this opening. I shred her barrier and pin her to the wall by her throat, lashing her in place with ropes of twilight dark.

Maria laughs, loud and a little mad, as she crushes the parasite. Decisive: its head then its segmented body, and then she traps the entire thing in a bubble of the blackest seawater—I can feel, even from here, the deep-sea pressure, the implosive force in which no insects are meant to survive.

Cecilie howls. The chamber fills with her swarms.

There's something to be said for repeating a trick, to refining it. At my thought, the pact materializes Yves at my side, and together we plunge. With the spider lily joined to me, it's easier than ever to bring forth a piece of hell—like at the gala, but more, greater; hell has come to earth, and I am its anchor. The temperature shifts. The ground beneath us fissures.

I leap onto Cecilie. I pummel her skull; I rip her throat apart with my bare hands. In my fist her eyeballs burst and under my hand her intestines crisp, and even then I know it's not enough—we have trapped her in hell, but the parts of her are scattering, slipping wetly through my grasp, even now searching for a way out. I turn black fire into arrows, into bars that close in around the constituent bugs, and still more burn themselves to escape...

Everything fades to white. Or rather—

Looking up I find myself confronted with row after row of bone, the lines of them joined in sinuous lengths. In *serpentine* lengths. Each vertebra is enormous, each web of cartilage glistening, covered here and there by blue-black scales. The eyes—more than I can count, each nearly the size of my fists—are sun-gold.

I am looking at Yves—Yves as she was born, as she grew into herself, the form folded and hidden away by the human seeming she shows me, by the mass of shadow that she sometimes becomes. Her truest form, if any may be called that: a leviathan poised to devour the stars, perhaps the inspiration for the myths of beasts that will wrap their tail around and swallow the world. She is a vision that must've caused religious ecstasy throughout the ages, or driven prophets mad, and she is *mine*.

Her great maw opens. It takes into itself the trillion pieces of Cecilie Kristiansen, and one by one breaks her.

The fragment of hell is gone. Yves is beside me, on two legs and clad in that light-eating suit she likes so much. We stand in the ruins of my office, the arctic howling beyond the circle of shadow I've erected.

"Well," I say, folding the spider lily back into just a flower again, "I knew a little about demon biology, but *that* was an education."

Her smile is faint. "Are you going to raise objections to me being a reptile, Ms. Hua?"

I take hold of the back of her skull, making her bend until I can kiss her on the mouth. "Hardly. Actually, I think that was magnificent. You're exquisite like that. I've fallen for you all over again."

She blinks. "Even among warlocks, you're unusual. I shall not complain."

Dallas and Chang'er are at Olesya's side, eagerly embracing the woman they both love. Maria limps over to us—I let her hold onto me for support; she's lost a good deal of blood ripping the parasite out of herself, and I respect the maneuver. Your enemy's downfall at any cost, fueled by sheer spite.

It's over. What remains of Cecilie Kristiansen is but ash, and her plans for dominion perish with her. Her minions, her catspaws—they died a long time ago, but what remains begins to slough and fail; there is nothing we can do for them as their flesh melts, carcasses run through and hollowed out by Cecilie's ravenous hunger.

It's a victory, as total as one could hope for. Even Mother's stone homunculus is here.

Wait. For all that it is semi-autonomous, there's something... organic about the way the homunculus moves, the way it is helping Olesya stand.

"A pleasure to see you again, Ms. Hua," the stone speaks, then gives a too-human bow. "Inspector Budak, of—formerly of Sealing and Containment."

It takes me a few seconds. "You... died, didn't you?"

"Very much so." She chuckles, and the stone groans with an embarrassed shrug. "But your mother felt strongly that she owed me a debt for saving both of your lives, a weight she said would take two lifetimes to repay. I just never thought she meant it so literally."

"Ah." There is a whole ocean of history and meaning in Budak's answer, and I want to ask after the pieces I don't yet have. But that's for later. "The emeralds capture your eyes well."

Olesya lays her hand on the construct's arm, beaming, and gives a kiss to the soot-covered alchemist at her side. "Chang'er made it, and even Fahriye is here!" Her voice is so bright, her face so radiant, and I realize how long it has been since I've seen her truly *happy*. "No one dies and everyone lives and—"

And then she coughs. My sister coughs, and she doesn't stop coughing, rich red splattering her hand and spilling down her chin. Her spine bends with the wracking force of it. Inspector Budak catches her as she falls; Dallas darts to her side.

The tiger clutches at Olesya, face pale. "It's going to be okay," she half-assures her, half-pleads. She wipes tears from my sister's eyes, smears blood across her face in crimson streaks.

I stand paralyzed and useless. All the might I demonstrated in breaking Cecilie now seems like nothing, a child's illusion. "What's happening, Yves?" I ask, trying to make sense of what I am seeing. We won, dammit. We won, and now we go home and laugh about how close we came to defeat, and how we triumphed against a world pitted against us. No one dies and everyone lives and Olesya grows old—

"She burned through the rest of her years to fight Kristiansen," Yves says, voice somber. "She shielded her women and struck down her enemies, fought hard and true with no regard for herself. Her wasting disease has metastasized."

Fury replaces confusion. "You knew?" It is unfair, it is awful—Yves could hardly have split herself to help my sister while Cecilie was pinning her down, and it was Olesya's sacrifice to make, but someone must be at fault. In this moment, victory snatched by the jaws of defeat. I cannot make myself reasonable. I cannot lose my sister.

In this moment, even Chang'er is more useful than me. She is kneeling beside Olesya, fighting through the tears as she pulls potions and healing reagents from her combat rigging.

Dallas looks up; I see in her gaze the panic of a tiger as the cage slams shut. "But Kristiansen is dead. Why isn't the curse broken?"

"Kristiansen created the curse," Yves answers. "But she created it from *me*—the stuff of unreality, eating away at the body each time magic is used. The curse will last as long as I do."

"I'm sorry, my tiger," Olesya says, her fingers feebly grasping at Dallas'. "I had my suspicions, but I couldn't just stand by and let you get hurt. Please don't be mad."

"Then... then we'll unsummon you, Yves!" Dallas suggests, grabbing at any straw she can find. "We'll dispel you, and the sickness will go away, and then we can summon you back!"

I have had this same thought before. Warlocks are nothing if not obsessed with theory. "It won't work. Yves must have already been dispelled by Kristiansen—I summoned her, after all—and yet Olesya has remained stricken for years."

Maria, next to me, stands apart and looks lost. "I would love to help in some way, but..."

"It's fine, it's fine," my sister says, face gray and voice weak. "I outlived Cecilie and avenged my family. It's a fate befitting a Hua."

"Please," Dallas whispers, "please, there must be something you can do, Yves."

My demon is quiet, her black smoke transmuting to unmoving obsidian. "Viveca," she says, and the world shrinks to just the two of us. "When we first met, you threatened me—you said that if I let you die, you would task your homunculus with destroying every instance of my True Name."

A knot of fear, vertiginous, seizes my chest. "What are you getting at, Yves?"

"Unsummon me. Unsummon every part of me—cast a spell that obliterates my name from every record. Cauterize this wound to reality; deny this stolen, bastardized part of me any purchase, in history or memory."

"Will that work?" the tiger asks, distant, confused as to how this is different from what she suggested.

"We'll forget your True Name," I say.

"Yes," Yves replies, simple.

Dallas finally catches up. "You'll be unsummoned, with no way back."

"True Names cannot be destroyed, Dallas, not forever. Someday, my name will reappear many generations hence, in tossed runestones or ancient tomes that rewrite themselves, and some other warlock will call me forth. So it is not a death, not like you know it."

"But it is a goodbye," I conclude, my voice muted.

"Oh, now that's some bullshit. You can't—" Olesya calls out, and then descends into what will be a final coughing fit.

"In their time, each Hua is presented with a choice, a great and impossible question," Inspector Budak murmurs, her stone voice like an avalanche. "And each time, they have answered correctly." She does not look up from Olesya.

I do not know the tiger, not how Olesya or Yves do. But her emotions are transparent, like glass—like glass, fracturing. Frantic and broken, a tiger ensnared in a trap she cannot escape. She wants to stand to confront Yves; she must keep holding Olesya.

It is Yves who bends to meet Dallas, who kneels beside the tiger and takes a blood-covered hand in hers. "Dallas, you are my oldest friend. But in all the time we have traveled together, I have never told you what you... that I—" She shudders, her composure cracking.

"Then don't. Not now," Dallas snarls, eyes wet. "Tell me when next we meet." Maybe that is possible. Very probably not—this version of Dallas will not survive a thousand years, ten thousand. But a tiger might dream as a human must.

"This sentimentality is killing me," Olesya croaks.

"She's clearly fine," I say, gallows humor steadying my voice. "Give her a moment, she'll be up on her feet."

Yves smiles, sad. "It's time for me to go, Xinyu Hua," she says, careful and precise, and in her use of my True Name I feel the depth and breadth of her feelings for me, the love and longing and understanding with which she treats me.

"I love you, ███ ," I reply.

It is the last time I ever say it.

As spells go, it's not particularly unique—a spell of finding and a spell of destruction, welded together toward a very precise end. And while the scope of the spell is global, it is not as if Yves chiseled her name in deep caves, or as if common textbooks report her most esoteric truths. I have her power through most of the spell, too—an enveloping warmth and a gentle strength, the comfort of a lover that trusts in me and my ability completely.

And then she's gone.

Almost immediately, Olesya's breath slows and becomes steady; I see her relax, pain-free for the first time in what must be years, years in which I could do nothing to help her. Chang'er ejects a cartridge from one of the weapons we brought: inert metal, no longer bane to magic.

Dallas hugs Olesya tight, then gently lays the sleeping woman down. Watches, for a moment, as color slowly returns to the face of one of the women she loves.

"Olesya is going to be fine," I say, resting a hand on Dallas' shoulder. "Mages are notoriously good at regenerating, and the healing arts she learned to slow her illness will help her recover."

The tiger staggers to her feet, then turns into my embrace and slumps heavily against me: we may only know each other so much—so little—but now we are joined in grief. Her face is drawn, and her eyes have a glassy, shell-shocked look to them.

"I can't remember her name," she murmurs, burying her head in my shoulder. "The demon… what was her *name?*"

And I feel it now, too. The taste of ash and petrichor, the charge in the air before a rain of fire—it's all there, except that in my head and in my heart is a hole, a gnawing chasm where a name and a life should be.

Epilogue

VIVECA

The red spider lily is as hale as the day she picked it and tucked it into my hair, the bloom still fresh, every tepal sheened with life. Probably it will always remain like that, outlasting my human expectancy. Fit for an heirloom, as she promised.

But I have kept it in a glass case. I don't keep it embedded within me, wear it as I once wore her. I tried that once. As potent as ever, as protective as she was, only there was no heat in it, no voice in my ear. It is not the person, the demon; it is a reminder. It is a tombstone that bears no name. I took it off and wept until I was sick, and then I became furious that she knew all along how it would end, and so left me this keepsake. A great gift, one any warlock—any mage—would covet. It cannot replace her.

Our enemy is vanquished, even if she leaves behind the question of what really happened to our mother. My sister is cured, able to thrive once more, the happiest and healthiest she's been in years. Sealing and Containment is gone, and my name is for all intents and purposes cleared. I have restored my tower, repairing the damage inflicted by the battle and by Cecilie, clearing out insect corpses. There are many causes for celebration, and yet all I can do is pace my chambers, sink myself deep into the tomes and manuscripts of the family library. There are social functions I'm obliged to attend; I tell Olesya and Chang'er to go in my place.

My sister is understanding, at least, and she has been holed up in her estate too long. Now is the time for her to shine as a Hua, her opportunity in the sun with a stunning woman on each arm, when she can persuade Dallas to be at her elbow. The tiger is loyal, and she loves Olesya—

—but she is distracted, like I am, obsessed. I find her in my library—my private library—a week after our victory. It ought to be sealed to everyone but me, and even Cecilie didn't breach it; Dallas has impossibly slipped through wards and traps to stand in my sanctum. She sets a satchel down on my desk. "It's the *Liber Juratus Honorii*," she says, without preamble. "Solomonic text, lots of bindings and stuff. It could help us."

I have no time or interest in the tiger's aid. I have only blinding resentment in my heart, anger where empathy might be: this woman had *a century* or more with my demon, and I had so little. Even Dallas' explanation reeks of buffoonery. "Of course I have a copy," I reply, "and there is no *us*."

"It's not a *copy*." The tiger looks at me, eyes unreadable. "And you're nothing like your sister."

She leaves before I can demand to know what *that* means.

And then she's back, two days later, sitting at my dining table. "How the fuck," I almost scream, "do you keep getting in?"

"Cats and dragging things," she says, brushing me off. There is a box of fresh donuts on the table. "What do you know about this place?" she asks, smearing sugar on an aged map she's unfurled. "Ancient site of Babylonian power, something about a shadow goddess. Maybe we can find a scrap of her name there."

"What the hell is your plan, Dallas, except to torment me?" I need solitude and space, not this beast.

"I'm going to re-write her name, of course." She seems confused by the question. "What are *you* doing?"

"Go home to my sister," I say, and teleport her away.

Fresh milk in the fridge, reads the note she's left on the donuts.

There is a hole where the demon's name should be, for both of us. The True Name was her anchor, of course, and what needed to be erased from this world to save Olesya. But my spell was thorough; *every* name and alias I called her is gone, every thread of identity severed, the collateral damage to Olesya's cure.

It is the same for Dallas, too; the wound is torn open each time I hear the tiger struggle and settle for saying "the demon." On occasion a seed of madness seizes me: I think of inviting the tiger to my bed. After all, don't we memorialize her—the demon, *our* demon—in our bodies? And I can even see an answering impulse in Dallas' face, rare but persistent; I know that she's considered it too, a stopgap, a means to give our common despair respite.

Neither of us goes through with it. How can we properly grieve or find catharsis, when we can't even speak her name?

My grief, I accept, might be eternal. But demons *are* eternal. They may be banished. They may be restrained from manifesting on this earth. To genuinely destroy them is near-impossible, and the wherewithal for such is most likely beyond any mortal. She's out there, and I just have to find her. My family has been warlocks, generation after generation. If there's a method to recreate a path for a specific demon to return to our realm, it would be hidden in one of our archives.

By the reckoning of mages, I am young yet, I am relentless, and I am alone; there will be no distractions. It could take decades, it could take half a century and more, but I will find a way. Even if it requires the rest of my life.

I welcome no visitors, save my sister. Dallas continues to come anyway.

Her tenth visit, and she's snoring on my couch when I find her. The noise is insufferable; she only wakes when I pull a slab of raw meat from the fridge and leave it on the table.

"I'm close to finding the bracelet," she says, voice and face strained by lack of sleep. "It was in one of Cecilie's vaults, I know that much. I tracked down the mercenary company that raided the vault after her fall—they're all dead now, you can thank me later—and I got—"

"You look like shit," I interrupt. I've long since passed any threshold of decorum around Dallas; I'd curse more if it meant I would see her less. "And what the fuck are you on about?"

She stares at her empty plate, contemplating the bloody residue, the liquid remains of a once-life. "When she and I traveled together, she was bound to a silver bracelet. She could move independently—would, sometimes for years at a time—but it was her anchor to this world. We... I grew tired of that weight, and one day threw it away. I've tried to find it before, but the effort has taken on a more pressing nature these past weeks."

"You also have the support of a powerful benefactor now," I add dryly.

"I know it probably won't help." It's the first time I've heard her express doubt; I prickle at the tone of her voice, the slump of her shoulders. "But I have to try. I have to. She spent years under torture, and I..." She fixes me with a look. "I sometimes think her name is right on the tip of my tongue—that if I could just stop thinking about it for one moment and relax my jaw, it would come spilling out. We're close, Viveca. I know we're close."

"That makes one of us." Harsh, unfair, true; there is no reason to hide from the reality of the situation. And then I surprise myself: "Go get cleaned up in the shower." It will take days to get all her hair out of the drain. "In the meantime, I'll make a phone call about your damn bangle."

Fahriye Budak comes to my door, once, the one guest other than Olesya I'm prepared to receive; when someone saved your life from vampires, you make exceptions. She tells me that she's going to restore the Scottish cabin.

The sight of Mother's homunculus speaking and moving with its—her—own volition is startling; it could speak before Mother's death, but not like this, so fluid and conversant. The construct itself has shifted in appearance, too, beginning to match the soul it now contains, the face more lined and the complexion much darker than before. Incomplete as yet; eventually it will perfectly reproduce how the inspector looked in life. This is also not a capability I knew the construct to have.

That Mother modified the homunculus to prepare for this, to accommodate a human soul, speaks of her regard for Fahriye. That she kept it a secret from us speaks of something else. Endangerment to Fahriye's previous career, perhaps. Not wanting us children involved in her personal affairs; wanting something private for herself alone.

I could ask. I don't. It's not as though I cannot already guess.

187

"How are you acclimating to the homunculus, Inspector?" I say, to keep up the polite fiction that I want to receive guests at all, that I want to do anything but devote myself to my life's work in the library. In sending forth demons to search archeological sites, obscure collections, dust-thick archives.

Fahriye looks at me with her jewel eyes. "Slowly. It's... Master Elizaveta was a peerless mage. The act of capturing a soul in the moment of death is unique enough, and to transfer it into a vessel that adapts to it, too—your mother, Ms. Viveca, deserved her title in all ways."

I want to tell her that I do miss my mother, and does she miss my mother too—but those are a child's questions. "And you're comfortable?"

Her laugh rumbles, sand on granite. "Not everyone gets a second chance, do they? I'll make do. I'm not even uncomfortable—it's *strange*, but not exactly an ordeal. As for the cabin, Olesya will be doing most of the heavy lifting. I didn't realize she excelled at transfiguration."

"The entire mage-killer moniker rather eclipsed everything else. But yes. She's actually a fantastic sorceress. About time she's accorded the proper respect." Maybe she will be the one to produce the next generation of heirs, with weretiger contribution or otherwise. I'll become the aunt who always smells of old paper and clay tablets.

"You're very fond of each other." Fahriye smiles. "That's good. I used to worry you might grow up like a lot of mage siblings, the ones who fight to the death over who gets to inherit. Your mother would, I think, have been proud of you."

These are comments one might expect of a close relative, a doting aunt, not a near-stranger who pretends she has no relationship with our mother beyond the most professional and distant. "Is that so?" I needle a little. "Did she tell you that?"

The homunculus body lacks cardiovascular functions, and little reaction shows on her face, but she's caught out, defensive. "I'm just guessing, Ms. Viveca. She adored her daughters, I understand."

"She didn't talk about us to just anyone, you know."

If she had the means, Fahriye would be flushing. "I suppose that she did not. You'd know best. The cabin—will you come by?"

That place is important to me, too. Once it felt the safest sanctum in the world. "I'm in the middle of some crucial research."

"The demon?"

Someone must've told her. That, and she watched Dallas and I make our farewells to—to the one whose name has slipped clear of memory. "The demon." My voice is flat. I will not cry in front of her. "It's like you said—the Hua warlock is presented with an impossible question every generation, and we have always answered correctly. But this answer? It's killing me."

"I..." Fahriye starts. She pauses, licks her lips, starts again: "It was a thing that was, and then it was a thing that wasn't. Your mother and I, we saved Hong Kong together, more times than I can count. The world, once or twice. We... perhaps you do not want me to share this?"

"Ms. Budak. *Fahriye*." It is the first time I have smiled in months. It hurts. "I've known about you both since I was twelve."

"The—oh gods, when you caught me at the fridge."

"Yes. I absolutely did not believe that Sealing and Containment needed to guard our fridge at two in the morning."

The former inspector leans back, mortified. "And your sister—?"

"She absolutely still believes that Sealing and Containment needed to guard our fridge at two in the morning."

"It was really good chocolate milk!" Fahriye justifies, and we laugh, hard. Finally, slowly, Fahriye opens up about the woman I called Mother, and whom she came to know as Liz—she may be the only person alive Mother ever allowed to call her that.

"We did our best to be discreet," she goes on, "careful, never formally acknowledging any sort of lasting obligation between us. And in any other relationship, I think a distance like this would have been the coldest poison. But with your mother..."

"She was a warlock," I finish. "She trafficked in deals, bound people and demons to her on flights of fancy and in plots of timeless calculation. To not be one of those people... you were unique."

"And then she was just gone. Dead, apparently, at the hands of Cecilie Kristiansen. I—" She stumbles, tongue suddenly tied. With the body she

189

has, it seems she's returned to inanimation entirely, no alimentary signs, no movement at all—of the eyelids, of the lungs, nothing.

"If it helps: Cecilie didn't kill her. She wanted us to believe she did, but she never manifested any of my mother's power, or her knowledge." A pause. "When I came to tell you of my mother's passing, I said that she wanted you to live your own life, that revenge could be ably pursued by my sister and I. That was ten years past, and we have not succeeded. We would... *I* would welcome the assistance of Sealing and Containment's last, best inspector."

Fahriye grimaces. "I will try. It's... it's hard."

I nod. "God, it's so *fucking* hard."

"I will not say," Fahriye murmurs, "that you must move on eventually and live your own life. It's a fresh thing, and I am one to talk—I never quite managed to move on, myself. But more than that, I believe you will be able to accomplish this. Out of all mages, the Huas are the most adept at the impossible. I am living proof of that."

There's some sort of gala—I don't know whom for or why; I have not been paying attention. This is, in absolute terms, a mistake; I should be side-by-side with Olesya, securing our foothold and taking advantage of our enemies' destruction, both Cecilie and Sealing and Containment. Or, barring that, I should be investigating the actual murderer of our mother.

Instead I watch myself, as if through a mirror, pull on a black dress that makes my skin itch, draw on jewelry that lacks the luster of golden eyes. There is dross for conversation—incredibly important, new powers feeling each other out—and I listen with the attentiveness one might pay the hum of traffic, doing my best to read signals and make the appropriate turns.

Dallas manhandles some ambassador or another out of the way; the tiger has an unhealthy pallor and a crumpled suit that looks incongruously stunning. "I have a new lead—fossils in the Antarctic."

I grab her elbow and pull her into an adjoining sitting room; the hall is lousy with locations for people to step aside and plan secret deals with each other, no doubt eavesdropped on by my sister. Whatever; they can't speak the one name that matters.

"That sounds stupid," I say. "What are you thinking? Where's the bracelet?"

"I'm working on that." Her face clouds, then clears; she flows like water around her problems and her emotions, wearing one down with time while concentrating on another. "So I was thinking, fossils are basically relics of antediluvian provenance, right? And the demon is basically a primordial leviathan? So what if—"

"You know about that?" I hang on to this fact, that someone else knew the demon as more than a human shape of smoke and fire.

"You don't spend two centuries with someone and not see who they really are, out of the corner of your eye."

"Ah." I suddenly feel exhausted, and slump on a couch. "Fossils? We're getting really far afield. Did your Sumerian angle work out?" It sounds almost like we are working together, so I add, "It was a stupid long shot anyways."

Dallas lands, heavy, beside me. "We're *technically* the third and fourth authors on an archeological paper about Bronze Age kingship, but no."

We sit in silence for a moment. Then I say, "The demon pulled a little plot of earth to her reality—used it as a garden and a forge, as best I can tell. Filled with red spider lilies. Inauspicious, associated with death. But I only saw the beauty of it. And I can't help but think she is waiting for me there, in those flowers. Like a corpse, I guess. I can't find a way back there. Did she ever make you something like that?"

Dallas settles against me, and only then do I realize she has fallen asleep, mouth open in a snore. Her head is on my shoulder. Inconvenient, trapping me here like a sleeping housecat—and me, a crazed cat lady, bleeding my emotions everywhere. But I stay my hand from waking her. The tiger has been running herself ragged, like I have, and she smells good enough. A short nap won't hurt her.

We cause a whole security fiasco after that. It takes Olesya forty-five minutes and a building lockdown to find us snoring, propped up against each other in the sitting room.

And then, of course, Olesya has to arrive at my home.

"You've always said you don't love Hong Kong's air," I tell her when I find her in my parlor one day. She didn't knock, either, and didn't send a message to herald her. Simply she is here. Familial entitlement.

She has ensconced herself on the sofa, a piece of furniture that belonged to our mother—we split the items of decor and so on evenly, so that there are pieces of Elizaveta Hua both in her estate and mine. Or there were, before she incinerated her place.

Olesya has brought a slim suitcase with her, but it's probably an item that holds more than it has any right to. She's come in a dress of antique gold and lake green, mermaid silhouette; her favorite sort. Perfectly made up, adorned by precious things—emeralds that hold echoes of deep, Mesolithic shadows; gold that has been exhumed from Etruscan vaults and restored. A perfume that radiates the freshness of sea breezes, mingled with a note of spice. Custom-made, probably by Chang'er; that girl dabbles, has a fox's nose for fragrance.

Next to her I must look like I've been nesting in a compost heap. If she's noticed how musty my parlor smells, she has not commented on it.

"That reception we attended," she says. Hesitates. "I'm worried about you, Viveca."

I already know that. Of course she's worried. But at the same time: she does not understand. In every way, she has emerged from the battle whole. She has her women and her magic is back, and I—

I have nothing. I am trying to have something again, and toward that end I must dedicate my every waking breath, every hour and second. She does not understand that.

Olesya crosses her legs. "And I needed to apologize."

For half a moment I think she means to apologize for her cure demanding the disappearance of my demon. Then I realize that is not what she means. "You have nothing to apologize for." My voice is flat. I'm no good at pretending at sisterly reconciliation today.

"For years, I didn't tell you about the poison. I didn't want to make you worry; I didn't want to become a hostage against your good behavior, if that's what it came to. And I didn't know what caused it." Her hands fold in her lap. "I felt it was my responsibility, as the elder, to not only assist but protect you. I couldn't replace Mother, but I wanted..."

"It's fine." I am brusque: it is armor, of a sort. "It's all past. I would have liked to know, but it's as they say about wishes and horses." And during those years, was it not she who had nothing? Was I not the one in the light, the daughter who had it all while she languished inside the cage of her misery? What can I do but forgive; what can I say but *All bygones, sister.*

A frown indents her brow. Then she sighs. "I brought material." The suitcase opens—she can perform sorcery again, and seems apt to use it for every minor matter. Understandable.

Inside, bolts of fabric, in shimmering black and the complex red of good claret. Oxblood and burgundy. My colors.

"I don't need new dresses." Maybe what I wore to the gala struck her as dowdy, behind the season.

"You could use a wardrobe refresh. One does not need a reason for it. Pick what you like and I'll create you something elegant, in a style you'll enjoy. I know your tastes."

For so long, I did *not* need wardrobe refreshes. I wore what I already had in casual or professional contexts. For events, I wore...

The tears come before I'm fully conscious of them. And once they begin, I can't stop. The noises I make are so ugly. The force of grief bows my spine.

Olesya takes me into her arms—I mutter that I'll ruin her dress, and she says she can make a thousand more—and for the first time since I was in my preteens, I cry into my sister's chest.

It has been four months, verging on five since Cecilie's defeat, when the tiger actually *knocks.*

Her presence is an intrusion, as it ever is. I'm perusing a tablet etched in Sumerian—Dallas was right about something, a tiny bit—haltingly translated for me by a spirit; some warlock or priest in Uruk or Akkad was able to manipulate the contract between worlds, perform an invocation that did not rely on True Names. It was with the aid of a supposed divine being, but it was still possible, and in such antiquity. Our art has come a long way since, but much has been lost, too.

Grudgingly I set aside the tablet and dismiss the spirit. The banging on the door won't stop. Dallas is lucky I have modified my wards to include her, instead of strengthening them.

I don't bother dressing up or tidying my hair as I get to the parlor and wave the door open. Dallas stands at the threshold, as disheveled as I am, wilder-looking if possible, apparently frantic enough that she can only barge her way in this time, not sneak. Her mane of hair is horribly unkempt, black and gold standing up in tufts. Olesya must be irate. She's told me about the expensive brushes she purchased just for her tiger's hair- and fur-care.

There's appeal, I'll admit, to the untamed look though. And I've gotten used to her scent, the primal beast's.

"I found it." Dallas thrusts something at me—a band of silver, thick and antique, much tarnished. *"I found it."*

Confusion, then comprehension. It is the bangle she talked about and left weeks ago to find. Old silver, etched deep not in space but time and in power, resonating with a hum I can intimately recall. Still: "Well, congratulations. But it's not going to—"

"No, not just this. I remember her name. Yves. It's *Yves*, gods dammit."

My throat closes. My heart flutters between hope and despair. To finally be able to think a name about her; an almost-joy. I recognize; I cannot believe.

I reject. "It's… it's just the alias we called her, Dallas. It's not her True Name."

She grabs my hands. Clutching them hard enough to bruise. "It's more than we have had for months. It might work. It's got to work. Do you have anything else of hers?"

I open my mouth. I close it. The thought of this failing is nearly too much to bear. That is why I have researched and researched, I realize, without putting any of it into practice—because everything I've found is so flimsy, impossible to replicate, or unlikely. I have not wanted to attempt only to fail, to stare down the increasing unlikelihood that we'll meet the demon—*Yves*, dammit!—again. "I do." My voice hitches. "She gave me a flower."

There's something to the thought of summoning through affinity: the spider lily, the bracelet, even Dallas and me as catalysts. The companion who was with her the longest, the warlock who bound her through flesh and blood—it might work. I take the flower and lead Dallas to the office in which I first made Yves materialize, the one where the windows look out to the Antarctic, the one where we slew Cecilie.

The tiger eyes the surfaces I've restored and faultlessly kept clean, the inscribed circle on the floor built to contain, the near-invisible lines painstakingly carved into the ceiling for the same. She looks uneasy, perhaps because cages are so repellent to her, and what are these if not more iron bars? She doesn't seem to like the wintry decor any better.

"When she's back," says Dallas, "how are you going to anchor her?"

As if success is an inevitability; her confidence is almost heartening, even charming. "The same way as before. It's better than objects." For reasons that should be, to her, perfectly clear. I try not to be resentful of their past or of what she did to Yves. Perhaps if she hadn't carelessly discarded the bracelet, I might never have met my demon. And I have watched her, for months now; I could not possibly hate her more than she hates herself.

"Is it possible to split it?"

"So you would bear her as well?" I widen my eyes at her, mostly to distract from my own nerves.

"Just think of it as insurance, for you and for her," she quickly continues.

Her reaction makes me smirk. "That's like marriage, and Yves our wedding ring. Olesya would be so angry if she knew you're proposing to me."

"You—" She sighs. "You must have given Yves the most trying time."

"Not as trying as you." We are each whistling past the graveyard. I sober up. "I'm going to start."

At the age of ten, I performed my first functional summoning. It was just a wisp of spirit, barely more powerful than a housecat, but Mother was there with me and I wanted to do her proud, to prove that I could measure up to being the heir. I was nervous; it seemed life-or-death at the time, my single chance at this, even though Mother made it clear I would have many. My previous efforts had not gone well.

And now I'm staring down at a ritual that means even more, that could spell either the end or the beginning. Yes: I can try again even if it fails, but this rite fizzling out would tell me either the method or catalyst has proven flawed. And if this name doesn't work—and I have no reason to believe it shall—then we would be left with ashes in our hands, grasping at thin air again.

But I set all that aside. I will not falter. To have tried will be better than not at all. One of Mother's lessons, and one that's served me well.

I prick my finger, igniting the inscriptions with blood. At the heart of it, the actual rite is simple; what is crucial is the warlock's will and discipline. I form the words of binding, the words of seeking, incorporating into them what I learned from that Sumerian tablet. This is the law of the worlds, and I challenge it; this is the path by which those of the infernal realm may cross into our earth, and I hold sway over it. This is the balance, and my thumb is on the scale. I shall be the compass, the wedge that holds open the thinnest place in the veils...

And then, her name: "Yves."

Nothing, at first; the air is still, the room is quiet save for the muted howl of subzero winds. The seconds tick by. I hold myself tense, every muscle in me tight as bowstrings.

Then it comes, that familiar whisper of inferno, the warmth of distant conflagration. Every centimeter of my skin pricks. Dallas makes a small gasp. One of her hands twitches as if she's burning to reach out, to grasp what is inside the summoning circle.

I hear a cry: not mine, not hers. Not anything mortal's. It is the noise of more than one demon—a chorus of demands, of entities attempting to cross through the gate I've erected into their realm, one I imagine shimmering on their end with power and promise—of what they can have, once here; of the deeds they'll achieve to their glory, of tributes offered.

I repeat her name. "Yves. Come to me. *Come to us.*"

The screams grow in proximity and intensity. The windowpanes creak;

the air itself warps and splits, and a blue, clawed hand reaches through—

It is snatched back. Something screeches, a cacophony of voices. And then, Yves materializes.

The outline of her is frayed; even her substance is translucent—I can see the wall through her. "Anchor me, warlock," she snarls. "Quickly."

I do, a spell that's second nature to me, complicated by two anchors but no less simple to cast. Half in me, half in the tiger. Yves coalesces kneeling, her suit torn, her face scraped but already smoothing out.

Dallas is on her before the demon is even corporeal. "I looked for you, I swear I looked for you," she cries, oblivious to any decorum or tact. "I tore through every one of Cecilie's vaults to find the bangle, tore through every memory to recall your name, any name—" She begins to sob next, wracked by months of pent-up emotion.

I am the opposite: dumbstruck, unable to process what I am seeing. "It worked?"

Yves smiles—broad and genuine, relaxed in a way I have never seen her before. "Well, a wise tiger once told me that names were supposed to change over time—you give away parts of yourself, and gain the parts of others, and who you are grows." Dallas has turned into her tiger form, still tangled in shirt and pants, licking Yves' face; the demon squeezes and scratches back, like she is playing with a massive housecat. "I guess I am Yves now, in the truest sense possible."

My brain is slowly beginning to regain function. "And that blue claw we saw?"

"Ah. *That*. The summons of a Hua is a clarion call in my world—and with your victory over Kristiansen, your star is the highest it has ever been. Your expressed wishes were quite clear, but the number of upstart demons willing to gamble on being the first to answer your summons was, quite literally, legion." Her smile takes on a wolfish look. "It wasn't a fair fight."

That handsome face, its easy confidence and dangerous charm, draws from me an answering grin. "Oh? You'll have to tell me how many battalions you conquered to make your way back to me, all your brave and mighty deeds."

"I will." She takes my hand and kisses my knuckles. "I'm home, Ms. Hua."

Dallas stays over for dinner. She's visited often enough that I have learned well her carnivorous habits—I eat about the same quantity of meat as any human, but her portion requirements are a good deal greater; I've had to stock up enough to feed an entire wolf pack. Oddly, when she's not drinking dime-store coffee or eating day-old donuts, her manners at meals are surprisingly refined, likely honed over centuries of sitting at the tables of royalty and aristocracy.

I watch Dallas watch my demon. There's tenderness in her every gesture, every look. I must ask her for stories someday; where she has been, what lives she's led. What she and Yves did together, adventuring across the globe.

"I'm surprised to find your place so empty," Yves remarks to me. "I would have thought you would have taken on... companions."

"You must think me very fickle. It's been half a year, Yves, not twenty." I put down my glass of caramel tea. Probably I should have poured wine for the occasion, but I don't often drink and Yves has no real preference in beverages. "What have you been up to?"

"Visiting family." This is said with a perfectly straight face. "And you, Ms. Hua?"

I shrug. "Advancing the warlock arts."

"She means," Dallas cuts in, meticulously wiping her mouth on a serviette that immediately turns pink, "spending her every waking hour looking for a way to bring you back."

They share a smirk. I try to hold onto my composure. "Well—I did want my finest armor back; any warlock would invest the time and energy."

"Of course." Yves' tone is bland. "I'm so pleased to be contracted to a woman of pure, ruthless calculation. I adore being objectified as a mere instrument of combat. Don't you agree I would be the envy of any demon, Dallas?"

The tiger bites down on her lip, keeping back her laughter. "Don't bring me into it. Watch out, your warlock's going to use a spell to shut you up."

"Yes, let me get right on that." I grab Yves' tie and drag her toward me, then kiss her full on the mouth.

The warmth that suffuses me is instant. It's like lighting a fuse. My own desire and hers, mingling, looping through our bond. At once I think, it's been a season and more, during which I missed her desperately; at once I remember our glade, where she spread out under me, where she professed that I was the heart of our haven, the heart of her…

Dallas clears her throat. "I believe I should be making myself scarce."

I almost ask her to stay. Olesya called on me and Fahriye Budak offered her condolences, but it was Dallas who best understood me, this past season of suffering. There is real attraction here, real appreciation for more than her looks; she helped me when no other soul could, believed in me when I did not believe in myself.

But Yves stands before I can speak, steps around the table to embrace her oldest friend—hugs her tight, then slips a hand into Dallas' thick hair to pull her into a kiss. Finally, they rest their foreheads together, eyes closed, simply enjoying each other's proximity.

"I'm not running away again," Dallas murmurs, diffident, answering some accusation that only she can hear. "It's just… it's just that Olesya has given me something that isn't mine to give away."

The demon pulls back to look at her, then laughs. "You—you remember what I said!"

Dallas glares at her with faux annoyance. "Yves, I remember everything you've ever said to me. I only act like I don't."

Yves' smile falls. "In all our time together, I have never once told you that I loved you."

"You and I, we've never been one for words—we let our actions speak for us. And who can blame us? Human speech is not our native tongue." She shrugs. "But maybe we've each figured out that love requires both word and deed. And maybe we'll get it better next time."

Yves nods and relents, and Dallas turns to wink at me. "Yves is a very sensitive soul stuck with a very serious face. Respect and appreciate her, more than I have." She shows herself out after that, but not before I hear her rustle in the fridge a final time. "A steak for the road!" she shouts back. "I've eaten like shit for *months...*"

And then it's just the two of us.

I am, against all reason, suddenly shy. Perhaps it is the experience of having observed their intimacy; perhaps it is the fact I am still shocked that we succeeded in bringing Yves back to us. I remain seated at the dining table, awkward, unsure what to do with myself or how to venture next.

What does one say at a time like this? How do you preserve the sanctity of this reunion and ensure this moment—and the next, and the next after that—remains perfect? And can I compare, really, to the easy camaraderie they have shared, the centuries-old companionship that arose from more than carnal impulses and warlock clauses?

"Ms. Hua." Her voice nearly makes me jump. "What would you like to do? I can clear the table."

The thought is so mundane it's a little funny: that the first thing I have Yves perform, upon her miraculous return, is a domestic chore. "The table can wait. Let us," I add, with more courage than I feel, "retire to the bedroom."

"Retire it is." She bends to kiss my forehead, and then sweeps me into her arms.

My pulse hammers behind my ribs. She must hear it, too, because she laughs a little and murmurs, "My warlock bride."

A few words, and none of them especially filthy. It's like a conflagration has been set off, and when she deposits me on the indigo sheets I sit for several moments, again dumbstruck. To think I was the first to ask her into my bed, and now I've been robbed of all initiative, all propulsion—Yves, indisputably, has the upper hand this evening.

She unhooks the back of my dress, peeling off one shoulder then the other. The motion is considered, as if she's about to see me naked for the first time. Two hands cup my hips, measuring the span of them, and then my waist, as though she means to tailor me a bespoke dress. A third hand begins to work on my bra. With Yves, more hands than the human usual is to be expected. But I've shut my eyes without realizing it, and when I open them I realize this is not quite the usual.

The mirror above the bed—I'm allowed my minor perversions—shows rather more Yves than I'd expect. There being two of her, each human-shaped, one behind and another before me. One mouth kissing my nape, the other kissing my clavicle. Both of her glisten, here and there, with blue-black scales.

"Given the occasion," one of them says against that little nub of collarbone, "I thought I would do something a little different."

My imagination races ahead of my actual, physical reality. "Well." I try to make my tone smoky and sultry, the consummate seductress', but my mouth is too dry with excitement. "The demon advantage."

"And you're both the most powerful living warlock, and the most adventurous one."

I rest my hand on the base of Yves' skull. The Yves in front of me, at any rate. "Show me," I say, and finally find the exact tone I want.

Her tongue grazes the line of my jugular, and I wonder how much she wants to break the skin, to sip at something she's gone so long without. A sacred ambrosia to her palate. I think of her leviathan form and shiver; Yves rewards me by sending twin coils of serpentine smoke around my ankles and wrists.

"I'm about to ask of you a great deal of trust. There's two of me, and…" One palm rubs, slow, against my coccyx. "How would you like to, temporarily, have a second part where you may be pleasured?"

I spend a few seconds trying to make sense of that. One of her tongues trailing a path down my spine is distracting. "You mean you're—rearranging my anatomy." Literally. "Giving me a second—"

"For the duration of our tryst. Functionally it won't affect the rest of you; it's extra-dimensional. It's not as though I intend to displace your ribcage." She presses her mouth to my brow. "You know I will never bring you harm, not in any way."

The idea shouldn't sound this intriguing. "Why, first I was your bride, now I'm to be your whore?"

Her laugh gusts. "Your vulgar tongue, Ms. Hua. Is it a yes?"

"Yes." Now I grin. "Do make me your whore."

Yves *tsks*, with both mouths. She has slid down my dress until it puddles around my waist. A hand cups my breast, her thumb teasing my nipple. With her other hand she palms my abdomen. The sensation as she changes me there is odd, new flesh blooming inside me, lightly tickling. It is not an injury, and when she touches me there I gasp with the sensitivity of new nerves, her fingers very gentle as she parts and caresses.

I don't quite look down as I wiggle out of my dress—the sight of Yves' creation would be a little much—and attempt to position myself to give both bodies access. It really is something else to look over my shoulder and find a mirror image of the lover in front of me; nor have I ever taken more than one partner to bed before, so even the physical element is novel.

A rustle of fabric, and then the metallic click of a belt buckle. For the first time I am watching Yves strip the outer shadow of herself, to bare to me a manifestation of naked flesh. And what flesh it is: she has chosen a strong, broad physique, but I've only ever seen its outline—no more than her bare arms, sleeves (her own skin, again) rolled up. I have seen the cords of muscle.

But, oh, this vision she has chosen to reveal: small, pale breasts—hanging a little heavier than one would expect, tipped in nipples that startle me with their vividness. The gorgeous stomach that looks as though it has been chiseled by a master, the hard lines of muscle that move with her (simulated, yes, but) breath. The way all of this descends into the sort of thighs immortalized in statuary. A ragged scar winds its way around one hip. There is no softness here, except what she offers to me in symbolism, the heart and the glade.

Resting where her genitals might be is a pool of shadow, shifting and forming. Tendrils, at first, knitting into a thick length. By its shape, I know the fit will be just right.

I turn and kiss the Yves at my back. She tucks me against her abdomen, then busies her hands with my breasts. Her erection—the duplicate of what I'm seeing before me—rests warm against my back.

Fingers, first. Yves delves into the opening she's made, proving quickly that it is strikingly analogous to the one I normally sport, inside and out. In my wildest sexual fantasies, I did not account for the idea of possessing two clitorises, one for each lover.

We quickly turn from exploratory to voracious. I bite Yves on the mouth. One of her shifts me onto her lap and enters me from the back while the other slides into me from the front. I shut my eyes. I exhale. I do not romanticize or exaggerate: I have, in the most literal sense, never been this filled.

When a hand grips my breast, I hiss, "Rougher." Fingers twist at my nipples. Pain, to contrast with the rest.

Yves' organs can manifest anywhere on her and she makes full use of that advantage. Mouths latching on as she finds her pace inside me, both her instances reaching something like a difficult orchestra—the back and forth, the give and take, my body their shared chalice. I hold on to my demon, bracing myself for each thrust, my nails digging in hard enough to shred Yves' substance.

It is agonizingly slow; it is excruciatingly fast. Her hips jerk against me. Her grip on my waist is bruising and when she sinks her teeth into me, I nearly scream—too much, all of this at once, Yves' tongues seemingly everywhere that I can be touched, reached, tasted.

I crane my neck up to watch us in the mirror. Three bodies. Myself bracketed, driving and being driven, coiled within the rhythm's demands.

And then one of her comes, or at least twitches and fills me with warmth. The motion pushes me onto the other appendage—impaled—the final beat that at last makes us arch together, crying out, wild and desperate.

I slump against Yves, shaking; there are tears in my eyes, sweat streaking down my brow. All of me is raw, sundered by the force of climax. Very distantly I feel her pull out and pass her hand over my front, making my stomach just my stomach again.

"Gods," I say, when I can find language.

"Demons, surely." Yves chuckles. "Though I've been worshiped as a deity, now and again."

"You smug..." Her mouth is red, and my shoulder is bleeding. The wound's already closing, but I almost want it not to. I want her to keep licking and sucking.

"Well, was it good for you?"

I bring one of her hands between my thighs. I rub myself against it, tempting fate when I'm already so sensitive. "We must do this again."

"Planning the next bout already. You're insatiable, Ms. Hua."

"Isn't that why you came at my summons?" I pinch Yves on the bicep.

We settle into the comfort of the bed, both bodies holding me between them. I curl up against them, resisting the urge to doze off, murmuring softly when she takes the spider lily from the nightstand and places it in my hair.

"While we were parted, I spoke to… you'd consider them my great-aunt, though we're not the same species." Yves shifts to let me draw closer, the sheets dry on her side of the bed. "They were familiar with a previous Hua warlock. From what I told them, you remind them of her a lot."

I'm not quite sure where this is going. I wrap my legs around her anyway. "I hope I've met with your relative's approval."

The shadow of her substance pools gently across me, in lieu of a blanket. "Our families don't quite work like that. There's not much of a tie, it's just that in this case my great-aunt has very specific expertise. Your forebears have made an impression. What is the closest bond you would consider having with a demon, Ms. Hua?"

My confusion grows. I touch the spider lily tucked behind my ear. "Don't we already have one? I can feel your emotions, probably tap into some of your memories."

"Humans marry, don't they?"

"Well, sure, but I don't see…" I blink. Then I flush. When she called me her warlock bride, I thought that merely foreplay. "Oh."

Her expression grows solemn. "I know you place a great deal of importance upon carrying on the Hua lineage. It's why I spoke to my great-aunt and got the idea that perhaps the Huas wouldn't *mind* a little demon in the genome… but if not, you could take a human partner with whom you could produce completely human offspring. I'll not take offense. That is, if you'd consider my suit to start with."

"Oh." My mouth seems stuck on that one monosyllable. Even with no certainty, no evidence that I could triumph over the impossible, she had faith she would return to me—spoke with acquaintances, made plans to take her place by my side again, wed to me. I scrunch the bedsheet in my fist. All of me is running too warm, for reasons that have nothing to do with our coital sport. "What about Dallas?"

"She has her priorities. I have mine. We'll always be entangled and, yes, lovers. But tigers have one mate at a time." Yves combs her fingers through my hair, careful not to dislodge the flower. "I will devote myself to you foremost. As my warlock, my beloved, my…"

"Bride," I supply, then laugh—finding my voice on the edge of breaking, my eyes warm with tears. "I accept your suit. I will be your wife, as you will be mine."

"What is it that humans say? Till death do us part." She sweeps her hand over and drapes me, for once, in a color other than black: a gown of gold-lined red, the wedding colors of my house. "Till the worlds do us part, Xinyu Hua, I shall honor you, cherish you, and defend you from all ills."

I am the first Hua heir to officially wed a demon, not that I require anyone's approval. Though I have not announced the union to mage society at large, henceforward I have every intention of introducing Yves as my wife.

We receive gifts from Olesya's household, Fahriye, and a mysterious sender. The last is addressed to "the fourteenth warlock of Hua."

"Ah," Yves says, eyeing the package, "that will be from the great-aunt I told you of."

It has come in a case of obsidian, seamless on the outside. I hold and heft it, trying to guess at what is inside, if anything. "You said they knew one of my ancestors."

"Helped raise your ancestor. They were very fond—when she passed, peacefully in her old age, my great-aunt mourned for several centuries. Here." She touches a catch in the obsidian that I can't see, and the lid springs open.

Inside lies a knife in a bed of velvet, the handle made of black wood, the blade a peculiar alloy: slate-gray shot through with gold, the hue of Yves' eyes. When I hold the weapon, the grip warms and fits my hand perfectly.

"My great-aunt crafted it very specifically, apparently over the course of centuries." Yves wraps her hand around mine so that we hold the blade together. "I may be your armor, but they evidently think you need a sword, too. This has been imbued with a potent premise—I will not call it a spell; this bends reality itself. The blade will slay the one who ended your mother, the thirteenth warlock of Hua."

The one puzzle that Cecilie's death failed to solve. "I like your great-aunt. You have to tell me more about what they're like."

My demon makes a face. "They'll pay us a visit eventually. I'll remind them to be courteous."

"I look forward to it." Then, wryly I add, "So—what are your plans for our first days as newlyweds?"

Yves plants a kiss on the back of my neck. "I've been led to understand that humans have this tradition called the honeymoon. After that…"

It is testament to our connection that she knows what I want to do after, and I know that she knows. I don't need us to complete each other's sentences, but the effortless communication has its perks. "After that, I'll find out who killed my mother."

"And do what must be done, both for love and as the duty of your station." She gathers me closer to her. The geometry of my dress shifts and thickens into armor. "When that time comes, I will—as always—be your shield."

Perhaps that enemy shall be the one who exceeds my capability. Perhaps I will discover secrets too terrible to confront. But either way, I am sure of this: Yves will never fail me, nor I her.

Till the worlds, as she said, do us part.

Something Wicked This Way Comes

Cecilie Kristiansen rages from the confines of her single body.

She will destroy them all for this indignity. She will rip their bodies apart, and their minds, and their very existences, and she'll do it slowly and methodically after pinning that fucking warlock and her demon pet to the inside of their own skulls, wear them like puppets, kill everything they love with their own hands. She will make them suffer. Make them see it coming, unable to stop it, unable to halt her revenge. She'll be their final nightmare.

The idiots think they are safe. They think they've destroyed all of her, but there is always more of her. She folded herself into the one bug the warlock and her demon missed. When she realized they were closing in, she had one of herself tear out of the former Michael Pritchard's throat and hide herself, no longer a person, just a nameless store of Cecilie for later. (She did it in front of the former-Michael's family at dinner, spraying blood and mucus on them as the empty husk stopped pretending to be a person, clawed its own throat open, and died. But that only mattered in as much as their horror amused her a little in the ruin of her empire, the wreckage of her plans.) She crawled through apartment walls and empty building spaces, waiting. A few days and they'll stop looking for more of her. She will find a new human, take everything from them—even their name—and begin to rebuild: and then the house of Hua will fall.

She's already found her prey. A young woman, probably in her first apartment away from home. A lovely body, young and fresh and attractive: it could be useful in so many ways. Elizabeth Zhang. A delicious name, too, that will be her own name soon, cutting her off completely from that old existence, nothing brought over but her deep, unslaked, unslakable hunger for revenge. What a delightful coincidence the name resembles Elizaveta's so much.

In the meantime, she has alleviated her hunger on the regular roaches in the apartment walls. Pretending each one is Viveca or the demon as she rips them apart, devours their chitin and ichor and tiny insect lives, growing a little each time. She can't speak Elizabeth Zhang's True Name in this form, and needs to be stronger to drive her way into the girl's flesh and selfhood by force. Well, soon she'll be big enough: already, her body has more legs and more claws, can consume the other insects in a few bites. The roaches are fleeing her instead of fighting back: the way she likes it, powerful, impossible to resist. She'll take Elizabeth Zhang by terror and without resistance too, soon.

This roach is dead. Freshly dead. She's eaten it—her hunger as all-consuming as she is—before the fact really registers. Roaches die all the time, although she likes killing them herself when she can. There is another corpse nearby: a lot of dead or dying insects near her now. She scuttles over to examine it.

The bug's legs and head are lightly dusted with a grayish-white powder. It takes her a long time to place it, dredging up stolen memories so useless in her era of power as to be almost buried and forgotten. It is diatomaceous earth. Cents per kilo at any home maintenance store. Lay it down when you have bugs; Elizabeth Zhang must have seen the roaches and bought some. The bug tracks through it, and the sharp fossilized shells of ancient microscopic sea life slice up its exoskeleton; it bleeds out and dies.

And then other roaches—cannibals all—eat its body, and eat the dust with it, and they die, too.

As she stands there, staring at the poisonous corpses all around her, her guts begin to itch.

There is, of course, the mystery of the thirteenth Hua. She carried the weight of her lineage with grace, made allies in unexpected places—was, by some measure, even heroic. But she remembered the promise of the first Hua, and in time came to believe that the success of her family rested on maintaining that oath, sworn so long ago.

So she set her mind to the restoration of this long-lost artifact, a birthright lost to her line, knowing that it would inevitably lead to confronting the eldritch being contained within.

The details of her success or failure are not my ken—this story is scarcely legend, scarcely cold in the ground, not even history. But this much is certain: the thirteenth Hua was destroyed in her pursuit of this ancient promise, and the artifact has now escaped back into the world, no doubt promising great power to whomever will wield it in violence against its once-captors.

- Lussadh al-Kattan

About the Author

Maria Ying is both a fictional character and the joint pseudonym of Devi Lacroix and Benjanun Sriduangkaew.

Devi Lacroix can be found on https://devilacroix.com/

Benjanun Sriduangkaew can be found on https://beekian.wordpress.com/

For this outing, they were joined by Julian Norton, who wrote the prologue and 'Something Wicked This Way Comes'. Thank you for making Cecilie such a scary villain! Follow him on Twitter at https://twitter.com/zyzzyva1 936

Acknowledgments

Special thanks to Isabelle Thorne for providing the book's naughtiest idea.

We'd both like to thank Rien Gray for inspiring this book with a Halloween special AU of their assassin romance series *Fatal Fidelity*.

Thank you Jill, who has believed in us from the beginning, and to Diana, who always has the right Mountain Goats song.

Other Works by the Author

Those Who Bear Arms

The Gunrunner and Her Hound

The Spy and Her Serpent

Those Who Break Chains

The Grace of Sorcerers

The Might of Monsters

Printed in Great Britain
by Amazon

41579215R00128